the scattering winds

Arc of the Oracles
Book Two

gordon bonnet

Then the beasts go into their lairs, and remain in their dens;
from its chamber comes the whirlwind, and cold from the
scattering winds.
— Job 37:8-9

part one
the foundling

The women and men came from the ruins of the former world, and those who were righteous stood safe though the stone edifices and marble monuments collapsed around them. Finally they stood atop a hill watching the lake rise up to take them as well, leaving none alive. But Blessed Soren turned as the flood rose higher, and stretched out his right hand, defying the power of the water, saying, You shall have none of these. They are under my protection.

And the water dared not touch those who stood behind him, but receded from the devastated land, uncovering the bodies of the thousands who were not standing guarded in his shadow, but who perished when the land tilted and the seas rose up. Thus was the Earth cleansed of the evil that had grown up within it, She of the Unspeakable Name and the ones who followed her to their own destruction, as was foreseen by the Four Sacred Oracles by whom our people were led forth unscathed.

—from The Founders' Tale

one

. . .

The nine statues in the Hall of Images gazed down at Syra Cheraskin, and for once, she tried to meet their eyes. The light of the Eternal Flame flickered over their solemn faces, making the carved wooden folds of their clothing seem to move.

Leda Banfield, the twenty-sixth oracle of the lineage of the Blessed Martyr Mary of the Bridge, was one of the longest-lived oracles since the Fall and the establishment of the community of Klen over six hundred years ago. Syra had been her apprentice for almost fifty years, so she'd seen the statues daily for as long as she could recall. By now, she was so used to the position of apprentice that she had given up thinking about when she might become Guardian of the Word in her own right.

She looked from one of the statues to the next. Beautiful work, and old. No one knew how old. Were they carved from life? Did the images actually look like the people they had been created to represent? They resembled the faded paintings stored carefully with the other relics of the Flight, which were supposedly painted by the Blessed Brandon himself—but no one knew if that was true or only a legend.

Syra kept her skepticism to herself. It wouldn't do for people to think the future Guardian of the Word had her doubts about whether any of it was true.

The only one of the images that was smiling was the Blessed Mary of the Bridge herself. Her countenance seemed to glow with welcome and good cheer, one arm outstretched toward Syra as if saying, *Take my hand. I will guide you where you want to go.*

Which was odd in and of itself, because if the legends were true, Mary of the Bridge was the only one of the nine founders who died without ever reaching safety. Despite that, her face radiated happiness.

Syra was glad she belonged to Mary's lineage. She'd always liked her best, even when she was little and had no idea she'd be chosen as apprentice. The other faces seemed aloof, distant, almost inaccessible. She looked up at the nearest, the statue of Blessed Finn. He stood, broad-chested and upright, strength radiating from every inch of his powerful frame, gazing down at her with stern pity. He held one hand up, palm toward her. Whether this gesture was intended as a greeting or a warning was impossible to know. His other arm was at his side, the fingertips just touching the hand of the statue next to him, Blessed Soren, the next of Mary's line after Mary herself died on the bridge during the Flight. Syra remembered when she first learned why Soren and Finn's hands touched like that, when all the others stood alone and separate.

They were lovers in real life. Soren saved Finn's life, and brought them safely above the flood waters, both his beloved and the rest of the ancestors. Without Blessed Soren, there would have been no Founders, no oracles, no Klen at all. Soren and Finn deserved that, to have the hands of their images gently touching, as they had in real life. She liked that thought. It made them more human.

She shook herself out of her reverie and returned to her duties, anointing each statue's feet with scented oil, then tending the fire. The silence echoed around her, magnifying every little sound of her movement. She was always cautious and deliberate in this holy place, but today it was as if everyone and everything was holding its breath.

Syra knew why, as did everyone in Klen. Today was the day that Leda Banfield would die. Then after the three-day period of mourning, Syra would be invested as the twenty-seventh oracle in the lineage of the Blessed Mary of the Bridge. Leda of course knew when she was going to die, and had given Syra and everyone else plenty of warning, but the status quo had been unchanged for so long it didn't seem real.

Syra sensed it the moment it happened, as Leda said she would. Her hand stopped halfway to adding a cedar branch to the fire to make the smoke smell sweet, the knowledge of Leda's death hitting her like a physical blow. She took a step back, giving a sharp intake of breath. The flames flickered and crackled, the firelight playing over the carved faces of the nine Founders standing in a semicircle around it. They seemed to be watching her to see what she'd do next.

She heard it, almost as if someone had spoken the words aloud—*You are one of us now.*

After a moment, Syra took a deep breath and added the cedar branch to the fire. She watched it crackle and burst into flame, then took unsteady steps away from the brazier and sat down, her back against the wall, trying to regain her equilibrium.

Leda had told her what it was like, long ago. Syra herself was only about fifteen at the time, just become apprentice— such a lot yet to learn—but the memory was undimmed with time.

"Your mind expands in all directions," Leda said, one

long, graceful hand sweeping through the air, her eyes focused somewhere far distant. "The future becomes as clear as the past. It isn't like the oracles of the other lineages, where the knowledge comes in interior voices or prophetic pronouncements or brightly-colored pictures. It is all one piece, the past and present and future all laid out before you, and everything you have experienced or will experience is silent and unmoving and unchangeable. Bubbles frozen into a block of ice. Look at it from this way and that—your perspective changes, but the events never do. You see it all at once."

Syra hadn't understood what she meant then, but she did now. There was the sudden and disorienting sensation of watching her own life from above, seeing the whole thing spread out like the pieces on a game board. Things she knew were in the past—her childhood, her choice of Eliane Shimada as a partner, Eliane's death from a sudden illness six years ago. Things that were in the future—the solemn burial ceremony for Leda Banfield, Syra's installation as Guardian of the Word, choosing a new apprentice, who that apprentice would be.

Syra's own death. The oracular gift of the lineage of Mary of the Bridge conferred a knowledge of one's own mortality but at the same time a complete loss of fear. Once you know something will happen, that it's a fixed point in space and time, it is very much like it's already happened. There was some sadness at the knowledge that her lifespan was limited, but truthfully, wasn't everyone's? That she knew when it was going to happen was the only difference. It was all part of the beautiful, never-changing frozen landscape that was the reality of time.

After a few moments, the dizziness passed. The sensation of what Leda called "all-in-one" didn't diminish. It just was. It always had been there. Until she received the gift at Leda's death, she just didn't see it.

She stood slowly, and when she was convinced she could

walk without staggering too obviously, made her way out of the Hall of Images. She needed to talk to the other three oracles immediately. Certainly they knew that Leda was going to die today, but they may not have been aware the instant it happened. The oracular gifts were unpredictable, but they had always proven true in the past. And whether they knew or not, she needed to give them formal notice so that the three-day ritual of burial, investiture, and appointment of a new apprentice could begin.

"Are you ready to accept your role?" Garlin Abraham caught Syra's gaze, concern in his dark eyes. He was of the lineage of the Blessed Brandon, so the yearly repainting of the statues in the Hall of Images was his duty, as was creating whatever new inspiration came from his visions.

"I don't think it matters if I'm ready. The gift happens when it happens. We can't control that."

Garlin was only thirty, and it hadn't been long since his own investiture. "Of course. I know that. It was a foolish thing to ask."

"It's all right. It's been a bit of a shock. Even knowing Leda was ill—and that she'd told me when she would die—it felt impossible. It's like when you're little. It seems like it'll be that way forever. Your parents will always be alive and will always care for you. Then one day, you realize that it's all changed."

Bastian Nguyen, the oracle in the lineage of the Blessed Julia, gave her a raised eyebrow. "That is true, but there's also readiness in a practical sense. You have the prayers memorized? You'll need to be able to recite them by heart."

Syra allowed herself a quick frown. "Of course I do. I've had long enough to learn them, haven't I?"

Bastian's lips tightened, but he didn't respond. Syra was

apparently not the only one with some adjustment to do, and she'd always sensed that Bastian didn't like her much. In one step she'd risen from a mere apprentice to being one of the four sacred oracles. The fact that she might have to fight to achieve the level of respect the others got automatically had never crossed her mind.

She could just barely recall the grumbling when she was appointed apprentice, at age fourteen. She was naïve enough at the time not to understand it completely. Leda shielded her from the worst of it—the Guardian was a tough-minded and demanding woman, right from the beginning, determined that her apprentice would not have to deal with ignorant bigotry as well as all of the other difficulties that came naturally with the position. But Syra had still been aware, even so.

"Why couldn't she have chosen someone who was one of us?" an old woman said in a loud whisper, at the annual celebration of the Founders' escape from destruction and death, the year after her investiture as apprentice. At the time, Syra thought the old woman didn't know she was there, sitting quietly only two rows back, and could hear everything she said. In the five decades since, she'd become convinced the woman knew perfectly well Syra was within earshot, and didn't care—or, perhaps, was glad for the opportunity to let Syra know what she thought while still giving the impression of a private conversation.

"She's one of us," the old woman's companion said. "Sort of."

The woman made a scoffing noise. "Half. Her mother was an outsider. Pale skin, hair that was nearly white. Abnormal, I call that. Why her father took up with that woman I'll never know. Against all the rules, yet he got away with it somehow."

"The Guardian allowed it." His voice sounded reluctant, almost apologetic, as if he didn't want to be in this conversation but didn't have a graceful way to end it.

Another snort. "Said he foresaw it would be good for Klen. Well, it's fifteen years since, and I don't see any good that's come of it. And now she's not only allowed to be here and take part in what is rightly for true community members, but she's been appointed as apprentice to the most important office in Klen." A pause, then she continued in a sneering tone. "The girl takes after her mother, too. You'd never know she was one of us by looking."

"Hopefully Leda will have a long life as the Guardian. Syra might be nothing more than an apprentice for decades."

"Perhaps she'll die first." The old woman's voice was nearly a snarl. "Then Leda can rectify her mistake and choose someone who is suitable."

Then the recital of the prayers started, and the two fell silent. But Syra never forgot it.

Perhaps she'll die first.

She never told Leda about the overheard conversation, at first out of shame, then because she grew to trust that the Guardian knew what she was doing. If Leda chose her, it was because she foresaw that Syra was the next in the lineage, that it wouldn't matter what the grumblers and bigots thought.

But now, fifty years later, with Leda dead and a three-day mourning period and an investiture ceremony between Syra and becoming the Guardian of the Word in her own right, it was a slap in the face to see the doubt in Bastian Nguyen's eyes, to find that the old prejudice was still there.

And from one of the other oracles, no less.

Syra knew the prayers by heart. All the rituals, orders, legends of the Founders, knowledge stretching back six hundred years. She was fluent in the sacred language, had every pronunciation and inflection so deeply within her that she sometimes dreamed in it. Those dreams were often of an elderly man, tall and thin but vital, who spoke to her in the sacred language as easily as if it were common speech. Through cautious questioning of the other oracles, she was convinced this man was the Blessed Quaice, who had written the language himself six centuries ago. The man in her dream certainly resembled Quaice's statue in the Hall of Images, but there was a big difference between a living man and a wooden statue, however beautifully-made.

The Blessed Quaice—if that was who the dream-man was—reassured her each time that everything was happening as it should. Her self-doubts were nothing to fear. She would prove herself, and the naysayers would have no choice but to accept her.

Of course, Quaice himself had not been not an oracle, however important he was as one of the Founders of Klen. So his words of encouragement might not mean much, might not be any more than her own subconscious engaging in wishful thinking.

Syra sighed. Three days till her investiture as Guardian of the Word. Three days during which she would be going over and over the prayers, making sure to have every word perfect. Perhaps others had the freedom to make the occasional mistake. Even Leda Banfield had sometimes, and had always accepted her own fallibility with a shrug and a smile.

Syra didn't have that latitude.

And before then, she would have to talk to the young man who would be her apprentice. At least there could be no criticism of his appointment, not that Syra had a choice in the matter. The oracular knowledge informed her of who the next apprentice would be, and that was that. But still, it was a relief when she learned his identity.

Unlike her, he was of Klen ancestry through to the bone. Which, she realized, would make his decisions—his life, even—more of a shock to the community. They had expected Syra to do something outlandish, half-outlander that she was, and she had responded by trying to prove herself a woman of Klen every time she had a chance.

Her apprentice?

She smiled.

He would be the opposite. If they blamed her for his heresy and transgressions to come, that'd simply be the way it was. She could no more change that than she could change anything else—past, present, or future.

two

· · ·

Kallian Dorn stood, brushing the dirt from his hands and giving a little smile of satisfaction at the pile of weeds he'd uprooted from the vegetable garden. It was a hot, sunny day, something to be appreciated in this climate where the winters were long and wet, and sometimes the snows reached downward from the mountains to the east and blanketed them in white.

But today was perfect. A perfect day, and his chores were done, leaving him the rest of the afternoon free. He grabbed his shirt from where he'd hung it on the fence, but didn't bother putting it back on.

Every moment of sun on bare skin was to be relished.

First he'd go for a swim, then do some exploring. There was a little lake only a quarter of a mile from the settlement, but still within the boundary fences. It was a beautiful spot, the water limpid and cool, and usually there were at least a few other swimmers. But today, despite the excellent weather, it was deserted.

He stripped, tossing his clothes under a nearby tree, and walked to the edge, out on a rock that projected just beyond where the deep water began. Without hesitation, he dove in, leaving a trail of silver bubbles in his wake.

The feeling of the water sliding past his body, washing away the sweat and the garden dirt, was delicious. He only got out when he started to feel chilled. The lake never really got warm, even in blistering hot weather, and he could only swim comfortably for twenty minutes or so before starting to shiver. He pulled himself out onto the rock, and for a while just sat with his eyes closed, toes just barely touching the water's surface, letting himself dry off in the sunshine.

After a while he stood, stretched, and shading his eyes with his hand, looked around. Still no one else there. Excellent. It wasn't that he minded if someone saw him naked—it would be far from the first time that had happened—but Kallian was an introvert by nature, happiest when left alone with his own thoughts. He recognized that in his nineteen years he'd made no real friends, not in the deepest sense of the word. He was liked by just about everyone, and really understood by absolutely no one, not even his parents. He didn't set out to be secretive. It came naturally, and he had no real inclination to share his thoughts, his fears, and his loves with anyone else. He had a superstitious concern that to give voice to what was in his mind would be to damage it beyond repair, to give someone else part ownership over his soul.

There was no doubt he sometimes felt lonely, and ever since he was little a part of him had wished there was someone he could be close to. Ever since puberty hit him like a sledgehammer about five years earlier, there was the addition of the physical craving, something that sometimes swamped his mind and made thinking nearly impossible.

But he felt no particular attraction to any of the girls in the settlement, so he took care of that need by himself, too.

He dressed slowly, easing his muscular frame into clothes that were a bit too small for him. He'd grown another inch and a half in the previous year, but he hadn't wanted to trouble his parents with a request for new clothes, so he made do with what he had.

Where to now? He knew where his feet would take him unless he deliberately steered them somewhere else. Uphill, around east of the lake and into the trees. Another quarter of a mile to the double line of fences that surrounded the entirety of the settlement of Klen.

The fences that demarcated where Klen ended, and the wilderness began.

They'd first been built something like six hundred years earlier, when the plague came. After the disastrous earthquake and flood that precipitated the founding of Klen, the ragged remnants huddled together to survive, and for a while, welcomed in other stragglers. But then the sweating sickness came—a disease that took its victims from healthy and full of life, through fever and delirium and copious, drenching sweats, to coma and death in a space of forty-eight hours. The four oracles at the time declared that Klen needed to be shut off, that the contagion had come in from outside, and that once it ran its course within the settlement, the remainder would be all right as long as no one new came in, carrying the plague back in from elsewhere.

It worked. Over half the settlement's population died of the sweating sickness by the time the epidemic faded, but with the fence, there was no second wave. No one was allowed to come in from outside. No one left. After a time, a second ring of fences was built, about a hundred feet inside the first, creating a strip of land in a rough circle where no one, insider or outsider, set foot. The fences were made of wood wrapped with barbed wire—the latter made from the long cables, strung from wooden poles, that had been everywhere in the former world—but it still took three violent skirmishes with outsiders attempting to get in to dissuade them from trying.

After that, Klen had been an entirely self-contained community.

Well, almost entirely. There'd been one person who had made it in, and for some reason been allowed to stay. She'd been emaciated and covered with cuts and scratches, but somehow had gotten through both the outer and the inner fences without being seen, only to collapse unconscious a few hundred feet from the nearest house. This had all happened long before Kallian was born, but he'd heard the story many times. Thea Cheraskin's arrival had sent shock waves through the settlement, but after she found support from all four oracles, the community had reluctantly let her stay. When she arrived, she'd spoken a strange mix of common speech and words from the sacred language, laced with utterances that appeared to come from neither. She was grateful to be allowed to remain, and in her halting tongue told them she would be killed if they sent her away.

She showed herself eager to learn the ways of Klen, leaving behind what she'd known and seemingly never looking back. She'd partnered with a young man named Davran Keene, and they'd had one child, Syra. Thea hadn't lived long afterward, dying of some wasting disease only eight months after her daughter's birth. But—so Kallian had been told—Syra Cheraskin was so much like her mother in both appearance and personality that it seemed she lived on. Odd-looking woman, her pale skin, light blue eyes, and blonde hair standing out in a community where just about everyone had dusky skin, brown eyes, and dark hair.

But Kallian saw the attraction, imagining what Syra had looked like when she was young. She didn't have a partner. She'd had one when she was younger, but after her death Syra had never partnered again. Even at sixty-five, she still had an exotic beauty. Perhaps where her mother came from, there'd been more light-skinned, light-haired people. Here, her appearance was fascinatingly unique.

A half-hour's leisurely walk through the woods brought Kallian to the first fence. He looked across the gap, and in the shadow of the trees could only dimly glimpse the line of the outer boundary. He'd been drawn to the edge since he was a child, and he peered into the wilderness beyond with longing.

"There's nothing out there besides wild animals, starvation, and the Border Runners," his mother told him, when he was about ten and had spent all day daydreaming while looking across the no-man's-land between the fences. "Everything you need is here. Step outside, you wouldn't last long. None of us would."

That, of course, simply increased the attraction. Most of the time he only saw trees, sometimes the occasional squirrel or deer. But once—only once—he'd caught a glimpse of one of the Border Runners. The boy looked to be about Kallian's age—fifteen, at the time. He was naked except for a loin cloth, carrying a wooden spear tipped with a sharpened stone arrowhead. The boy's face was wild, feral, and when he caught sight of Kallian he'd run to the fence, making noises in a guttural language of some sort. Kallian didn't understand a single word. His heart pounding, he backed away from the fence. There was no way the boy could have hit him with the spear from that distance, but the grinning, savage face was terrifying.

Moments later, the Runner had disappeared into the shadows. He'd made no attempt to get across the fence, fortunately. Perhaps the Runners had taboos about crossing as well. But whatever the reason, Kallian had never seen the boy since—nor anyone else outside the perimeter, for that matter. As far as he could see, it might have been mile after mile of trackless forest, with no inhabitants except for one half-naked boy with a spear, and the legends of the fierce tribes of Border Runners nothing more than that—a legend.

Today, all was quiet. He peered into the darkness, between the trunks of massive firs. He brushed a still-damp lock of hair out of his eyes, then stepped forward till he was almost touching the inner fence.

Part of his fascination with the outside came from the tales his father had told him when he was little—that long ago, before the Flight and the arrival of the Founders and their followers in Klen, there had been a massive civilization capable of all sorts of incredible things. Vehicles that zoomed along the roads, faster than the wind, or actually flew through the air. Devices that gave them the ability to communicate instantly with anyone else in the world, no matter how far away. Magical medicines that could cure any disease, and gave them lifespans of centuries or longer. But it had all collapsed—brought down by evil men and women led by She of the Unspeakable Name—a proud civilization left in rubble. The wires of the fences, his father had told him, had once stretched from poles that lined every road, and those had been how the communication devices connected to each other over long distances. But how they might have worked, no one now knew. The rumor was that west of Klen, perhaps a day's walk, there was the ruin of one of the great cities of the former world, now abandoned, a wasteland of fallen stonework that had been swallowed up by forest. It was haunted, the legends said, stalked by the specters of the thousands of people who had drowned when the seas rose up to defeat the evil and let the Founders escape.

But neither Kallian's father, nor anyone else in Klen, had ever seen it.

His musings were interrupted by a soft voice.

"I'm sorry to disturb you… they said you might be here."

Kallian turned. There was a girl standing a few feet away, looking at him with a wistful expression in her brown eyes. Lexa Sahin. He'd grown up with Lexa. She was only a year younger than him, and only recently had he become uncomfortable around her. She was attracted to him—every word, every glance told him that much—but he couldn't reciprocate.

She was pretty, kind, and gentle, but he felt none of the draw to her that she evidently felt toward him.

The thought crossed his mind that she probably would have been delighted if he'd responded by stepping forward and kissing her. Kallian had a normal sex drive for a nineteen-year-old male, but for some reason, it felt completely wrong to pursue her.

Or, more accurately, to encourage her to pursue him. Not that she'd need much encouragement.

"Hi," he said, trying for a smile and mostly succeeding.

"I came to find you because… you're needed back in the village. Now. Syra sent me to find you."

Syra? Why on earth would she care where he was? In his memory, the odd, distant apprentice to the Guardian of the Word had never so much as spoken directly to him. She was cool, cautious, and reserved with everyone, of course, seldom speaking unless spoken to, apparently content with her role as an apprentice to the strong, capable, outspoken Leda Banfield.

"What does she want?" Kallian asked.

"She didn't say. Only that you should come quickly." Lexa paused. "I'm sorry, I wish I could tell you more."

"That's all right. I'm sure she'll explain once I get there." Kallian walked away in the direction of the village. The thought crossed his mind that his words to Lexa had been brusque, almost rude, and he added as an afterthought, "Thank you for bringing me the message."

"It's no problem," Lexa said, following him.

They circled past the lake where he'd gone swimming, and he was glad that she hadn't happened upon him while he was naked. Things were awkward enough.

As soon as he got near the village, he knew something important had happened. People were walking with purposeful strides and serious expressions. They spoke in hushed tones. He saw a man comforting his wife, who was crying.

"What's going on?" Kallian said to Lexa, half pivoting toward her.

She opened her mouth to speak, but before she could answer, someone spoke.

"Kallian. Good. You need to come with me. Thank you, Lexa."

It was obviously a dismissal, and Lexa turned away, disappointment in her face. Syra Cheraskin was approaching him, and to his surprise, she held out one hand for him to take.

Mutely, he accepted, then went with her toward the Hall of Images. He rarely went inside there except on days of observance. Honestly, the silent, brooding statues had scared him since he was a child. Even the smiling figure of Blessed Mary of the Bridge seemed uncanny. Her outstretched arm—the exact gesture Syra had just used—said, "Take my hand… but if you do, you won't ever be able to let go."

He looked downward at his own powerful hand, clasped in Syra's smaller and more delicate one, and had the sudden realization that any opportunity to avoid that fate had passed as soon as they'd clasped. Somehow, Syra *was* Blessed Mary of the Bridge, no longer simply an apprentice of her lineage… and he was about to be swept away.

They entered the Hall of Images. Three of the oracles were seated in chairs that faced the statues of the Founders. One chair was empty.

He looked up into Syra's face, their eyes connecting for the first time. In them he saw understanding, compassion… and pity.

"Here he is," she said to the other oracles, who nodded solemnly.

"But what…" he began, then faltered.

"The Guardian of the Word is dead. I will succeed to her

place as the oracle in the lineage of the Blessed Mary. And you… you are to be my apprentice."

Whatever he'd expected her to say, it wasn't that.

He'd heard that Leda Banfield was about to die. Everyone in Klen knew that, although the ramifications hadn't been apparent to him. The idea that he'd become the new apprentice to the Guardian had not entered his wildest imaginings.

"I'm not…" He stopped, swallowed. "I'm not an oracle."

Syra gave him a quick smile, there and gone in an instant. "Not yet."

"But I don't have any skill at—" he gestured around him —"all this."

"Not yet," Syra said again.

"But why me?"

"There's no real answer to that question." Syra sat in the empty seat, and even she looked a bit uncomfortable, as if she were taking a liberty she should not. "Or, if there is an answer, it's beyond our knowing. But as far as your being the apprentice, that is certain. Regardless what doubts you might have about your fitness." Another smile. "Believe me, I've had fifty years of those doubts about myself. You are hardly alone in feeling inadequate."

"We all felt that way at first," said Garlin Abraham, oracle of the lineage of the Blessed Brandon. "It's a deep commitment. One that lasts a lifetime."

"What if I refuse?"

The words came out before he could stop them. He didn't want to be an oracle, or even an apprentice. He wanted things to be as they had been. Caring for the vegetable gardens, spending his time daydreaming and wandering and skinny-dipping in the lake. No way did he want that kind of responsibility, even if he felt worthy of it, which he didn't.

He expected Syra, or the other oracles, to respond sternly. To his surprise, they laughed, not in mockery but in understanding.

"It's not that you *couldn't* refuse, Kallian," Syra said, her voice gentle. "It's just that you *don't*."

"You know what I'll do?"

She nodded.

"So you're forcing me to become the apprentice." A sense of desperation rose in him, a desire to flee, not just from this shadowed room with its eerie statues, but from Klen itself. Climb the fences, escape alone into the wilderness beyond. Taking his chances with what lay out there seemed infinitely preferable to this. "If you know what I'll do, isn't that the same thing as my having no choice?"

"I know it seems that way. But witnessing a man act, and forcing him to act, aren't the same thing. The distinction might seem unimportant. Either way, the action is accomplished. But to the man himself, there is an enormous difference. All the difference in the world."

three

. . .

T he night after Syra's investiture as the Guardian of the Word, she lay in bed, sleepless, pondering the day's events.

It had all gone off without a stumble. Despite her nerves, she recited the prayers in the sacred language, performed the rituals flawlessly, and when she sat in the Guardian's chair in the Hall of Images—still feeling like a usurper—she looked out at the people in the room, and to her surprise saw that most were smiling.

Maybe she wasn't as much of an outsider as she'd thought.

Kallian, though, had looked downright overwhelmed at this sudden change in his life, as if he expected the entire scene to dissolve like a dream upon waking. He went through the whole ceremony with wide and unbelieving eyes, starting with the prayers for the peaceful repose of Leda Banfield, through Syra's receiving the blessing and anointment with holy oil from the other Oracles, to the announcement of his being chosen as apprentice and his own blessing and anointment. Kallian's parents were glowing with pride. Kallian himself looked as if he were a hair's breadth from running out of the room and away from Klen and never looking back.

But he didn't. Afterward, as he went back home to gather his belongings to move permanently into the home of the Guardian, he seemed more resigned than afraid. By the time he returned, carrying two satchels containing everything he owned, he appeared to be so exhausted that Syra showed him to his quarters, told him to settle in and sleep well, and left him to his own thoughts.

Now, she lay there considering how best to put the young man at his ease. She recalled Leda doing the same thing for her, fifty years ago, but honestly, the reassurances hadn't helped much. It took the distraction of getting down to the real work of learning everything the Guardian needed to know before Syra felt herself relaxing into the role.

He would, as well. It would take time. But he would be a fine apprentice, and a powerful and wise Guardian once Syra was gone.

Now, the task was getting him to believe that.

As winter closed in on the settlement, the harvest brought in, and preparations made for the cold, rainy season, Kallian proved himself to be a hard worker and a diligent and quick learner. He already knew the rudiments of the sacred language, so he wasn't starting from nothing, in that regard at least. Who he'd learned it from, she had no idea. A lot of people in Klen knew a smattering of it, so he could have picked it up anywhere. He showed a real talent at memorizing the legends and tales of the Founders, the prayers and rituals, and the history of Klen. He was especially curious about what lay outside the boundary of the settlement, even though there was very little she, or anyone else in Klen, could tell him.

"Who are the Border Runners?" he asked her over their evening meal, on a chilly night just past the Winter Solstice, as the rain slashed against the roof and the wind moaned in the branches of the fir trees.

Syra frowned thoughtfully. "We have no real information about them. Nothing, at least, that is at all certain."

"Who do you think they are?"

"My belief is that they're the descendants of people who lived here before the flood that drove our ancestors to this place. Nowhere does it say that our forebears found this land unoccupied. The Runners may be the children's children's children of the people who once lived here."

"So the Founders just… took the land from them?"

She paused to take another bite of food and to ponder how to answer this. Criticizing any of the Founders' acts was considered close to sacrilege, and she had no wish to pass on her own doubts to her young apprentice, who had enough to worry about.

"No one knows," she finally said. "It may be that the land was empty, and the Border Runners came in later, and from elsewhere. It may be that for a time our ancestors and the ancestors of the Runners shared the land, and only parted ways later, perhaps when the Great Plague struck. It may be that the Founders fought for this land, and defeated its original owners. The truth is, it is not recorded in any of the legends or histories, so we don't know and have no way of knowing."

He digested this in silence.

"Why are you so curious about the Runners?"

He looked up at her, his brown eyes filled with a strange longing. "I saw one, once. I was near the fence, and I saw one. A boy, who shouted at me in some odd language and shook a spear in my direction, then disappeared into the trees. Ever since, I've wondered about who they are."

"They're not evil spirits or demons, although you'll hear

some people talk like that. They're humans just like you and me. I'm not saying they aren't hostile. My guess is if you were to leave the boundary fences and get captured, they wouldn't treat you kindly. Whatever the truth of how they, and we, got here, there's no doubt they hold us in no high regard. I'm glad you didn't let your curiosity lead you to find a way through the fences."

Kallian nodded. "I've heard your mother was a Runner."

Ah, so that was it. It was bound to come up sooner or later. "I don't know, Kallian, and that's the truth."

"You've said that a lot this evening."

Syra laughed. "That's part of being the Guardian of the Word. It's as important to be honest about what you don't know as it is to remember what you do know. My mother was from outside, there's no doubting that. Whether she was a Runner, or from somewhere else, I never found out. She died when I was very little. I've heard rumors that several days' march south of here there are other settlements, perhaps even territories many times larger than Klen, with kings who live in great stone palaces, built from the wreckage of the former age. Or maybe those are just wild tales with no truth to them. When I was younger I used to fantasize that my mother was a princess who had run away from one of the kingdoms in the south, and found her way here."

"But you don't know."

She shook her head. "No. As a young woman, those ideas seemed very real to me, but with time I've come to believe they are probably just wild imaginings."

"You do look different than other people in Klen."

"You think I don't know that?" She immediately regretted her sharp tone, but Kallian shrugged, and took another bite of food.

"I figured you did. Do people treat you badly because of it?"

Something about his openness was disarming, and she

forced herself to relax. There was no need to be on guard around this young man, but old habits were hard to break.

"Sometimes, yes. Well, *treated badly* may be an overstatement. I certainly didn't get the automatic trust I would have gotten if I had your brown hair, brown eyes, and darker skin. But despite looking different, I became the Guardian, so that has to count for something."

"You probably didn't have a choice in the matter, any more than I did."

Syra stared at him for a moment, then began to laugh. "No, you're right. Choice really didn't come into it. But all told, my life has been good. I am an integral part of the community, and most people rely on me to keep the knowledge of Klen safe. I had a lover who was dear to me, and even if she was taken far sooner than I wanted, love can't be measured by a duration of years. I've been lucky."

"Will I be as well?"

"You will walk the road that lies before your feet, the same as all of us. And good or bad, when you get to the end of it you will look back and see that you couldn't have taken any other path."

Winter passed, and spring crept in on stealthy feet. The days lengthened, the air warmed little by little. Then, as if some signal had been given, plants leafed out, flowers opened, and the air was filled with bird song.

Syra watched her apprentice from the front porch of the Guardian's house. He was hoeing up the stubble of the rye they'd sown over the fallow vegetable garden to keep the winter rains from eroding the soil, all the time singing softly to himself, seemingly unaware of her presence. He never balked at a single chore he was given.

How different she'd been in her early years as apprentice

—always trying to speed through the tasks she was given, whether they were physical chores or mental ones, so she could have more time free to spend with the friend who would one day become her partner. Leda Banfield had to chide her regularly that her first duty was to the collected knowledge of the settlement. She was no longer her own person, and never would be again. It wasn't that she was prevented from being happy, but that her happiness came second to her role as apprentice.

Kallian was different. Everything was met with placid acceptance. The physical chores delighted him, even tedious and tiring ones like hauling water from the nearby stream. She found herself piling on the work just to see when he would finally object or refuse outright, but he never did.

And he didn't seem to have any need of companionship with young people of his own age. He was friendly to everyone but close to nobody, one of those rare people who really are happiest when left to themselves.

She smiled to herself. That was an outlook on life that worked fine—until it didn't anymore. She just hoped that when changes came, as they certainly would, he would have the courage to face them.

It was shortly after the equinox that Syra received the summons. She knew it was coming, of course, but these things had to play out in their own way. Anticipating them accomplished nothing.

A young woman named Lexa delivered it. She told Kallian, who was out in the garden, and Kallian relayed it to Syra. Lexa could have come straight to her, of course, but used it as an opportunity to talk to the handsome young apprentice.

Another thing that would play out in its own way.

She got up from the chair where she'd been sitting, sorting through squash seeds from the previous year's harvest and throwing away any that were shriveled or had been nibbled by mice, when Kallian came indoors.

"The other oracles need you,." His voice was tinged with worry. "I don't know what it's about."

Syra nodded, and brushed her hands on the cloth of her skirt. "You needn't be concerned. It's nothing dire." She gave him what she hoped was a reassuring smile, and left the house for the Hall of Images where they were waiting for her.

All three turned serious faces toward her as she came into the shadowed room, lit only by the flames in the brazier. Garlin Abraham, of Brandon's line. Bastian Nguyen, of Julia's. Elen Alleman, of Perry's. Since Syra's investiture, all three had accepted her place as Guardian of the Word and oracle in Mary's line, but she still got the sense they didn't entirely trust her. Garlin accepted her the most, and Bastian the least—but it had been months since her investiture, and whenever there was a conflict, it usually devolved into three against one.

Which became apparent with the first words spoken.

"Why didn't you tell us what your apprentice is planning?" Bastian scowled at her. "You must have known it couldn't remain a secret."

"Of course I knew."

"Then why didn't you tell us?"

"Two reasons. First, it wasn't time. Kallian himself doesn't know yet, so it wasn't my place to usurp his right to direct his own future. Second, I knew you'd find out on your own in due time."

Bastian gave a harsh sigh. "Kallian Dorn gave up the right to direct his own future when he accepted the role of apprentice. He belongs to the community, not himself."

"And if what he is planning is in the best interest of the community?"

Bastian's lips tightened, but he didn't respond.

"Syra, why don't you tell us what you know?" Garlin said. "Bastian learned about it through his own oracular voice, but there was not much in the way of details. Neither Elen nor I have heard a word of it. But whether you were right or wrong not to tell us yourself, surely you must agree—now that we know, this is too big to keep to yourself."

Syra nodded, trying to compose her thoughts. "I will tell you what I can."

"No," Bastian snapped. "Enough of the secrecy. Tell us all of it."

"I can only tell you what I know myself," Syra fired back. "Unless you want me to give you a plausible lie just to satisfy your curiosity."

Syra had so seldom raised her voice that the other three oracles didn't respond, merely looked at her in some amazement.

"My apologies," she went on, in a calmer voice. "That was poorly spoken. I know you have no wish for me to tell you anything but the truth."

Bastian gave her a stiff nod, and she continued.

"Very well. This summer, shortly before the solstice, Kallian will leave the settlement of Klen. It will come about because of finding someone who is lost, and trying to right a very old wrong. He will go south, past the ruins of the ancient city. Along the way, there will be hardship and pain… and loss. But eventually he will find there, far south of the ruined city, a settlement, much larger than Klen. When he arrives Kallian will risk his life to protect people who otherwise would die horrible deaths. He will succeed that far. After that…"

"After that?" Bastian said.

"After that, I don't know. After that, I see nothing at all."

Elen, a slender, gray-haired woman only a few years

younger than Syra, said in a hesitant voice, "You do know what that is likely to mean."

"Of course I do."

"And he is prepared to face whatever comes to accomplish this… task? Whatever it is?" She paused. "As are you?"

"It will happen, whether we are prepared or not. But as far as that goes, yes, I know what I have to do, which is to give Kallian as much help as I can provide."

"Toward what end?" Bastian at least was keeping his temper in check, but the question was still tinged with hostility.

"Toward whatever end must be. And I'm not simply being vague or stubborn. It's just that I don't know." She took a deep breath. "You mustn't tell Kallian about this. Not a word. I see pieces of the future, as the three of you do. I once thought of it as a gift, but truly, it is a burden. Some might even call it a curse. He will come into his place as an oracle after me when the time is right, and at that point he will have to accustom himself to bearing that burden. Until then, it's better that he not know what his future holds."

Bastian gave her a grudging nod. "Of course. We only share what we learn as oracles with the people who need to know. And only when they need to know it."

Syra gave him a faint smile. "Which, Bastian, was exactly what I was doing."

He opened his mouth to speak, then closed it again, and to her amazement he chuckled. "Very well. You've made your point. But I wish you trusted us fully."

Her gaze met his without flinching. "When you trust me fully, I will certainly reciprocate."

four

. . .

K allian felt growing restiveness in his heart and mind as spring drifted toward summer. He put as much of himself into his chores and the tasks of learning the collected knowledge of the community as he had before, but over and over he had to drag his mind back from wandering and stop his body from squirming nervously. He was happiest when he had physical work to do. Perhaps it wasn't interesting, but it burned off some of the jittery energy welling up within him that kept him from sleep, sometimes far past midnight.

Over and over he was drawn to the lake where he'd liked to swim, and to the section of the boundary fences only a short walk beyond it. Now that the weather was warming, he sometimes saw people swimming—today, three boys only a couple of years younger than he was, naked and shivering but laughing as they splashed and wrestled in the shallows. He had no desire to join them. His position as apprentice to the Guardian had simultaneously raised him above the people he had once known, and set him apart from them. The thought made him a little sad. He'd always been quiet and introverted, but there was a difference between solitude being by choice, and it being because everyone suddenly saw you as a different person.

He passed the lake, leaving the noise and laughter of the swimmers behind, and walked deeper into the forest. The shadows of ancient fir trees made the trail as dark as twilight, and even the usual noises of birds and small mammals were hushed. There had been clouds on the horizon that morning —rain coming in—and perhaps that was why the whole place felt like it was holding its breath.

He approached the first line of the fence, walking as silently as he could for no very obvious reason. A light breeze ruffled his hair, still carrying the cool moisture of the spring they'd just left behind. The barbed wire line was hard to see in the dim light. An unwary walker might run right into it, five dark strands spaced close enough that crawling through would be difficult, the top one at shoulder height. Each was laden with twisted spikes ready to catch clothing and tear skin.

He looked beyond the inner fence line across the no-man's land to the outer fence, wondering as he had done since he was a child what lay outside its boundary, simultaneously questioning why even now, as a young adult, he was still drawn to the place.

That was when he saw something huddled on the ground near the outer fence.

He moved as close as he could to the inner boundary line, squinting into the dimness. The breadth of the no-man's land had been deliberately chosen to exceed the reach of an easy bowshot or spear-throw. The distance made whatever it was even more uncertain. It was of no obviously recognizable shape—mostly white or gray, a crumpled, irregular blob that certainly hadn't been there the last time.

He stared at it, frowning, for several minutes.

Then it moved.

Kallian startled and stumbled backward, even though the

thing was far away and there were two lines of fences between him and it. Recovering his composure, he moved forward again, and this time his squinting eyes were able to resolve what it was.

It was a child.

As he watched, the child raised its head, moved it a little from side to side, then it settled back into immobility. The motion was slow, cautious, weary, the movement of someone nearing the end of their strength.

"Hey!" he called across the space in between, immediately questioning whether it was prudent.

The child's body jerked and its head came up again. He could just barely make out its features. Its posture was once again still, but this was the stillness of terror. Frozen panic radiated from it, evident even at this distance.

"Do you need help?"

Stupid question. A lone child collapsed on the boundary line? Of course it needed help.

He carefully began to maneuver his way through the inner fence. The wires were taut, and the barbs plucked at his clothes. One caught in a lock of his curly hair, but he was able to free himself. Finally he was on the other side, and he stood, brushing the debris off.

Kallian was now farther away from his birthplace than he had ever been.

He looked around. Somehow, he had the expectation that it would feel different, that the gravitas of his moving beyond the boundary that had been the perimeter of his entire life would express itself in mysteries and portents, promises of excitement and adventure, signs of danger. But everything looked the same on the other side of the fence. Fir trees, scrubby undergrowth that soon would be laden with sweet huckleberries, springy leaf litter underfoot from the needle-fall of uncounted years. Even so, he still couldn't shake the feeling of moving outside the walls of safety that surrounded

Klen, leaving behind the security he'd known for twenty years.

And once you did that, anything could happen.

He cautiously walked forward toward the child, who had again laid its head down. As he got closer, he saw that it was a little girl, perhaps six or seven years old, with tangled and dirty blonde hair, wearing a filthy and torn dress. It took him only five minutes to cross. He'd always seen the boundary as more substantial, but now he realized that it was only a thin strip of land forming the edge of his known world.

Anyone sufficiently motivated could cross it easily. Maybe the threat of the Border Runners wasn't as dire as it had always seemed.

But that would be something to think about later.

He came up to the outside fence and knelt only a few feet away from where the girl lay.

"Hi," he said, in as gentle a tone as he could manage. "I'm not going to hurt you."

The girl startled, her eyes wide and terrified, and she made a groaning, half-feral noise and tried to stand. Her leg buckled under her and she cried out in pain, but continued to try to edge away from Kallian on all fours, her movements stiff and crab-like.

He held up both hands. "Wait! I'm trying to help you."

The girl moaned again, and stopped crawling, but her eyes were still locked on Kallian's.

"Do you understand what I'm saying?"

Nothing but fear and incomprehension.

He said it again, speaking slowly.

Nothing.

Then an idea occurred to him. He said, in a quiet tone, "*Médvar ké dolar thót.*"

I want to help you.

She stared at him, breathing in sharp, painful-sounding

gasps, and at first he thought she wouldn't answer. Then she said in a thin voice, *"Thó labar, aps slotar két."*

Her pronunciation was odd, a little nasal, but understandable. She was speaking the sacred language.

Please don't hurt me.

He shook his head, and told her again he wanted to help her, then said she needed to cross through the fence so he could get her to safety. All that came back was puzzlement. He wondered about his own use of the language—he'd only been working at learning it for a year—perhaps he hadn't used the right words. Or perhaps, where this girl came from, they spoke it differently.

But figuring that out could come later. All of a sudden, Kallian got the impression of being watched. He looked past the girl, scanning for movement among the tree trunks, and saw nothing. The hairs on the back of his neck prickled.

He reached out one hand. *"Thó lóga."*

Come.

That much she understood. After a moment's teetering indecision, she lurched forward and grabbed his hand. He pulled up on the wire of the fence to give her as much space to squeeze through as possible, but even so, one of the barbs caught the back of her dress and tore a great rent in it.

She didn't seem to notice.

Once through, she tried to stand, and failed again, falling into Kallian's arms. He picked her up. She felt like she weighed almost nothing. How long had she been alone and starving in the forest? Back to the inner fence, another struggle with getting them both through without being gouged or scratched.

He picked her up again, and took off for the settlement at a jog.

Syra looked up when he entered the house bearing his burden. There was no surprise in her eyes, not even a quick eyebrow raise.

"Help her into the chair," she said, gesturing. "I'll get a blanket."

Of course she'd known. She'd seen it happen. Not for the first time, he wondered how on earth he was going to stand knowing his own future, and the futures of everyone around him, when he succeeded to the Guardianship. He didn't like uncertainty, had often thought he'd like to know how this or that would turn out, but the idea of seeing *everything* before it happened was nothing less than terrifying.

As Syra returned with a woolen blanket, he said, "She seems only to speak the sacred language."

Syra nodded, and tucked the blanket around the girl's thin frame. "What is your name?" she asked gently, switching over from common speech fluidly.

The girl stared at her, her eyes huge. "Lanya," she whispered.

"Where have you come from?"

No response except for perplexity.

"Did you run away alone, Lanya? Or were you traveling with others?"

Her mouth quivered, and her eyes filled with tears. She was completely silent as she cried.

"Never mind," she whispered, and stroked her hair. The first touch made her flinch, but then she leaned into the caress. How long had it been since anyone had touched her in love and affection? "We can talk later. Kallian, will you get her food and water? Small amounts of both, and for the food, something easy on the stomach. Cut up an apple. If she keeps that down, we can get her something more substantial."

He went into the kitchen, pared and cut up an apple into chunks, and filled a cup with water from the bucket he had brought in early that morning. When he returned to the sitting room, Syra still knelt on the floor, and was holding Lanya's hand.

"Thank you." Syra took the bowl and cup. "Lanya, here is some food and water. I know you're hungry and thirsty, but you must eat and drink slowly or it might give you a stomach ache. We have plenty more for you if you want it, so you needn't fear this will be your only meal. Do you understand?"

The girl nodded, then reached out timidly for the cup.

Minutes later, the cup and bowl were empty, and that little bit of comfort eased her enough that exhaustion over-whelmed her. Her eyes were drooping, but she kept startling, trying desperately not to sleep.

"Don't be afraid," Syra said. "You're safe here. You can sleep as long as you want. When you wake, you can have more food and water. No one here will harm you, I promise."

By the time she finished speaking, Lanya was already asleep.

Syra stood quietly, and motioned for Kallian to follow her out onto the front porch.

"Where did she come from?" Kallian said in a near-whisper.

"Outside," Syra responded.

"I know that. I found her on the other side of the outer perimeter fence." He frowned. "Don't you already know all about her?"

She gave him a quick smile, there and gone in a second. "Some, yes. No one ever knows all about anyone."

"Can you tell me?"

"I'll let Lanya do that. Which she will. One thing I've learned as Guardian is that people still have the right to tell their own stories in their own time."

"Can you at least tell me how she comes to speak our sacred language?"

Syra looked off into the distance, her expression thoughtful. "She lived for a time with the Border Runners. That's their speech."

Kallian goggled at her. "The Runners speak our sacred language?"

"Well, it's not *our* language, or at least, we can't claim that it's ours alone. The Blessed Quaice brought it to our ancestors, but remember that before the plague struck, we were a much larger community and had no boundary fences to keep us in and others out. We know some people in Klen left, for a variety of reasons, and I believe that either they met the ancestors of the Runners and taught them the sacred language, or perhaps the group that left *were* the Runners' ancestors. In any case, yes, the Runners speak Kalila."

"You said your mother arrived knowing some of the sacred language, too."

She nodded. "That is what I've been told, but I don't know how she learned it. My belief is that she lived for a time with the Runners, just as this girl did, and learned some of it from them. When she got here, she didn't know which language to speak, nor how much to trust the people in the community. When you're in a dangerous situation, sometimes it pays to pretend to less knowledge than you actually have."

"But why…"

Syra shook her head, and he closed his mouth.

"As I said, Lanya will explain once she's rested and no longer starving. Wait for her to tell us."

Kallian nodded.

"Until then, busy yourself in the garden. This time of year, there are always weeds to pull, and there may still be some of the pea vines that have pods." She smiled. "Patience. It's not easy, but it's an important skill to cultivate."

This was obviously a dismissal, and he descended the two steps down into the front yard, then crossed it toward the huge vegetable garden. His mood had turned sullen, something not usual for him.

It was easy enough for Syra to tell him to practice patience. She already knew all the answers. The physical and mental restlessness he'd been feeling for months didn't make it any easier. He wanted to *do* something, find something out, not cool his heels in the garden. After all, he was the one who'd rescued the girl. Surely he had a right to know whatever Syra could tell him about her.

Ordinarily, he enjoyed the physical labor of gardening, but today, every tenacious weed and stone in the soil irritated him further. The afternoon dragged by, and by dinnertime, he had worked himself into a genuinely foul mood.

He came inside after going to the creek for a quick wash-up, and found Lanya sitting at the table, Syra across from her. The girl was eating a bowl of oatmeal. She startled at the noise of the door opening, but seemed to relax when she saw it was him.

"How is she?" Kallian asked in common speech, trying to keep the annoyance out of his voice.

Syra responded in Kalila. "Lanya will be fine. A few days of rest and good food is all she needs."

Lanya looked from one of them to the other, and said nothing.

Kallian sat down, pushing back his irritation and mostly succeeding. "Hi," he said to her, switching over to the sacred language, his lack of knowledge making his speech slow and halting. "I'm Kallian. I'm the one who found you in the woods."

"I know."

"Where did you come from?"

She shrugged and took another mouthful of oatmeal.

"How did you find your way here?"

"I ran away. They left me in the house by myself, and when I saw that no one was looking, I ran." Her speech had an odd accent, and one or two words were unfamiliar, but he understood her with little difficulty.

"Who?"

Shrug. "The people."

"Your family?"

This got a quick furrowing of her brow. "No. The people we were with."

"The Runners?"

A frown of incomprehension.

"Even if that's who she was with," Syra said, "I doubt that's what they call themselves. She might not know the name."

Kallian nodded. "But that's not where you came from. Before."

"No. My mother told me about it. She and my father and I came from a long way. I don't remember it. I was too little. But she said it was far away, south of where the people lived, by the water. Salty water, she said, too salty to drink. They were in danger so they ran, and we got captured by the people. They killed my father, and my mother and I lived with them."

"Why did your parents leave where they were and go out into the forest?"

"My mother said that if we returned, we'd be killed. So living with the people was bad, but not as bad as going back." She took another bite and chewed, her face thoughtful. "My mother became the wife of the leader. She was going to have a baby, but then when it was her time, something happened. She and the baby both died. It was last winter. Since then, I knew I had to run away. The way the people looked at me was different after my mother died. It scared me."

"So you ran."

She nodded. "But I didn't have any food with me. I had to run when I had the chance, so I didn't have time. And if I'd been wearing a pack, people would have seen me and known I was running away. Without it, I thought that if they caught me, I could tell them I was just playing. But no one caught me."

Kallian wondered if once Lanya's mother died, they didn't have any reason to value her, and might have been just as glad to let her go.

"How long were you in the woods before you got here?"

"I don't know. A few days. I didn't count."

"Thanks for talking to me. I'll let you eat now, and we can talk more later." He switched over to the common speech, and said to Syra, "What else has she told you?"

She smiled. "Honestly, she told you more than she told me."

"Has it occurred to you…" Kallian trailed off, frowning.

"Has what occurred to me?"

"That this is very much like what happened to your mother."

"Of course it's occurred to me. The parallels are obvious."

"Do you think she came from the same people as your mother's family?"

"It's possible, but I don't know how we'd find that out. She said she'd lived with the Runners since she was very young, so she probably doesn't know any of her family other than her mother and father." She took a deep breath. "But it's uncanny, I have to admit. My mother didn't speak much about her past, or at least that's what my father claimed. Perhaps once she was gone, he didn't want to tell her secrets. Or maybe what he knew was painful and he didn't want me to know what my mother had endured. In either case, I don't know." Syra looked at the child, who was obviously listening to their conversation closely—whether with any comprehension was impossible to tell. "There's also the blonde hair."

"It could be common in other places."

"That's true." She paused. "Wouldn't that be a strange thought, that my mother arrives here, and seven decades later, another foundling from the same place ends up on our doorstep."

"Maybe she's a relative of yours."

"I suppose it could be." Switching over to Kalila, she said, "Lanya, do you have a last name?"

She nodded. "Desorla. I'm Lanya Desorla."

"It's a pretty name." Syra's gaze flickered over to her apprentice's.

"Sound familiar?" Kallian asked.

The older woman shook her head. "Not in the slightest."

"At least we found her before she starved."

Syra looked at the girl thoughtfully. "Yes. Now, I just have to convince the other oracles that the right thing to do is let her stay."

five

. . .

Gaining the support of the other three oracles turned out to be easier than Syra had anticipated. Bastian took Syra's side immediately, much to her surprise.

"We can't simply put an orphaned child back outside the perimeter and say, 'Go on your way.' It'd be tantamount to killing her outright."

Elen frowned. "What if she carries disease? That was why the fences went up in the first place. I understand your desire to be kind, but the settlement's safety comes first."

"She isn't ill," Syra said. "Just starved, footsore, and lonely. She didn't bring anything dangerous into Klen."

This wasn't quite true, and the thought flashed across her mind that disease wasn't the only dangerous thing a stranger could bring in.

There are also ideas. Sometimes the most dangerous thing of all.

But she didn't say that. She glanced from one face to the other, and said, "Shall we put it up to a vote?"

"No need, I think," Bastian said. "Elen, do you have serious concerns about letting her stay?"

Elen gave a quick shake of the head. "No. The Guardian

would know if she posed a threat. It's just not a question we've had to face in a very long time."

"Since my mother arrived." Syra knew they were thinking it, may as well have it out in the open.

"Do you think the girl came from the same place?" Garlin asked.

"Kallian wondered the same thing. No way to know, I would guess. Wherever she's from originally, she lived with the Runners for most of her life. She was young enough when she and her parents were captured that she doesn't remember much from before it. Only that her mother told her their original home was a long way away, and they couldn't go back, because they'd be killed." She paused. "Are all in agreement that we should let the girl stay? Does anyone have an objection or concern?"

No one spoke.

"Thank you. She'll stay with Kallian and me for the time being. She seems to have formed a special bond with Kallian. Understandable, since if it hadn't been for him, she'd still be starving in the forest. I'll have him start teaching her the common speech. It won't do if she can only communicate in the sacred language."

Syra asked families who had older daughters if they still had any clothes suitable for children, and found a hand-me-down dress that fit Lanya well. Her old dress was so frayed and torn that it was unsalvageable for anything besides rags for tying up the pole beans and tomatoes. The girl showed remarkable resilience, considering what she'd been through, and although still showed shy around strangers, she followed Kallian around like a puppy.

Good for Lanya, and also good for Kallian. Syra knew that her apprentice was becoming increasingly restive, and his former placid temperament was being roiled by forces he couldn't yet put a name on. A distraction was nice, even if temporary. Having the responsibility of looking after the little girl took his mind off his frustration. He jumped into teaching her common speech with enthusiasm, and spent hours doing his chores while holding objects up, saying their names, and letting Lanya repeat the word.

It was only three weeks after her rescue that when Syra gave her a plate of food for dinner—fish baked in the wood-stoked oven, sliced cucumbers, and crusty bread given to them by a neighbor—the little girl said, haltingly, "Thank you."

Syra beamed at her. "You're welcome, Lanya." She switched over to Kalila. "You're learning fast."

"Kallian is a good teacher."

"I expect he is."

Kallian brought his own plate to the table, and sat down with a smile. "Soon she'll speak the common language better than I do the sacred language."

"Children learn fast. A pity adults lose that facility, but inevitable, I'm afraid."

Dinner proceeded in silence, and it was only after the food was gone that Lanya looked up. She said, "Do you have books?"

Syra looked at Kallian, who shrugged, a mystified expression on his face. The Kalila word Lanya had used for *books* was not unknown to them, but it was mostly used to mean *marks*—like the scratches left on a wooden surface from a carelessly-handled knife.

"What do you mean, Lanya?" Syra said.

"Books." She looked from one to the other. "My mother had some, but I don't know what happened to them. I was learning from her how to read them."

Another odd word choice. *Read.* Kallian looked at Syra in

perplexity, and said in the common speech, "Why would you have to learn how to look closely at something?"

Syra shook her head. "I honestly have no idea." Reverting to Kalila, she said to Lanya, "Tell me more about these books."

"They had stories written in them. Stories from the place my parents came from. My mother said I learned fast, and I'd become a good reader one day if I kept practicing. But she only had four, I think. They weren't in the language the people spoke, but my mother wanted to teach me because it's how they spoke in her home place. I only learned a little, because she said the people would take the books and destroy them if they heard us talking in a language they didn't know."

Syra and Kallian exchanged glances, but let Lanya continue.

"My mother said where she grew up, there were so many books they had entire buildings filled with them. If you wanted to know something, you could find it in there, written down in a book."

Kallian frowned. "They don't have a Guardian? Someone who knows all the history and stories, who keeps them safe?"

"Why would they need one?" She looked as puzzled as Kallian did. "If you write something down, you don't need to remember it."

Syra steered the conversation into trivia after that, but later that evening, after Lanya was asleep, she felt compelled to talk to her apprentice again about the girl's odd question.

"Kallian, what did you think about what Lanya told us?"

His dark eyebrows rose. "Didn't you already know about it?"

"A little. I knew she was going to talk to us about it, but that doesn't mean I can explain what she was referring to."

He absorbed this in silence.

"What it made me wonder is how old these books she was

talking about actually are. Maybe not the ones her mother had, but the ones in the place they came from."

Kallian looked at her with dawning understanding. "Maybe… you're thinking they came from the former world? From the Before Time?"

"I think it's possible. And you see what that means."

"That we might be able to have access to all of the knowledge our ancestors had."

"Perhaps not all. But certainly more than we have. You know the legends, right? What they say our forebears were able to do?"

He nodded. "I thought they were just stories."

"Maybe some of them are. But if there are records that came from the Before Time, we might be able to recapture some of the knowledge that we thought was lost forever."

"I've heard that the people then could cure any disease. They had vehicles that could go over land, water, and even in the air, moving so fast the eye could barely keep up. They had the ability to send their voices over long distances. Their weapons could kill from far away. I've heard they cooked their food without fire, and had machines to keep them cool in the summer and warm in the winter."

She nodded. "I've heard the same. Like you, I don't know how much of it is true, how much exaggeration, and how much flat fabrication. I've often pondered on how we could relearn some of what our ancestors knew, but I always believed that knowledge was lost forever. If what Lanya's mother told her is true…" She held both hands palms-upward.

Kallian gave her a thoughtful look. "But even if we found the books she spoke of, and they did tell of how our forebears lived, how could we understand them? If the people here in Klen ever had that skill, it's been lost for centuries."

Syra smiled. "You forget. We have Lanya."

"Do you think she knows enough?"

"We can find out. We should ask Lanya if she'll teach us how to decipher the books she's spoken of. She said she was on the way to becoming a reader—even with allowances for the fact that she's a child and her mother was no doubt encouraging her, I'll bet she could show us the basics. Certainly more than we know."

"Why do you think our ancestors lost this skill? Did they simply forget about it?"

"It's hard to say. If I had to guess, it probably happened because especially at the beginning, they had the raw demands of survival to deal with. Then the plague came. After all that... well, all it would take is a single generation not being taught for the skill to be gone. Especially if there were no books to keep it in people's minds. That kind of knowledge is remarkably fragile." She met his eyes steadily. "But if even one person still knows, it can be relearned."

He grinned at her. "So I'll go from teacher to pupil."

"Well, so will I. We can study it together."

"But..." He stopped, bit his lip. "What good will it do us to have the knowledge of reading the marks, when we don't have books ourselves?"

"We don't have books *yet*."

"But that would mean..." He gave her an incredulous look. "Are you suggesting what it sounds like?"

"At the moment, I'm not suggesting anything. However, it would be best to prepare for any eventuality. We should certainly have Lanya teach us what she knows, however, and soon. If we wait too long, she may forget enough of her skill that anything she could show us would be incomplete and possibly inaccurate. We may not get any opportunity to use it for years."

"Or perhaps much sooner," Kallian said in a thoughtful voice.

Lanya was delighted by her sudden elevation from student to teacher, and every evening they sat and watched while she drew letters on a flat piece of wood. All they had to write with was a straight, sharpened twig dipped in a mixture of the black soot from the wood stove and a little bit of oil, which worked well enough but was messy and slow. Perhaps they should talk to Garlin Abraham, whose role as oracle in Brandon's line meant he had paints and brushes. Those could be used for writing, if they could convince him to part with some of them.

The first night, she carefully wrote out "L-A-N-Y-A D-E-S-O-R-L-A," and then sounded it out for them.

"My name," she said proudly.

"So each character stands for a particular sound?" Kallian asked.

She nodded, then frowned. "Usually. Sometimes. There are some characters that can make more than one sound, and sometimes they aren't pronounced at all."

"Why? That's an odd way to do it, isn't it?"

Lanya shrugged. "I asked my mother that. She didn't know either. She just said that the rules were complicated, and there were all kinds of exceptions."

"What language was used in writing and reading the books?" Syra asked.

Lanya frowned.

"You said that it wasn't the language we're speaking."

"Oh. No. My mother taught me to sound words out, and then told me what the words mean. She said they were in the language she and my father spoke, before they ran away. She was going to teach me how to read and speak it, but she was only able to teach me a little before she died."

"Is it the same language Kallian is teaching you?"

"I don't know. I don't remember a lot of the words I learned, I'm sorry."

"You needn't apologize. I'm simply curious." She looked

up at Kallian. "Here's another mystery. The Runners speak Kalila, but where Lanya's parents came from, they had another language entirely."

"The common speech?"

"Possibly. The legends say that people everywhere spoke in the common speech in the Before Time. When Blessed Quaice gave our ancestors the sacred language, they learned it and passed it down. It may be that in other places, they only have one way of speaking."

"At least if we were to go there, we might have a way of being understood." Kallian's dark eyes were looking into the middle distance, unfocused, as if his mind were already far away from the little community where he'd spent his entire life. Dreaming of voyages and adventures—and books. Books that could bring back the knowledge of a lost civilization.

<hr>

From words for everyday objects and activities, Lanya moved on to more unfamiliar or complex ideas. Her mastery of the common speech grew day by day, and she was soon able to carry on halting conversations. Her curiosity and drive to learn was impressive. And she reciprocated by teaching Syra and Kallian to write and to sound out words using the alphabet she'd taught them.

One rainy day, Syra was preparing their meal while Kallian and Lanya sat at the table, taking turns writing on a piece of scrap wood now so covered in marks it was nearly useless for the purpose. They were both laughing uproariously, the silliness easing some of the tension Kallian had carried for months, as if he'd reverted to the carefree child he was before his selection as apprentice. The game had gone on to names of animals, and for some reason, Lanya found his attempts to spell words like *squirrel* and *chipmunk* hilarious.

Syra's ears perked up, however, when Kallian spelled *bear* as "ber"—and Lanya said, "That's not right."

"That's what it sounds like," Kallian said, still smiling broadly.

Lanya's face became serious. "I know. But it isn't right. That's a word that was in one my mother's books. It's spelled B-E-A-R."

Syra looked over from the pile of green beans she was cutting. "Are you sure, Lanya?"

The girl nodded. "I don't remember many words, but I remember that one. I remember it because the day my mother taught it to me, a real bear knocked in a door—not where we lived, but near—and ate every bit of food in the house. My mother said she should be careful what she taught me, because she didn't want to make anything else appear."

"I don't think she made the bear appear," Kallian said.

Lanya rolled her eyes. "I know that. She was joking."

"But this confirms it," Syra said. "The books were written in the common speech."

"So that's what they speak, where her family came from."

"It would seem so."

Lanya looked from one of them to the other. "Why does it matter how they talk there?"

Their gazes met for a moment.

"Lanya," Syra said, "did your mother tell you anything— anything at all—about where your family came from?"

"Not much. A little. It was a long way away, she said. There's a big river, and if you follow it downstream, eventually there's a huge lake of water that's salty. She said that the big lake flooded part of the city a long time ago, but that it was rebuilt, and the people live in houses made of stone. And that the chief person there is a very wicked man, who would kill us if we ever went back."

"And she also told you about the books."

Lanya nodded.

Syra digested this for a moment, and it was Kallian who spoke first.

"I wonder if the flood her mother told her about is the same one our ancestors escaped from."

"It's a possibility."

"So that would mean it can't be that far away."

She looked at Kallian in silence for a moment, and finally said in a quiet voice, "It's not."

"You know where it is?"

"More or less."

"But then... we should go there."

Lanya's eyes flew open wide. "No, you mustn't!"

"Think about how much we could learn."

"The chief man there is wicked! My mother said so! Kallian, you can't."

He took a deep breath. "I'm not... Lanya, I'm not planning on running right out of the door today. But still, don't you..." He turned to Syra, his eyes as earnest and eager as a little child's. "Don't you think it would be worth it? Even if we only recaptured a fraction of what our ancestors knew. Think about what we could bring back to Klen. How much we could improve our lives and the lives of our friends and families."

Lanya seemed near tears. "But Kallian, it won't help anyone if they kill you. You'll never get home."

"Relax, Lanya," Syra said in a soothing voice. "We won't go if it isn't safe."

"It *isn't* safe. My mother told me that. I must never try to go back, even after she was gone. It would never be safe. Don't go, Kallian, please tell me you won't."

He sat silent, looking at the girl, his face set in a frown.

Some of the watchful wariness of her first few days in Klen was back full-force. She looked as if she were ready to run herself, but away—in any direction but toward the fearful city with its stone buildings and wicked ruler. Kallian opened his mouth to speak, but Syra met his eyes and gave him a tiny shake of the head. Continuing the conversation at this point would only agitate the girl further.

But she read in her apprentice's face the signs of his thoughts, and saw there a plan set in motion, a plan she couldn't have halted even if she'd wanted to. The girl's arrival in Klen was like dropping a small pebble into a still pond. The ripples spread out across the water's mirrored surface, eventually reaching the edges, touching everything within it. But here, the waves weren't diminishing, and the pond settling back into its previous tranquility.

These waves would rise, higher and higher, as unstoppable as the great flood that had driven their ancestors to this place six centuries earlier. Kallian was already being carried by them, even though he had only begun to recognize it.

And the crest of those waves would determine the trajectory of his life, driving him farther away from home than he could ever have dreamed.

six

. . .

K allian approached the Hall of Images slowly, feet dragging, heart pounding against his ribcage. He knew what he had to do, but was terrified to do it. The urge to run—what he'd felt the day of his investiture as apprentice to the Guardian—swelled in him, making it hard to breathe. A bead of sweat trickled from his armpit down his side, and his shirt already had dark patches where it had soaked through.

It was a hot day. Maybe the oracles would attribute it to that. He didn't want them to think he was a scared child. This question had to be asked as a rational, reasonable request from an adult to other adults, not as the wild dreams of a willful, reckless youth just out of his teenage years.

The truth, though, was that his drive to do something that no one in Klen had done for six hundred years had nothing to do with rationality, and his fear nothing to do with reverence for the authority of the oracles. He was in the grip of a compulsion with a power he'd never experienced before. If they denied him, he would defy their command and do it anyway, even if it meant being banned from the community for life.

It felt very much like standing on the edge of a precipice so high he couldn't see the bottom.

"Can't you ask them?" Kallian had asked Syra the previous evening, after Layna was asleep. Any mention of the City of the Books, as Kallian had come to think of it, upset her, so he'd ceased asking her about it or even mentioning it in front of her. He'd have to broach the topic again, but no sense in distressing her ahead of time.

"This is your quest," Syra answered.

"But you approve of it."

"Yes. I approve, but I can't go along. While the other three oracles might well agree to your leaving Klen, there is no way they'd agree to my coming along. In fact, I can't even ask them to do so. In becoming Guardian, I accepted my role as the repository of knowledge of the settlement and its history. It sounds arrogant to say it, but it is nothing less than the truth. I am too valuable to risk. You are learning a great deal, but your training is still far from complete. If I were to die before passing along to you what I know, there would be no way to recover it."

"There are the books."

"We don't know what they contain. All we're judging by is the memory of what a six-year-old was told by her mother, and her scanty familiarity with the four books she actually had. I hardly need point out that the rooms full of records Lanya told us about could be an exaggeration. And even if they exist, there's no guarantee what kind of information they contain." She shook her head. "Kallian, I will not deny that my heart very much urges me to go. Even the possibility of such knowledge—to someone who has devoted her entire life to remembering everything our people know, all our history and rituals and traditions—you surely realize how attractive it is. And not just, as Lanya pointed out, that having access to written records, and learning how to decipher them, would mean we wouldn't have to put as much faith in one person's memories. I'm as excited as you are by the possibility of learning what our ancestors knew, what we thought had been lost forever."

"But you already know what is going to happen." A stubborn note came into Kallian's voice. "What's the risk if you know ahead of time what the dangers are?"

Syra gave him a long look. "It doesn't work like that."

He looked at her in complete incomprehension.

"The path is laid out in front of me. In front of all of us, really, it's just that I'm in the position of seeing it. Even so, I only see the part of it that I'm going to live through in some way. If an event is truly outside my experience—past or future—I have no way of knowing about it, and am in the dark as much as everyone else."

"So you know if the oracles will approve my leaving?"

She nodded.

"Then tell me."

She smiled and placed one hand on top of his. "Kallian. My friend. I know how hard it is. I felt the same thing when I was apprentice. But Leda told me that the most important thing about being Guardian is knowing when to share knowledge of future events with another. And, she said, it very seldom is the right thing to do. She told me once—I can't have been much older than you are—that seeing the future isn't such a special thing, because all of us will see the future ourselves if we wait long enough. Seeing it ahead of time isn't the gift you might think it is." She paused. "Try to temper your impatience and anger, and know that I felt all that when I was at your stage of things. All that and more. Our temperaments are different. I was fiery, stubborn, and quick to anger, and what I had to learn was to quell that, not only because I was apprentice but because of the natural bigotry I faced because of who my mother was."

"I don't see anything natural about it."

"It's not kind, it's not pleasant, but it *is* natural, especially when you realize that our community has been completely closed for hundreds of years. It took me a long time to accept that. Longer, in fact, than it did for the community to accept me. You're starting from a different place. Your nature is to be self-contained and independent. Until I got to know you better, you seemed to be all smooth surfaces, nothing to catch hold of, content in your own self and meeting your own needs. Your task is learning to assert yourself, to reach out to others and accept their help, affection, and love, to recognize that you're not alone in this world."

"I asked you to come along with me."

She laughed. "Which tells me how strongly you feel about this quest, and how determined you are to succeed."

"Will I succeed?"

Their eyes met, and she didn't respond for a moment. Finally she said, "Let me ask you this. Suppose I say, 'You will not bring home any information we didn't already know.' Would it dissuade you from going?"

He shook his head.

"Why not?"

"Because I have to do this. I feel like my entire life has brought me to this point. This is what it all meant, all the staring across the fences, all the dreaming about what was out there. Even if I come back empty-handed, I won't be the same person when I get back home."

"And if I told you you would never return to Klen?"

A longer pause. "That doesn't change my answer. My feet are already on the path. Maybe they always have been."

She nodded. "Then go tomorrow and speak to the oracles, and don't be afraid. What must happen will happen. As it always does, whatever our hopes and fears may tell us."

So now Kallian approached the door of the Hall of Images, his shirt streaked with sweat, his hands trembling. Syra had left before him—as one of the oracles, she had to take her place in the Guardian's seat to hear his request, even though she knew what it was—and he felt uniquely alone as he pulled open the wooden door.

The interior, lit only with the flickering light from the brazier, was dim, with moving shadows that seemed like the ghosts of all the other oracles who had sat in those seats, an unbroken lineage going back over six hundred years. The sweet scent of cedar smoke hung on the air. The faces of the four were grave, the firelight casting a ruddy glow on their skin. Three with dusky skin like Kallian's own, and one pale, with long, straw-blonde hair. He'd seen the four of them together before, but today Syra's otherness leapt out at him.

Half of her ancestry came from outside the perimeter fences, in that great, trackless, unknown wilderness. But today, she represented the community of Klen, and her differences wouldn't change the way things played out. He had an inkling of what it was like for Syra—what it would, one day, be like for him—the sense that the die was already cast, and all he was doing was playing the role, letting a future come that he had no power to change.

He bowed down to each of the oracles in turn, then stood facing them, silent, waiting to be invited to speak.

Elen Alleman said, in her quiet, steady voice, "Kallian Dorn. You come to us with a request. Let us hear it now."

He took a deep breath of air, and let it out slowly, hoping the trembling of his body would not be immediately obvious when he spoke.

"Yes, Oracle. I have a request. You know of the girl Lanya Desorla, who came to us from the outside three months ago."

No one spoke.

"When she arrived here, she spoke only the sacred language, which she apparently learned during the time she stayed with the Border Runners. But I... we... discovered a few nights ago that where her parents came from, they spoke the common speech. And we learned that in that place, there are many—we don't know how many—records from the past.

Possibly the distant past, from the Before Time. Before the flood."

He paused.

"Go on," Garlin Abraham said.

"If we could study those records, perhaps even bring them back to Klen, we could learn about what's been lost. Regain the knowledge our ancestors had."

"How would you study them?" Elen asked. "If our ancestors even had that skill, it was lost long ago. Lost so deeply that no trace of it remains."

"Lanya has taught Syra and me the rudiments. She was learning it herself. Her mother was teaching her."

"How much does she know?" Bastian Nguyen regarded him with a frown. "Surely a child would not have complete mastery of something so complex."

"No. Certainly not. In fact, she did not realize at first that the language in the books was the common speech. But the basics of reading are easy enough to learn. I have no doubt there are subtleties she doesn't know. But… if I were able to go there, go to the place where her parents came from, perhaps I could learn from the people there. They may welcome someone who wants to study what they have, even if I would not be allowed to bring the actual records back with me. Perhaps there is someone there who would be willing to teach me the skill of reading the records. Refusing such a request makes no sense. As the oracles understand, sharing knowledge doesn't diminish it. The more it is shared, the more it grows."

Bastian raised one eyebrow. Kallian wasn't sure if it was meant to communicate surprise at Kallian's insight, or merely skepticism. "And if they will not allow you to study the records?"

"Then I return empty-handed, and we are no worse off than we were."

"You understand the risk to yourself personally," Garlin said.

"Completely."

"Do you understand, however," Bastian said, "the risk of your loss to the community? You have already been apprentice for a year, and have learned a great deal. Were you not to return, that motion forward would be fruitless, and the Guardian would have to select a new apprentice, beginning again from nothing."

"I do understand. It is why I must go alone. The risk to myself is considerable, and I accept that risk. But isn't that why an apprentice is chosen as soon as the former Guardian dies? The knowledge we have is too valuable to place into one single mind. There never is a guarantee that the apprentice will live long enough to succeed to the Guardianship. Nor that the Guardian will live long enough to teach the apprentice everything she knows. Everything is a risk. Stepping outside your front door in the morning is a risk. What you must decide is which risks are worth taking." He took a deep breath. "You're right, I've learned some, and I value my role as apprentice. But I'm not irreplaceable. The greater part of the risk is to me alone. And what could be gained is incalculable."

The four oracles were silent, as still as the statues of the nine Founders that stood behind him. Had he impressed them? It was impossible to tell. At least he hadn't stumbled over his words, as he'd feared. And they hadn't denied him outright.

Finally, Syra said, "Thank you, Kallian. We understand your request. We will discuss it further, and will inform you when we have come to a decision."

It was clearly a dismissal. He gave another respectful bow, and left the Hall of Images, blinking as his eyes were struck by the harsh sunlight after the cool dimness of the interior.

Discuss it? For how long? The issue was plain enough.

What was there to discuss? But he quelled his impatience, and returned to the Guardian's dwelling,

When he arrived, Lanya was in the vegetable garden, picking ripe tomatoes and peppers and tucking them into the pocket of her apron. When she saw him coming, she reached in and held up one of her harvested vegetables.

"Cucumber!" she said, in the common speech.

"Well done." The compliment sounded half-hearted in his own ears.

"It's a funny word. Where were you? I got up, and the house was empty."

"Did you eat the breakfast I left for you?"

She nodded. "Where were you?" she repeated.

"I was speaking to the oracles."

"About what?"

"I'd rather not say. It may come to nothing. If I'm wrong about that, I'll tell you then. In any case, it's nothing to worry about."

Lanya gave him a quick frown. In the past weeks, they had studiously avoided discussing the distant city, and Kallian's desire to go there, but it was obvious she suspected what his conversation with the oracles had been about.

However, despite her obvious curiosity, she respected his answer and did not press further.

Whatever Kallian's assessment of there being little to discuss, the oracles didn't summon him back until late afternoon. He was finishing up his chores in the garden and giving thought to preparing some dinner for himself and Lanya when someone called to him.

Lexa Sahin stood on the path leading from the house to the garden, her face set in its usual eager expression.

When would she give up on her infatuation for him?

Every muscle in her body expressed longing—she was leaning slightly forward, as if she were having to restrain herself from moving much closer. A quick thought crossed his mind that maybe he should give in and reciprocate her interest—he certainly felt the physical need he knew she'd be glad to satisfy, and she was a kind enough and attractive enough young woman—but that quick musing was so antithetical to what he wanted that the idea was nearly repellent.

Even though he wouldn't have been able to put into words what he *did* want.

He forced a smile and said, "Hello, Lexa."

She smiled back at him. "The oracles… they sent me to find you. They said to tell you they're ready."

He had to stifle a sigh. Did she wait outside the Hall of Images until there was some message that needed to be delivered to him? It didn't seem outside the realm of possibility.

"All right, thank you. I'll go as soon as I wash up."

He walked past her into the house, feeling her eyes on him the entire way. Once inside, with the door shut, he stripped off his sweaty, grimy shirt and trousers, did a cursory wash with the bucket of water he'd hauled from the creek earlier, and pulled on fresh clothing. He ran his hands through his tousled mop of curly, deep brown hair, then decided any further neatening up wouldn't affect the outcome one way or the other—and his need to know their decision as soon as possible took precedence.

He opened the door slowly, looked around.

Lexa was nowhere to be seen. He'd half expected she'd have waited to escort him to the Hall of Images.

He only saw a few people on the five-minute walk. Most were finishing up outdoor chores and heading inside for mealtime. He got a couple of cursory waves, but no one spoke to him as for the second time that day he approached the heavy wooden door of the Hall of Images and pulled it open.

Once again he bowed to each of the oracles, then stood,

his hands clasped in front of him, waiting for their decision. His heart hammered in his chest, and he was trembling. The sense returned of being on the edge of a cliff, but now was the moment to leap—or not. Once he leapt, there would be no turning back. His life would forever be shaped by what happened in the next five minutes.

The first to speak was Bastian Nguyen. He'd always been a little afraid of Bastian, both because he was stern and seldom smiled, but because Syra had her share of clashes with him. Syra had once said not to sink into dislike for the man—that he wanted what was best for Klen just as Syra and Kallian both did. He might disagree on how to achieve that, but that could be discussed. His fundamental goodness and loyalty to the settlement were beyond question.

And when he spoke, it was in far gentler and more sympathetic tones than he expected.

"Kallian Dorn, we have considered your request. I will be frank with you—the request is the first of its kind, as far back as our collective memory runs, and that alone biased us to deny you, simply by virtue of it being too rife with unknowns to be safe."

Kallian opened his mouth to speak, but the older man held up one finger, and he closed his mouth again.

"That said, you spoke eloquently on your own behalf this morning, and after much discussion, we have come to the conclusion that—as you yourself pointed out—the potential gains outweigh the overall risk. I have myself wondered, for as far back as I could consider the question, whether it would ever be possible to recover what was lost from the former world. Or, more accurately, even to determine which of those distant and dimly-remembered legends were true, and which simply wild imaginings. You seem to be aware of the dangers that might lie outside the perimeter fences. Once you step outside the boundary, you will truly be on your own."

"I know that."

"You said this morning that even if you knew ahead of time that you would bring back no new information, you would still go. Might I ask why that is?"

Kallian cleared his throat, trying to steady his voice. "If no records remain in Lanya's home city—or if what records there are contain no information that would be useful to us—I still will return with knowledge of what lies outside of Klen. There is other information to be learned besides what records might still persist from the Before Time." He took a deep breath. "There is the knowledge that we are not alone in the wide world."

Bastian gave him a small nod. "I thought you would respond that way." The oracle looked to one side and the other, meeting the eyes of the other three with a fleeting glance. "On that basis, we grant your request to seek out what is to be found in the outside world. And may the blessings of our ancestors guide your every step, and bring you safely back home."

Kallian choked out the words, "Thank you," and then with no warning, all the pent-up emotion of the past day overflowed in a torrent, overwhelming him.

He burst into tears.

seven

· · ·

"I knew it!" Lanya shouted. Her face was drawn with fear. The girl looked as panic-stricken as she had the day Kallian found her. "I knew you wanted to go! You can't, you can't!"

"I have to." Kallian's voice was a dull monotone.

Lanya looked from him to Syra, as if desperately trying to find support from someone, anyone. "They'll kill you."

Syra spoke gently. "You don't know that, Lanya. It may be that your parents' danger came from something that wouldn't threaten Kallian. It's been five years. Perhaps the people they fled from have themselves died. Things don't remain the same simply because we're not there to witness them."

Her face set in a stubborn frown. She merely breathed again, "You can't."

He went to the girl and knelt in front of where she sat. "Lanya, I know you don't understand. And I know you're afraid. But here... what we need is knowledge. Hundreds of years ago, our ancestors had knowledge we can only dream of, knowledge we thought was lost forever. Even that there's a possibility..."

"Knowledge isn't worth you dying."

"I can take care of myself."

She shook her head rapidly. "No. You don't know. You've never been out there. It's not just the ones in the city, the ones who wanted to kill my parents. There's the people, the ones we lived with. They don't even think outsiders are humans. They killed my father. My mother and I… they only let us live because the leader thought my mother was beautiful. He wanted to have her as his wife. When she died… I knew they would soon kill me, too. That's why I ran away." She swallowed hard. "It's not worth it, throwing your life away for a bunch of books."

"I have to. You don't understand…"

"Stop saying I don't understand! Just stop! I understand more than you do. I've been out there. You haven't."

Kallian gave a momentary wince. The comment had stung. "It's what I was born to do."

Her voice rose to near hysteria. "What does that even mean? No one is born to do something. My mother used to tell me we're born, and we die, and all of us are just trying to keep as much time between the two as we can. If you go out into the forest, we'll never see you again."

Kallian looked over to Syra, and gave her a helpless shrug.

"Some risks are worth taking," Syra said. "Sometimes we need to do what's hard, or dangerous, because it's the right thing to do."

The girl shook her head, and dissolved into tears.

Kallian put one hand on her shoulder, but she shook it off with an angry gesture. He opened his mouth, then closed it again, silently stood, and went outside into the cool, twilit evening.

After a minute, Syra whispered to her, "I'll be right back."

Lanya looked up, her face filled with betrayal, but said nothing as Syra followed him outside.

"She'll be all right," Syra said as she walked up to where

Kallian was standing, silent, looking out into the rapidly darkening woods.

Without turning toward her, he said, "Are you saying that because you know the future?"

"No. Just because I know that hurts, whatever they are, don't last forever."

"I don't mean to hurt her."

"Of course not. Much of the harm in the world is accidental. We try our best, but when two people have different needs, it's often inevitable."

"Am I wrong to leave?"

"If I thought so, I would have told you when you first brought the idea up. The other oracles would have said so, too. You needn't question your motives." She paused, listening to the chorus of crickets and other quiet, soothing night noises, surrounding the sheltered little community like a protective blanket. "When do you want to leave?"

Now he turned toward her, his handsome face showing pain mixed with a deep, powerful longing. "As soon as possible. Now that I've decided, and been given leave, I want to go."

She nodded. "Wise. Summer is sliding by all too quickly. From Lanya's description, it sounds as if the city lies somewhere south of us, and near a large body of water, so winter travel might not be as treacherous as if it were up in the mountains to the east. But the chill and the rain would still make for an unpleasant journey. Making haste will give you a greater likelihood of walking in comfort."

He nodded. "What will you do while I'm gone?"

She smiled at him. "What I've always done. Tend to my duties as Guardian. Pronounce the rituals when it's time. Solemnize births and deaths when they occur. Continue to teach Lanya the common speech, and to learn from her what I can of reading and writing. Tend the vegetable garden. Keep vigil until you return."

"And as simple as that, I go beyond what anyone in our community has ever done."

"As simple as that." She laughed. "Did you think there'd be signs and portents? Lightning and thunder? The voices of our ancestors crying out from the heavens?"

This got a smile. "I'm not so important as all that."

"That's not what I meant. More, the most momentous choices we make sometimes amount to no more than setting our feet on the path. You've received the gift of knowing, knowing ahead of time, that what you are choosing will alter your life forever. Don't scorn that knowledge, which most of us only recognize in retrospect."

***

Preparations for leaving took only a day.

Much of it was taken up with saying farewell. By the morning of the day before his departure, the entire settlement knew about it. Some expressed excitement. Some were obviously envious of Kallian's receiving permission to do something no one else ever had. A few seemed convinced he was on a fool's errand and unlikely ever to return.

Lanya barely spoke to Kallian during that time. She alternately wept and raged at him, and nothing he or Syra said made the least difference. The other one who was clearly devastated was Lexa Sahin. Syra watched as Kallian bade farewell to his parents and his friends. Lexa stood to the side, tears streaming down her cheeks, but completely silent. Kallian, obviously uncomfortable, gave her an awkward hug and said something to her too quiet for Syra to hear.

The girl nodded once, said a word or two back, and Kallian turned away.

He pulled on his backpack, filled with food and personal necessities, then turned toward Syra.

"My blessings and the blessings of our ancestors go with you, Kallian."

He looked up, his dark eyes filled with tears. "Syra, be honest with me. Am I being a fool to do this?"

"I have never known you to do anything foolish."

"When I found out about the City of the Books, my heart pounded with excitement at the prospect of seeing it, studying the records, bringing back that knowledge to our people. Now that I am on the verge, all I feel is self-doubt."

"The hallmark of an actual fool is that he never doubts himself. Anyone in your position would be apprehensive."

He looked out in the direction of the perimeter fences, and was silent for a moment. Then he said, in a quiet voice, "Lexa said that she loves me."

"How did you respond to her?"

"What could I say? She's a kind person, and I like her, but I don't love her. I simply thanked her and said I'd talk more with her when I return."

Syra gave him a sad smile. "It's not what a young woman infatuated with a handsome young man wants to hear."

"I know." He cleared his throat. "Should I have lied? Said 'I love you, too?' Who knows how long I'll be gone, or if I'll ever return? Maybe it would be better to leave her with some hope instead of crushing it."

"No. Lying is never the right thing to do, especially not in matters of love. Like Lanya, Lexa will recover. It's time to turn your face outward toward the task ahead of you."

He nodded. "Will you come with me at least as far as the fence line?"

"Of course."

They set off, trudging through the forest, past the pond, and up to the first fence, nearly invisible in the shadows.

"So this is it."

She nodded, then enveloped him in a strong hug. "Be brave, Kallian. Take each adventure, each risk, as it comes.

Remember what the Blessed Julia taught—'take therefore no thought for the morrow: for the morrow shall take thought for the things of itself. Sufficient unto the day is the evil thereof.'"

"I've never really understood that teaching."

"Perhaps it will make better sense to you by the time you return. Sometimes words are empty until we've lived their meaning."

He nodded again. "Goodbye, Syra. Thank you for everything. For choosing me as apprentice. For teaching me so much. For giving me a home. Especially, for your kindness."

She smiled and hugged him again. "I will be waiting for you."

He took off his backpack, hefted it across the first fence, and dropped it to the ground. Then he maneuvered his way through the barbed wires, stood, went to the exterior fence, and repeated his actions. She watched as he pulled on his pack, then raised one hand in farewell.

She responded with a wave to him.

Then he turned and trudged off into the shadows, finally disappearing downhill past a pair of venerable old fir trees, and was lost to sight as he walked farther away from his birthplace than any inhabitant of Klen had for over six hundred years.

part two
cat-and-mouse

eight

. . .

His name was Gátra-Skómna, Leader of Falcons, but his secret name—known only to himself, his parents (now long dead), and his current lover—was Ádas-Dosan. Sky-Wing. Revealing his secret name to anyone with ill intent was a good way to be controlled, if not killed outright. If you know the true name of something, you own part of its soul, and Gátra, as all the members of the clan called him, would never let himself be owned by anyone. He even regretted telling one of his many lovers, but he was in the throes of passion at the time, and lust makes a man unwary.

As far as the clan themselves, they were simply known as Samada. The People. They had lived there, in the foothills of the mountain, for as long as collective memory stretched. The first of the People had come from the water, it was said—the great body of water two days' march to the west. Gátra had seen it only once, when he underwent the last of five trials for his elevation to the role of leader.

He'd been sent out, naked and carrying only a spear, away from the home of the People, to spend ten days alone and come back alive and with some new knowledge. In the days leading up to the beginning of the trial he'd made up his mind to set off toward the water, to see the ruins of the ancient city and beyond it the ocean from which his people had arisen.

He had seen all that and more, narrowly escaping being killed by a mountain lion that gave him slash-scars on his belly that he still carried. But nothing he saw could rival the vast expanse of ruined stonework, now green with vines and bushes, extending down to a sheet of restless, shimmering water.

When he saw that, he fell to his knees and touched his forehead to the ground, knowing he was in a holy place where none of the Samada now alive had ever stood.

He returned in triumph, proudly showing his scars and telling the awestruck People what he'd seen, as the priests solemnly dressed him in the garb of leadership. That was when he took his new name, Leader of Falcons. Before that, he'd been known only as Naté. Boy. Like the rest of the male youth. Once they came of age, their voices dropping, growing hair on their chests and groins and armpits, they too would be sent out on an ordeal to earn their names.

Half of them didn't return. Whether those ones died, or were too cowardly and shamed to return, no one knew and no one cared. If they'd died, it was while attempting something glorious. If they'd run away, they deserved to be forgotten. But he had succeeded as he knew he would, cheating death, bringing back the tale of seeing the ruined city and the waters that had given birth to the People long ago.

That was twelve years ago. Since then, he'd survived two attempts to kill him and usurp his place. Both had failed in short order, the would-be assassins ending up tied to trees and then pinned to them by a dozen arrows. He'd had his choice of lovers, although thus far, fathered no children who had survived. One of his lovers, an outsider who had been captured fleeing through the forest with her husband and child, he took as lover after killing the husband, but she'd died in childbirth less than a year ago, along with the baby she carried. Their daughter, at that point perhaps six years old, was kept alive, destined to become a sacrifice to the gods of the high mountains when she came of age. But she'd run away only a few months earlier, disappearing into the forest to the north, where she had no doubt either starved or been eaten by wild animals.

She was of no consequence, but he still had her caretaker beaten for letting her escape.

He often gave thought to where the girl's family had come from. The Samada had long believed that they were the only people in the world, and when the three of them stumbled into a hunting party, it had been such a shock they almost escaped capture. They only spoke their own savage tongue, but through gestures they communicated that their home lay far to the south.

Gátra instructed those who were with him as the strangers were being interrogated not to mention anything of their origin to the others. These kinds of stories begat curiosity, and that in turn begat rebellion. There was some talk and a few skew glances when he took the woman as lover, but his position was so well established by that point that no one dared question him.

Let them wonder why he desired to make love to a woman who wasn't even truly a person. Like the girl's escape, it was of no consequence.

So Gátra was soundly in command. He led hunting parties, made decisions for the People when there were disputes, demonstrated his strength in fights with other men who had earned their names, and publicly demonstrated his virility in the yearly Ceremony of Fertility on the Winter Solstice. Food, fighting, and fucking. As long as he could show his prowess in all three, he had nothing to worry about.

It was a warm, sunny day in late summer when the

outsider arrived. He had been alone, walking heedlessly through the woods as only a fool would, and the hunters tracked him easily. He showed no sign of wariness. When they sprang the trap, he had fought commendably, however —he was tougher than he'd seemed at first. But all he had as a weapon was a small knife, the kind used for cutting up food, and it was four against one in any case. They subdued him quickly, tied his hands behind his back, and none too gently brought him to the settlement. He was immediately brought into the leader's chambers. Everyone in the settlement knew that in such a circumstance, Gátra would want to see the interloper right away.

Gátra looked at the young man closely as he was brought up. He was perhaps twenty, tall, broad across the shoulders and chest, narrow-waisted, with fine features. His skin was darker than the Samada's, and showed a purpling bruise on one cheekbone. His hair was deep brown and curly, his eyes nearly black. They glittered with a combination of shrewdness and fury as he was forced to his knees.

"Why did you capture me?" he snarled out, to Gátra's surprise speaking the language of the Samada smoothly. His accent was a little odd, but completely understandable.

"Because you crossed into our land."

"I didn't know it was yours. And I'm not crossing in, I'm crossing through. Let me go and I'll be on my way, and with luck you'll never see me again."

Gátra laughed, as did some of the older men watching the proceedings. He approved of the young man's defiance—in a similar situation, he'd have been defiant, himself—but the captive needed to know who was in charge.

"You speak as if you have a choice in the matter. You are the one kneeling, with tied hands, not me. You are not in any position to make demands."

The dark eyes met Gátra's steadily. If he felt any fear, he

didn't show it. "I'm not demanding, I'm requesting. If I trespassed, I did not intend it and I ask forgiveness. I am no threat to you or your people."

"You're right about that."

More laughter from the other men in the room.

The young man bristled, but said nothing.

"What are you called?"

"Kallian. Kallian Dorn."

"What does that name mean?"

Kallian shrugged, his expression showing perplexity. "Mean? It doesn't mean anything. It's merely my name."

Gátra allowed himself a small frown. "Your people give their children meaningless names?"

The young man shook his head. "My last name comes from my father's ancestral line. It came from his father, who got it from his father. The women take their mother's last names in the same fashion. As far as my first name, if it has a meaning, I don't know what it is. My parents chose it, and it was added to the memory of the Guardian at the ritual following my birth. That's all I know."

Gátra nodded. This youngster was oddly forthcoming. Apparently unwariness was a habit with him. That might be of use. It might make sense to put him at his ease, lead him to believe that he was among friends. Kallian had been traveling from the north when he was spotted, the opposite direction from that which Gátra's lover and her family had come. This meant there were people on both sides of the Samada settlement. It would be wise to find out more about them while Kallian was still off his guard, before realized how dire his predicament was.

"I see. I am interested in finding out more about the customs of your people. It sounds as if they are quite different from ours. I am called Gátra-Skómna. Unlike your name, it does have a meaning. It means 'leader of falcons.' In address, you may simply call me Gátra. I would like the opportunity to speak to you further, and find out why you were trekking through the forest alone, away from your home place, and where you were going. We can learn from each other."

"I don't want to delay my journey."

Gátra gave a little shake of his head. "It would only be by a few days. Once we have learned from each other, we will provision you and see you safely on your way."

One or two of the men in the room smirked at this, and exchanged sly, sidewise glances, but Kallian had his back to them and didn't see. "I suppose that'd be all right."

Gátra was not used to having his authority questioned, even implicitly, and had to stop himself from reminding the young pup that his opinion on the matter was irrelevant. Instead he said, in as conciliatory a tone as he could manage, "Very well. We will make you welcome." He nodded to the man who stood nearest, one of the hunters who had captured Kallian. "Untie him and get him food and water, then show him to guest quarters. Then return here. There are other things we need to discuss."

The man obeyed silently, and once his hands were freed, Kallian stood, rubbed his wrists, and his captor guided him from the room. There was no need for Gátra to tell the hunter to guard Kallian's quarters and be ready to prevent an escape. As guileless as the young man seemed, there was nothing to be gained by blind trust. It was blind trust, and an assumption of naïveté, that had allowed the girl Lanya to escape.

She'd been of minimal utility, so that lapse of caution had been of minimal impact. Gátra had the impression, though, that Kallian could prove to be a great deal more useful than an ignorant six-year-old girl.

The man returned a few minutes later. His name was Thalaté, He-Who-Watches—given to him because of his keen eyesight and quick wit, and when he spoke he showed the name's aptness. He gave a glance around the room—the leader had dismissed the others, and an expression of pride crossed his face as he realized that what Gátra wished to say to him was for his ears alone.

"I took it upon myself, Gátra, to make the young man comfortable, but to order him quietly kept under guard. It seemed to me your desire would be to put him at his ease, and make him feel a guest rather than a captive."

"Excellent. You discerned my wishes exactly. You have done well." Gátra sat back, considering. "What do you think of our young captive?"

"How do you mean?"

"Does it not strike you as odd that a solitary, virtually unarmed young man was walking through the forest, heading neither up into the mountains to the east nor toward the ruined city in the west, but south?"

"I do not see its significance, Gátra. I await your clarifying your thoughts, so they become understandable to my poor intellect."

It was flattery. Thalaté's intellect was easily equal to his own, perhaps greater. But the deference still pleased him.

"When the woman, Azen, came here with her husband and child six years ago—you recall?—she came from the other direction, from the south."

"I do recall it well."

"I spoke to her about the place where she'd come from, and her description was clear, that it was a large settlement, many times larger than ours, and staunchly defended."

"I remember that as well. Might she have been lying, to give her home place higher standing in our eyes?"

"I considered that possibility, but there was no lie in her voice when she described it. As strange as it sounded to my ears, I believe there is a settlement with many people several days' march to the south."

Thalaté drew himself up. "They are not people."

Gátra smiled. He loathed being contradicted or corrected, but in this case it was to the glory of the Samada, and through them, to himself.

"Of course. I use the word loosely. My point, though, is that the settlement to the south is large enough, and well enough garrisoned, that there is no chance of our conquering it."

"Yes." Thalaté's brows drew together thoughtfully. "Do you think, Gátra, that is where the young man was heading when we intercepted him?"

"I believe it is likely. I doubt he would have cast off into the wilderness with no goal in mind, like an idler out on a pleasure walk. It is only a guess, but since he obviously did not know of our presence, it is a possibility."

"Perhaps he was simply exiled by his people for some crime."

"That could be. I will find that out. But from his bearing, and the way he spoke of his home, he did not sound like an exile. More like someone on a quest. But if he knows of the existence of the city to the south, do you realize what that means?"

There was silence in the room for a moment, and then Thalaté's eyes widened. "The girl."

"Precisely."

"You think that she reached their settlement, and told him about her parents' home place, and this boy is going there on some errand?"

"That is exactly what I think. This implies several things, then, all of which are important. First, there is a settlement north of us we did not know about. Second, the girl survived the forest, and was taken in by them, and she provided enough information about the city of her parents that this young man was sent out to go there." He paused. "Third— and I do not need to say this to you, Thalaté, you know my mind well, but this must not be repeated to any, not your brother, not your lover while you lie next to her at night—it has been in my thoughts for some time now that our people are becoming restless. It is long since they had a task to focus on. Restless men get ideas, and those ideas are seldom favorable to the leader and the ones who have the leader's ears. When rebellions are successful, the men who acted as advisors and confidantes are always the first ones to have their heads impaled on spikes."

That point went home. The other man simply nodded.

"If I find out from Kallian Dorn that his home place is small and poorly defended, I would like to put together a raiding party to attack it. The men would be hand-picked to be loyal—but also to include some of the restive young men who need to be taught the benefits of staying in my good favor. If successful, each man in the party would be given a share of the spoils and their choice of any women who are captured. Others, the men and children, could be killed or captured and brought back as slaves, as circumstances allow."

Thalaté took this in, frowning thoughtfully. "Why do you think the young man was heading, alone, toward a distant city, based only on what he'd learned from a little girl? It seems a foolish action. Virtually suicidal."

"As I said, I intend to find that out. It may be that his people are peace-loving and sent him out as an ambassador. He may be a spy, although his lack of caution in walking through the forest argues against that. It is certainly doubtful he could have learned anything from a six-year-old girl of sufficient value that he'd risk his life for it, especially since she hadn't seen the city itself since she was an infant and can't know much about it. Whatever his mission, it is most likely that he was sent out on it by the settlement's leader." A slow smile crossed Gátra's face. "In any case, his intent after his arrival at the city is irrelevant, as he will never get there. Once he has given me all the information he has that is of value to me, I will have him killed." He paused, and the smile widened, becoming almost predatory. "No. It is too long since I have had the pleasure. I will kill him myself."

nine

. . .

Kallian glanced around the dimly-lit interior of the rough cabin he'd been escorted to. The man who brought him there had said hardly a word, only indicating where he could rest until the leader summoned him, and saying that he'd soon be brought food and water.

His captor was a tall man, broad-shouldered and powerfully built, perhaps forty years old. He was beginning to show signs of baldness, but there was little other evidence of age in his face. His skin was smooth, and his green eyes had a shrewd, intelligent, and not especially friendly sparkle.

Kallian thanked him, which elicited nothing more than a nod. The man left, closing the door behind him.

Kallian watched his retreating figure through the small window in the front wall of the cabin. He paused to speak quickly to another man—Kallian recognized him as part of the hunting party that had captured him—and received a quick response that apparently met with a positive reaction. Then the man disappeared in the direction of the leader's quarters.

Kallian sat down on the cot, padded with a thin mattress made of some rough, tan-colored cloth. He had no doubt whatsoever that he was under guard, and any escape attempt would be short-lived. What reason they had to hold him was less clear. The leader's attempt at soothing words, about exchanging information about their people, had been misdirection, some sort of game, he had no doubt of that. There was a superior expression in Gátra's eyes that belied what he was saying. So until he knew why they wanted him, it was best to play along, to do his own share of misdirection and to keep the farce going as long as possible.

There were three possible reasons they might want to hold him, if he was correct that the leader's talk of a friendly cultural exchange was a lie. The first was that they were simply suspicious of outsiders, or had a particular hatred for trespassers. Upon reflection, this struck him as the least likely. If that had been the case, the hunting party would probably have killed him outright, and even if they hadn't, there'd have been no reason for the leader to feign friendship and cooperation. Second—perhaps they wanted to keep him docile for now because they had plans for him at a later time.

A sacrifice, perhaps? Who knew what kind of bloodthirsty gods they worshiped? One of the legends he'd learned as part of his training to eventually be the Guardian of the Word was a story about a trickster god who set up a test of loyalty and obedience in a man, ordering him to sacrifice his own son, and had only stayed the man's hand at the last moment. It had always struck him as a particularly repulsive story— surely any god who would demand a man sacrifice his son would not be worth worshiping, even if it did turn out to be only a test. But what it meant was there had been places where people engaged in human sacrifice, as horrible as that seemed.

It would be ironic to leave on a great quest, and end up as a sacrifice only two days' easy march from home.

The third possibility, though, was the most disturbing of all. Maybe the leader did want information from Kallian, but it wasn't the innocuous exchange he'd described. Maybe he thought Kallian could provide him with something valuable —perhaps information about his home. Why would he want that, though? Klen had nothing a man like Gátra would be likely to find valuable.

So, which was it? Or was it another reason he had yet to parse?

He decided that he would give Gátra as little as he could manage, and lie about as much as he could get away with and still maintain an appearance of innocent ignorance and some degree of plausibility. The longer Gátra thought he had fallen for the subterfuge, the more opportunity he'd have to find out what the man really wanted—or, possibly, to escape.

His thoughts were interrupted by the door opening to admit a woman in a drab-colored dress that nearly reached the floor. She had long, straight brown hair, and gray eyes that she kept focused downward. Every movement of her body radiated caution that bordered on fear. She carried a wooden tray with a bowl and a cup. She came a little way into the cabin then simply stood, silent.

"Hello?" Kallian finally ventured.

"I have brought you food," she said, in a low monotone.

"Thank you."

She didn't move. Finally she said, even more quietly, "Where would you like me to put it?"

Kallian stood, and reached to take the tray, but she flinched. A little of the water in the cup sloshed onto the tray.

"Please tell me where you would like it placed."

"Um… there?" He pointed to a little table in the corner of the room.

She nodded, still not meeting his eyes, placed the tray on the table, and silently left the cabin.

He stared at the closed door for some time afterward. Was she afraid of him because he was an outsider?

Or was she afraid of everyone for some reason?

Strange. He'd always pictured the Border Runners as living rough, little more than wild animals themselves. There was obviously much more to these people than a band of savages wearing loincloths.

Thus far, however, the bits and pieces of their culture he'd seen showed every sign of being repellant.

He lay down on the cot, and must have dozed a little, because when the door opened the light slanting in through it showed that it was late afternoon. He realized he hadn't touched the food the woman had brought him. Too preoccupied with his situation. The visitor was the balding man, who greeted him in civil tones.

"Kallian Dorn. The leader would like to speak to you. I trust you have refreshed yourself with food and rest?" The man glanced at the tray, and a faint smile touched his lips, there and gone in a moment.

"Sure."

"Excellent. Please come with me."

Kallian, trying to give every appearance of docility, followed the man back to the leader's quarters. Gátra sat in his chair, and standing to each side of him were other men, all stony-faced, watching Kallian's approach impassively. He was reminded of the wooden visages of the founders in the Hall of Images, stern and distant.

Except for the one he served, Blessed Mary of the Bridge. She was smiling, holding out her hand.

He took a deep breath. May she be watching over him today. He had the feeling he would need all her steadfast strength.

"Kallian Dorn," Gátra said. "I summoned you back because I wish to ask you some questions, and I am certain you have questions of your own for me. But first, are your quarters to your liking? I fear we have little better to offer, but we wish your stay here to be comfortable."

"They're fine." He smiled, hoping it didn't look forced. "In fact, I fell asleep."

Gátra laughed, but the men standing in a semicircle around him showed no change in their expressions.

"I am quite curious about where you come from, and why you were walking through the forest. We wish to learn more about what is out in the wide world, outside of our little settlement."

"I come from a place called Klen."

"And in Klen, they speak our language? We did not know that any others did."

It was hard to see how there could be any danger in answering this one honestly. "We speak two languages. The one we share is known to us as the sacred language, and it is used in our rituals, prayers, and ceremonies. The other we call the common language, and it is used for ordinary speech."

"Fascinating." Gátra didn't look particularly fascinated, but neither did he look overtly hostile. So far, so good. "For what reason were you traveling alone through the forest? Why had your leader sent you?"

"I wasn't sent. It was my decision. It was purely to gather information. We have known nothing of the outside world in the five centuries since Klen was founded, and it was thought prudent that we find out who, and what, are in the lands surrounding us. But the choice to go was my own. Our leader approved, but I would have gone with or without her permission."

For the first time, Gátra showed signs of shock. "Her? Your leader is a woman?"

Kallian frowned. "We have four leaders, who are responsible for our guidance. At present, two are men and two are women, but there is no reason that the roles couldn't be fulfilled by any mix of sexes. The highest position, that of the

Guardian, is currently held by a woman, and she is the one about whom I spoke."

Now Gátra's reaction spread to the onlookers, who showed varying emotions from surprise to outright disgust.

So there was the reason for the servile deference of the woman who had brought him food and water. And the reason that both times he had spoken to Gátra, there had been no women present.

Time to ask some questions of his own.

"So you have no women in positions of leadership?"

Gátra smirked. "Why would we take the advice of women, or worse, allow them the power of making men's decisions for them?"

"Perhaps they have knowledge or wisdom that could be valuable."

One of the onlookers snorted laughter, but quickly stifled his reaction when Gátra held up one hand. "Silence, Abo. You do our guest a discourtesy. Their customs are different from our own, which is to be expected. If they were exactly like us, there would be no need to discuss the matter with him. It seems that in Klen, their women have skills and abilities ours do not."

Now several of the onlookers smirked as well. They were ridiculing him, and by extension, all of his people. But he thought of Syra's quiet wisdom, and it struck him that if they were willing to throw away the talents of half of their people, it wasn't the men and women of Klen who were foolish.

He modulated his voice with an effort. "So, what roles do women play here?"

"They prepare food, keep our quarters clean, and satisfy our lust whenever it comes upon us. Nothing more."

Disgusting. But also not what he needed to know. Time to change the subject.

"What do you know of the city to the south?"

A quick narrowing of Gátra's eyes showed that the question had given the leader something he needed. But how? Confirmed a guess about Kallian's intentions, perhaps? Would Gátra have any comprehension of the real reason for Kallian's quest? He did not seem the type who would crave the knowledge books contain. When he spoke, though, it was in the same level, friendly tones as before.

"The ruined city, west of here? Near the water? I have seen it once. It covers the land as far as the eye can take in, stretching down to a vast sea. But seeing it, I knew it was haunted and desolate, uninhabited except for the spirits of the wilderness. Even I did not dare to go into it, but simply looked at it from a hilltop. What reason have you for going there?"

Kallian paused. He had no doubt whatsoever that Gátra knew he wasn't talking about the ruins, but about an inhabited city, and to the south, not the west. These people had almost certainly been the ones who had held Lanya and her mother captive and killed her father, and they would have known the family's origin. Kallian had the sense of being maneuvered into a trap, and could think of nothing to answer except the truth, or at least part of it.

"No, not the ruins, but a huge city with many people. We have heard rumors of it."

A quick curl of Gátra's mouth told Kallian that once again, he had given away more information than he intended.

"We have heard rumors as well. No more than that. It is curious it is your destination."

"I did not say it was my destination, I merely asked about it. As I said, I was sent out to gather information about the wide world, after our community having been isolated for so long. I have no business there except to learn about it, just as I wish to learn about you and your people."

Had that sounded like as much of a blatant lie in Gátra's ears as it had in Kallian's own? But the leader seemed to lose interest in the topic.

"And where is Klen? North of here, I would think, given the direction you were traveling when our hunting party came upon you."

Caution. Kallian had been waiting for this question to come up. But how to tell a convincing lie about places he'd never seen—to men who undoubtedly had wandered far and wide?

"It is about five days' march from here," he said, hoping that his confident tone gave his words more credence. "In a valley up in the mountains. The place is between two tall peaks, in a spot that is sheltered from winter storms and has fertile soil and abundant water."

Gátra nodded, but whether because he believed him or because he recognized it as a complete falsehood was impossible to tell.

"Fascinating," he said in a level tone. "We did not know any lived in the mountains. Surely the weather is bitterly cold in winter, too cold for any to survive? Or do your wise women know how to shield your menfolk from the frost?"

All right, that had been blatant mockery. Time to show his teeth a little.

"If a woman could do such a thing, who is the bigger fool? The man who takes advantage of her knowledge, or the one who ignores it and freezes to death?"

Gátra's gaze met his steadily for a moment. Had he provoked the leader too much, or earned some measure of respect by standing up for himself and his people?

Finally Gátra said, "If women had such knowledge, you would speak truly, but our women do not. Yours must be wiser."

Kallian had to stop himself from saying something conciliatory, such as *I meant no offense*. It would have been an expected sign of respect in Klen after an angry exchange. Here, it was more likely to have the effect of returning him to a position of weakness. In the end, he said nothing, just continued to meet Gátra's gaze without flinching.

It appeared to be the right decision. "There will be other chances for us to learn about each other. Tonight, there will be a feast in honor of our guest." He nodded toward Kallian. "You will see some of our customs on such an occasion. There will be plentiful food, and entertainment afterward that I have no doubt will be to your liking."

Shortly after sundown, a man—Kallian recognized him as one of the people who had watched while he and Gátra played their cat-and-mouse game that afternoon—came to his little cabin.

"The feast is beginning. Come with me."

A short distance from the leader's quarters, a fire crackled. On a spit above it was what looked like the carcass of a deer, roasting slowly, the juices sizzling as they dripped into the flames. Despite his caution, his stomach rumbled. However little he trusted these people, he wouldn't shy away from sharing their food if offered.

When Gátra saw him, he smiled broadly and made a beckoning gesture. The ruddy firelight caught the leader's skin and turned it bronze, and sitting upright in a chair surrounded by his retainers, he looked like a cast metal statue of one of the kings of old.

And powerful. He was in a sleeveless shirt that showed prodigiously muscled arms and shoulders. If Kallian was going to get out of this, it was going to be by brainpower, not brute strength.

But for now, Gátra seemed friendly enough.

"Kallian, our guest," he said in a commanding voice, and for a moment, every face turned to him.

He scanned the crowd of people. Not all the women

looked as downtrodden as the one who had brought him food and water that afternoon, but all were quiet, and in positions of obvious submission. The men clearly were in control here, and the stark contrast between this place and Klen explained Gátra's amused puzzlement at Kallian's description.

A woman carrying a platter served him food—slices of the roasted deer meat, bread, some sort of cooked greens, and a cup of what appeared to be beer. He hesitated at first, but when he saw a nearby man digging in after the woman served from the same platter, he ate hungrily.

He said little during the meal. Gátra kept up a steady stream of talk, mostly about his own exploits hunting and fighting and making love. The other men responded mostly in monosyllables of approval and the occasional fulsome compliment. The feast, obviously, was not in Kallian's honor so much as an opportunity for Gátra to demonstrate his strength and prowess, to make it obvious he was a leader to be reckoned with.

If Kallian hadn't seen the light of wily intelligence in Gátra's eyes earlier that day, he'd have believed his earlier assessment of the Runners being little more than human-like animals. But there was no doubt in his mind that these people were just as smart as his own, and that underestimating the leader's brains would be a mistake that might well turn out to be his last.

But there was no doubt that the Samada lived in the realm of the physical. After the feast there were staged fights between powerful young men stripped to their loincloths, contests that were evidently won by forcing the opponent to his knees or making him fall. Each victory elicited enthusiastic applause for the winner. After this, an older man sang a long, wandering song in praise of Gátra and his ancestors, using flowery and elaborate figures of speech and metaphors that were so abstruse Kallian stopped trying to figure them out.

Or perhaps it was the beer. It was potent stuff, and he'd lost track of the number of times his cup had been filled. Watching the spectacle unfold in front of him, he felt disembodied, almost like he was hearing about something that had happened to another man in another time, a tale of the long ago.

At the end—it must have been nearing midnight by that time—the women were finally involved as something other than servants, as they assembled into a swaying circular dance, accompanied by an older woman beating time on a frame drum. The men, still at the table, watched with obvious appreciation, but Kallian couldn't get past his revulsion at their subjugation. The dance was obviously meant to be enticing, but he couldn't watch it for long without feeling his gorge rise.

When it was done, there was some scattered applause, and Gátra turned to Kallian with a broad smile that flickered white in the light from the fire.

"Which one?" he said.

"Which one what?"

"Which one do you want? As our guest, you have your choice first. Do not hesitate."

Kallian struggled to keep the shock out of his face, with only limited success, and he couldn't stop himself from saying, "Without her consent?"

Gátra, and several men nearby, guffawed. "Do you ask the deer's consent before putting an arrow through its heart? This is only a different sort of arrow, one that is far more pleasant." He paused. "Unless you prefer to spend your seed on your own belly every night." He made an obscene gesture, and the laughter grew.

Kallian's face reddened, and he hoped it wasn't obvious in the firelight. "I… I mean no discourtesy. It is simply not the way of our people."

A hard glint entered Gátra's eyes. "But it is the way of

ours. Choose, or one will be chosen for you. It is discourteous to refuse a host's hospitality."

Kallian's heart gave an unsteady gallop. "I don't know," he said, his voice thin. "Her, I guess."

He pointed off toward the line of women in what he intended as no particular direction, but Gátra laughed again and shouted, "Shisla! You've been selected by our guest for the night. Pleasure him as many times as he needs." He grinned at Kallian's obvious discomfort. "You chose well. I've had her myself. You must tell us about it tomorrow morning."

Shisla, a tall woman not much older than Kallian, with straight brown hair and dark eyes, came to him and took his hand. Not knowing what else he could do, he rose, and she led him toward his cabin, and from behind him came the sounds of talking and bellows of laughter.

Obviously the whole thing had amused the men greatly. Kallian found his disgust turning to outrage.

Inside the cabin it was pitch dark, only enough light to make out the vague outlines of the furnishings. She led Kallian to the bed, and then slipped her hands under his shirt.

"Wait," he gasped out.

For the first time, she spoke. "Why?"

"Because this is wrong."

"Wrong how?"

"Do you want this?"

"What I want is unimportant."

He took her hands and drew them away from his skin. "It is to me. Your wishes are just as important as mine."

"That is what your people believe?"

"Yes. Fervently."

There was a long pause. "If I told you that I wished it, would it satisfy you?"

"If it was true."

"Do men and women not make love in your home place?"

"Of course they do." Kallian passed one hand across his

face. "But only if they both consent. There are few restrictions on who makes love to whom, or how often. The only requirement is that both consent, that both desire it."

She pulled him against her, once again pushing up his shirt and stroking his bare back. She tucked her face into his neck, and laughed softly. "It seems that you do desire it. Men cannot hide such things."

"I can't help how my body reacts," Kallian said, a little desperately. His emotions were whirling in his mind, a miasma of anger and lust and righteous outrage and desire and alcohol. She slipped her hand down the back of his pants, and taking one step backward lay down on the bed, pulling Kallian on top of her, and any resistance he felt was swamped beneath a flood of raw need.

ten

. . .

Thalaté had gotten to where he was—confidant to the leader, trusted friend, the unofficial second-in-command of the Samada—by being cautious, wary, and trusting absolutely no one.

His name meant He-Who-Watches, and when he earned that name after surviving his ordeal at age fifteen, it seemed almost prescient. He was given the appellation because of better than average eyesight, but it could well have been referring to other kinds of watching. It seemed to him sometimes that it was what he spent all his waking hours doing. Watching the others, at least the ones of any stature who could potentially be a threat. Analyzing and evaluating everything he saw and heard. Seeing something that needed to be done, and doing it before being asked, sometimes before anyone else had even noticed.

And most of all, waiting.

Gátra was no fool, that was certain. But he was also easy to win over. He had craved the role of leader because of what it brought him—the best food, the finest women, a continuous litany of compliments and flattery. Thalaté wondered if Gátra believed all the extravagant praise on his strength, his looks, his brains, his virility. Sometimes it appeared that he did, and sometimes he seemed to recognize it for the empty flattery it was. Thalaté added to it himself when he thought it was prudent, but he was known as a man who seldom spoke unless necessary, so there were only occasional situations when he had to lie and add his voice to those of the fawners.

It was obvious the situation couldn't go on for much longer. Not that Gátra would tire of it, or of him. Despite his powerful muscles, the leader was a fundamentally lazy man, who once he was in power wanted to stay there with as little additional effort as possible, reaping the rewards of the position without giving anything back in return. What would end soon was Thalaté's acceptance of his own subordinate role. It would come down to finding a way to catch Gátra off guard and killing him, and that wouldn't be easy. He would only get one chance. Fail—even wound rather than kill him—and by sundown Thalaté's naked body would be pinned to a fir trunk by a dozen arrows and left there to rot.

Thalaté was forty years old. He still was strong and healthy, with a mind as sharp as it was when he was twenty, but that wouldn't last forever. When he killed Gátra and took over as leader, he wanted to have a reasonable hope of being in that position for a long time. And, perhaps, doing what Gátra had never done—extending the reach, power, and wealth not just of the leader, but of the Samada as a people.

The arrival of the outsider had thrown an interesting and unexpected complication into the situation, but one that could well be twisted to his advantage. Gátra's attention was turned to making the young man's arrival—and his ultimate death—into as much of a spectacle as possible, while at the same time using every opportunity to ridicule him and reinforce his own stature. Even forcing the visitor to choose a woman at the feast the previous night had been staged to make him uncomfortable, although he'd acquiesced soon enough, and by the noises coming from his cabin not long afterward, it seemed like his reluctance had been short-lived.

But whatever move Thalaté made, the prudent thing would be to do it before Gátra tired of the game and had the outsider killed. Or, as the leader had said, did the deed himself. Knowing Gátra's attention span for anything that didn't directly benefit him, it needed to be within the next day or two. There was no knowing when he might have another opportunity when the leader was so distracted.

But it did leave him with little time to plan. There was nothing to be done about that, though. He would have to watch, wait, and take the opportunity when it came.

Gátra summoned him not long after breakfast. Despite long years of practice, Thalaté felt a momentary pang of fear that the leader had become aware of the treasonous thoughts that had occupied his mind that morning. With some effort he forced the emotion away. There was no way Gátra could know.

Thalaté, as always, had showed what was in his heart to no one.

Adjusting his face into a suitable expression of deference and subservience, he crossed to the leader's quarters, mounted the two steps to the door, and walked inside.

"I desire your advice," Gátra said, with no preamble. "About the matter of our young visitor."

Thalaté didn't respond at first. Giving the leader advice had to be handled delicately. If possible, it was best to see if he could determine what Gátra already wanted to do, and advise him to do that.

He finally said, "In what sense, leader?"

"I had hoped to gain more information from him about where his home place is, and how many people live there, but I fear he is more wary than I took him for at first. He evades those kinds of questions, giving vague answers that provide little."

"He did tell us that his village is a five-day march, and is up in the mountains."

"Did you believe that to be the truth?"

Gátra wouldn't have asked that question if he didn't think it was a lie, so it was probably safe to answer in the negative.

"It did not have the sound of truth to me."

"Nor me. And if he lied about that, there is no certainty about anything else he said. Worse, this indicates that he is suspicious of us, and may sense our actual intent. Worst of all, some of the people are favorably impressed by him. The woman I had last night told me this during our pillow talk before we slept. I told her not to fear speaking freely, but to tell me what people were saying about Kallian Dorn. She said that his handsome face had turned the heads of a number of the women, and that even some of the men thought he gave the impression of being worthy and honorable."

"This could be awkward."

"Awkward. Yes. But what it means is that we need to cut his stay short, before his presence causes more favor to turn in his direction. Do you agree?"

Thalaté nodded. "Any information he provides would be inconsequential balanced against the damage he could do if he sways people."

"My thoughts exactly. I am glad to find we are in such close agreement."

Had that been a jab at his servility? It would not do to be seen as an empty-minded sycophant. Time for something other than bland agreement.

Thalaté stroked his chin thoughtfully. "Perhaps, prior to his execution, we might take the opportunity to question him further, so that his stay here might prove to be of some value. I, for one, would like to know why he has set out for the city in the south. I did not believe his statement that he merely wanted to see the world, and the city was part of it. Unless I misjudge him entirely, he was heading for the city with some specific goal in mind."

"Again, I agree, and in fact had come to that conclusion myself. But what can he know about the city that would make him take the risk of going there unaccompanied? Until recently we ourselves have had only hints of the city's existence, from so long ago that many believed it was a legend. And the outsider's home place is even farther north and more distant from the city than we are. Wherever he comes from, it is north of here. That much was obvious from the direction he was traveling."

"As you pointed out, leader, it seems as if there is only one likely source—the girl Lanya. Although it could be that someone else from the city made their way to Kallian's home place without our knowing."

A quick frown crossed Gátra's face. "You think so?"

"I think it is possible, yes. Perhaps not likely, but possible. I do not think we can rule it out. We are not enough people to keep eyes on the paths through the woods. And there may be paths we do not use, perhaps nearer to the ruined city you saw in your youth."

The mention of Gátra's glorious vision on his ordeal had been prudent. The crease on his brow smoothed out.

"What you say is true. We are too few to guard the ways to the north and south. But even if you are correct, it means that there has been *some* communication between the city and Kallian's home place, and not long ago. Truthfully, it matters little whether it was from the girl or from some other traveler. Regardless, I am certain information reached their leaders about the city, and what it contains. Do you have any thoughts of what could be valuable enough to drive him there?"

"I think we can narrow it down, based upon the fact that they thought it reasonable to send out only one man alone. It cannot be material riches. Even if he were a master thief, and able to get into the city and out without being captured, there is a limit to what he could bring back. The idea that he is going there from hostile motives is patently ridiculous. A diplomatic mission of sorts is a possibility, as you mentioned to me yesterday. Maybe he is an ambassador or at least an errand-boy between his leaders and those in the city." Thalaté paused, frowning. "Perhaps his purpose isn't so far from what he told us—to gather information. But I refuse to believe that whatever information he might be after, it's as innocent as he claims, and a mere curiosity-driven wish to find out about the world. People do not undertake such risks, alone, unless the potential rewards are great."

Gátra nodded, and did not respond right away. Thalaté had a momentary qualm that he had said too much, or something wrong, or worded it in such a way as to draw suspicion. But when the leader spoke, it was in the same neutral tone as before, and he nodded.

"You speak wisely. And however the young man is winning our people's hearts, or even putting potentially dangerous ideas into their minds, before I kill him I want to know what he sought. If his leaders considered it to be worth the risks, it must have great value."

Thalaté thought, with an inward smirk, that this was almost precisely what he had just said, but he only raised his eyebrows a little.

"That is wise, Gátra. Perhaps whatever it is, it will turn out to be something valuable to our people, as well."

Gátra frowned, and seemed to come to a decision. "I am glad to see we have come to the same conclusions. And I have thought of an approach that might work. Since Kallian is already suspicious of me—that much is clear from his evasiveness—perhaps he will divulge more if he thinks he has an ally."

"An ally, leader?"

"Yes. Someone he believes he can trust. Someone who

warns him that our intentions are not as benevolent as they seem. No specific details, you understand. We do not want him to know our exact plans for him. Especially not that we will kill him as soon as his usefulness to us is over. I believe that you might be able to persuade him."

"Me, leader? I was part of the hunting party that caught him and brought him back here, captive. Why would he trust me any more than he trusts you?"

"Have you spoken to him since?"

"Only twice, and that in brief. When I conducted him to his cabin after he spoke to you upon his arrival, and again when you summoned him for questioning prior to mealtime. In both instances I said only a few words, merely what was necessary to communicate to him your wishes. And he said as little to me in return."

"Then as far as you know, he believes you to be entirely loyal to me."

"I do not see any reason that he would not."

Gátra nodded. "That will work in our favor. When people are surprised by something unexpected, they sometimes reveal more than they intend. I want you to win Kallian's confidence. Tell him that you are suspicious of my intentions for him, and warn him to be wary. Again, no specific details, and no indication of how near that fate is. Lead him to believe we intend to keep him here as a slave, but will treat him well and eventually he will become one of us. Whatever it takes to win his trust, confirm his suspicions about me, and persuade him to divulge as much information as you can."

Thalaté feigned dismay. "I do not want anyone to believe me disloyal, leader. Even a captive who is destined for execution."

Had that been obvious toadying? Or had his amusement shown through his words? But Gátra gave a dismissive gesture with one hand.

"You need not be concerned with that. After he discovers

his mistake, his remaining life span will be short enough. And if anyone else discovers the ruse—if, perhaps, Kallian speaks to a woman he spends the night with—it will become clear in short order. As far as your own personal distress, keep in mind that you are merely doing my bidding."

Thalaté cast his eyes downward. "I will try, leader."

"Excellent."

"When do you wish for me to speak to him?"

"As soon as may be. I do not know if he has roused himself yet, nor if Shisla is still with him." Gátra smirked. "I told her to pleasure him as many times as he desired, and knowing her, she may well have worn him out completely. The best option would be after Shisla leaves his cabin, but before he has done so. If he is still groggy with sleep and from the spending of his lust, he may be easier to dupe. If, on the other hand, he is already at breakfast, then merely find a time to ask him quietly to have a word in private."

Thalaté gave a little bow. "It shall be so."

"As soon as it is prudent, come back and tell me what you have learned."

"I will, leader."

Another quick gesture, this one of dismissal. Thalaté gave another bow, and exited the leader's quarters.

As he walked toward Kallian's cabin, Thalaté's mind was spinning.

He was astonished at how the opportunity he sensed in Kallian's presence had been magnified into something beyond any scheme he could have concocted. And, best of all, the idea had come from Gátra himself, with no prompting at all. Now, not only could he plan to betray Gátra, he had the freedom to do so without falling under suspicion of treason himself. Plus, if Gátra's idea worked, Thalaté would find out what valuables the city in the south held, and could potentially use that for his own gain when he became leader in Gátra's place.

If he had crafted the scenario himself, he could not have done better.

His step quickened as he approached the little cabin where the outsider was housed. When he looked up at it, he began to smile.

eleven

. . .

When Kallian woke up, he was sprawled, stark naked, face down on the bed, one arm hanging limply over the side, fingertips brushing the wooden floor. His brain was sludgy, blurred, unable to hang on to a thought long enough to make sense of it. Whether this was because of the alcohol he had consumed the previous night, or the fact that he and Shisla had sex four times—at least, so far as he remembered— was impossible to know.

He opened his eyes. Shisla, still naked herself, stood at the little window, running fingers through her long hair to pull the tangles out. He looked at the curves of her body, expecting a return of the desperate lust he'd felt for her the previous night, but nothing happened. She heard him stirring, though, and as he rolled over, groaning, she turned toward him with a smile.

"Finally awake, then?"

He cleared his throat. "Barely."

She chuckled and sat next to him on the bed, resting one hand on his bare chest. "Perhaps you spent yourself so much that it will take a while to recharge."

He looked up at her, trying to focus on her face and more or less managing. "Why did you do that?"

"Do what?"

"Make love to me."

She gave him a curious frown. "Because you chose me. Because Gátra commanded me to. Because I think you are beautiful, and I desired you. You regret it?"

"No." He paused, then said, more firmly, "No. I don't. Did you know it was my first time with a woman?"

"I wondered. There is no lover in your home place that you have left behind?"

"None. It's not something I really desired. I mean, I feel desire, just as much as any man, but there was no one I felt strongly enough about to form such a bond."

She laughed. "It needn't be a bond. You think we're bonded now?"

"I don't know."

"Sometimes there is nothing more to it than merely desiring release, and giving that release to another. Your people only make love if it results in dedicating yourselves to one person?"

"No." He shook his head, trying to clear away the confusion he still was mired in. "It's not that. As I said last night, as long as there's consent, there are no restrictions. A couple can make love once and go their separate ways, or commit to staying together permanently. It is entirely their choice."

"So why didn't you find someone? There must be at least one willing young woman."

Kallian immediately thought of Lexa Sahin, who almost certainly would have said yes had he asked her.

"I honestly don't know. It always felt like I was waiting for something or someone who wasn't there."

She stroked his skin. "A pity you waited in frustration for years."

"It never bothered me."

"Perhaps you didn't know what you were missing."

"Perhaps not."

She glanced toward the window, and her face became serious. "I would like to speak with you, however, about something else." Her mouth quirked upward in a smile. "Unless you wish to make love again."

"No. Not right now, at least. What did you want to say?"

The smile vanished. "Don't trust Gátra. He has no intention of letting you go, whatever he might have told you."

"I got that impression. It always seemed as if he was toying with me."

"That's what he does. There are only three groups of people to him—flatterers, enemies, and people he thinks aren't worth worrying about." She paused. "The first he tolerates as long as they remain loyal to him. The second he kills outright. The third he plays with until he tires of them, and then has them killed or kills them himself."

"It must make most people into flatterers."

"At least they pretend to. How many are sincerely loyal is questionable." She gave another of her faint smiles. "The men, at least, are one of those three. The women he ignores unless there is some need we can fulfill. Other than that, we are of no consequence. Of course, most of the Samada men share that attitude. It is a mistake, not that they recognize it as such. The men amongst the Samada believe that because they see women as unfit for anything but service, that we are fools. Their attempt to keep us in the dark doesn't mean we *are* in the dark. We see, and notice, and talk about far more than they realize."

"And you've seen him treat other outsiders this way?"

She nodded. "There aren't many, but yes. I remember when three people were captured, perhaps six years ago. They came from the city in the south. A man, his woman, and a baby girl. Gátra wanted the woman, so he let the baby live for her sake, but the man he sacrificed to the gods. I heard him say that even if outsiders looked human, only the Samada truly were. When he was asked, if so, why he let the woman live, he laughed and said, 'I don't intend to make her my advisor, I only intend to fuck her.'"

Kallian winced. Lanya's mother. That anyone could treat someone so cruelly was beyond his comprehension.

"And you think he intends to sacrifice me as well?"

"I believe so. Or, if he thinks you worthy, to face him in single combat."

"How can I escape?"

Her brows drew together. "I don't know. I'm not certain you can. But I couldn't let you talk to him again without knowing the truth, without knowing how wary you must be. Gátra only thinks about what brings him glory and what instills fear in everyone around him. If you see a chance to escape, take it. You may not get another."

"Aren't you taking a risk telling me this?"

"Of course. If Gátra knew, he would kill me immediately. But as I said, he discounts women except insofar as they can serve him. It would never occur to him to think that I see him as he actually is, much less that I would have the courage to speak to you about it." She smiled. "It's the problem with arrogance—you underestimate everyone."

"Thank you for telling me this."

She touched Kallian's face. "You seem an honest, good man, and I wanted you to know. You were gentle with me last night—your desire burned hot, but even so, you were kind. I have been with many of the Samada men, but you are the first man who has cared about my pleasure as well as his own. I don't know how the people are in your home place, but I would wager they treat each other far better than the Samada do. And are very likely happier." She smiled again. "And if you do escape here and make your way back, find a woman to love. The nights are cold with no one to share your bed."

Kallian nodded.

She glanced back toward the window. "I should go. It is not ordinary for a woman to spend time in conversation with a man. If we were overheard talking, it might rouse suspicion." She stood, picked up her light shift and long dress she'd worn the previous day from where they'd been dropped, and quickly donned them. She turned and gave Kallian a little smile. "I wish you good fortune."

Once she was gone, Kallian stood and dressed much more slowly, and was slipping on his shoes when there was a light knock on the door.

Frowning, he said, "Come in?"

The door opened to admit the tall balding man who had been his attendant to and from speaking with Gátra. The man glanced in, his expression a little furtive.

"Shisla is gone?"

"Yes."

"May I come in?" His voice was deep, smooth, uninflected. A neutral voice, hard to read. "I would like to speak with you."

"Okay."

He walked inside, closing the door behind him, his footsteps making the old floorboards creak. Once in the room he stopped, standing perfectly still, arms hanging straight by his side. His immobility reminded Kallian of the statues in the Hall of Images back in Klen.

"My name is Thalaté. I am here to ask some questions, and to give you some advice. If you answer me honestly, I can promise that I will advise you well."

"Okay," Kallian said again. He could hear the wariness in his own voice.

"First, what was your actual quest? I am disinclined to believe you left your home place, alone, simply to see the world."

Kallian met Thalaté's gaze and held it, but said nothing.

Thalaté gave him a thin smile, his mouth the only movement in his motionless body. Everything about the man radiated caution, as if even moving his hands could give away what he was thinking.

"Come now. You need my help. Perhaps you do not yet know how much. Not only is your situation more perilous than you may realize, you do not have all the time in the world." He paused. "In fact, your time left is measured in days or hours."

"You're trying to frighten me."

"Am I? You should be frightened."

This was so much like what Shisla had told him only minutes earlier that his heart stuttered in his chest for a moment.

"Very well." He tried to keep the quaver out of his voice. No sense letting the older man know his blow had struck home. "If I am in such a dire predicament, tell me why I should trust that you have my interests at heart."

Thalaté shrugged. "I do not see that you have many options. I can tell you outright that Gátra is not your friend. If your suspicions of me are justified, I don't see how you are any worse off. On the other hand, if I am telling you the truth, you have much to gain by trusting me."

There was a long moment when neither man spoke.

Finally Kallian said, "All right. I'm listening."

"Then answer my question."

He took a deep breath, his mind in turmoil, trying to figure out what this man could possibly have to gain by warning him. But there seemed nothing dangerous about admitting where he had been going, especially considering his current situation.

"I was heading toward the city in the south."

"Why?"

"Seeking information. No more than that. I hold no ill intent toward their people, nor yours."

Another flicker of a smile. "That was evident from the

outset. You weren't leading an armed attack force, and were barely armed yourself. What sort of information?"

"Information that has been lost for hundreds of years. Information our ancestors had, in the Before Time."

Thalaté's eyebrows rose, startling in that carven-from-stone face. Apparently this was not an answer he had considered.

"And you believe such information lies in the city to the south?"

"I think it may. I'm not certain. But our leaders thought it worth the gamble to send me to find out, and perhaps bring useful knowledge back."

"Your leaders must think such knowledge very valuable."

"They do. Or at least that it has potential value. That it was worth finding out."

"That has the ring of truth." Thalaté seemed satisfied, at least for now. "It is the first thing you have said that does, since your arrival here. I can guess how you had word that such knowledge was still kept alive in the city, but honestly, it is of no great concern whether or not my guess is correct. You maintain that your people had no hostile intent?"

"None. As I said, not toward you nor the people in the city. Indeed, we couldn't have had hostile intent toward you, because we didn't even know you were here."

Thalaté nodded. "It suffices that I am convinced you are no threat to us. How you deal with the people of the city, and the information they may or may not have, are your concerns, not mine. Which brings me to what I can offer to your benefit. If you do not heed what I say, the city in the south will never know of your existence, because you will die here."

"For what reason?"

"Because Gátra tires of you. You seem cautious enough. You must realize his friendliness toward you is a sham."

Again, very much what Shisla had said. "It didn't seem sincere."

"No, it is very far from it. In the next day or two Gátra will find a pretense to kill you. He intends to do it himself, for public show. He will challenge you to hand-to-hand combat, to the death. And though you seem a strong enough young man, you surely realize that Gátra is built far more powerfully than you are. Should it come to actual fighting, you are certain to lose."

"If I'm doomed, why are you telling me this?"

"Because if you agree to cooperate with me, I will see to it that his advantage is removed, or at least reduced. One of the women who cooks his meals has been a lover of mine, and she is well enough disposed toward me that she will do what I ask. She told me during an unguarded moment that she had been in Gátra's bed as well, and he had seemed to take delight in hurting her, so I don't doubt she will be glad of an opportunity for revenge. There is a plant that grows in the woods with leaves that contain a strong sedative. If it is possible, she will mix the finely-chopped leaves into Gátra's food or drink before the fight. It won't kill him, but it will destroy his agility and give you a chance."

"Why not put enough in his food to kill him?"

Another slight lift of the eyebrows. "If I poisoned him to death, it would be considered dishonorable. Whatever the other men think of Gátra, if I did that and it was discovered, I would be driven out into the wilderness, if they didn't simply kill me outright."

The reason for Thalaté's treason suddenly became obvious.

"You're planning a coup. Once Gátra is out of the way, you want to take his place."

"Of course. It is long since the Samada had a leader who was interested in more than self-aggrandizement. I want to make more than a show of leadership."

"And if I succeed, you will release me?"

"You have my word."

Something about the speed with which Thalaté said the words struck a chill in his heart. "But you've also given your word to Gátra to support him, haven't you? Why would you honor your word to me and not to him?"

Some measure of respect came into the older man's eyes.

"You are cleverer than you appeared at first. Yes, of course I swore an oath to Gátra. All of the Samada men pledge loyalty to the leader once they reach adulthood. But that oath was compelled. Had I refused, I would have been driven away or killed. An oath under duress is surely not binding. But giving my word to you? What possible motive would I have to lie to you? What could I gain by telling you this if I did not intend to honor it? You are powerless to help me— except in this one way. And if you succeed, I will reward you with your freedom."

There was another long silence. Finally Kallian said, "I suppose I believe you. I don't seem to have many choices."

"You have no other choice, as far as I can see. Unless you consider letting yourself be beaten to death a choice."

"Thank you for helping me."

Thalaté gave another shrug. "Do not thank me prematurely. There are any number of ways this plan might miscarry. He might not consume enough of the sedative to disable him. The woman whom I will instruct to tamper with his food might be seen doing it, and Gátra warned. Even sedated, Gátra might still overpower you. But I can give you my word this far—if you can cripple or kill Gátra, it will clear the way for my assuming the role of leader. And if that happens, I swear to you that I will set you free, either to continue your quest or to turn your face toward home, which- ever you choose."

Kallian swallowed hard. "When is he planning on fighting me?"

"I do not know. Probably either today or tomorrow. Certainly no more. These sorts of contests always happen after the evening meal, once the fire is lit." Thalaté's face became grim. "One more thing. Before the fight, Gátra will tell you the rules of the ritual—no weapons, stripped to the waist, nothing used other than hands and feet. However, you need to realize that he has no intention of following those rules himself. He will do whatever it takes to win, to kill you, and will have no hesitation in using whatever weapon comes to hand. You must do the same." Thalaté looked at Kallian steadily. "Know this going in. You will have to use any means you have, fair or not, because Gátra surely will do so himself. Like every other rule we Samada have, Gátra believes that they apply to everyone but him. Therefore the only rule you must keep in mind is that one way or the other, the contest is to the death—of him, or of you."

twelve

. . .

Gátra was just finishing his breakfast when Thalaté approached him. The older man, as usual, was stony-faced. There was no way to tell from his expression if his task to extract information from Kallian Dorn had been successful or not. It sometimes bothered Gátra that his advisor was so deadpan, so secretive, and occasionally—usually at night, as he lay sleepless in his bed—he toyed with the idea that the man was scheming against him. Thalaté certainly had that kind of mind. He was a wily fox, something Gátra had used to his benefit many times.

But whenever he took a hard, rational look at the possibility of the man's disloyalty—perhaps even outright treason —he dismissed it. Thalaté had always been scrupulously obedient, often anticipating his wishes before he voiced them, and always correctly. He had never been anything but completely respectful, never betrayed the slightest dissatisfaction or dislike, and had obeyed Gátra's commands to the letter.

No, even though the leader trusted no one completely, he came closer with Thalaté than anyone else. It was why he had to stifle a smile, thinking of what his advisor was trying to convince that gullible young outsider to believe. If anyone could hoodwink Kallian Dorn, it was Thalaté.

The older man gave a quick, deferential bow. "Leader, I have no wish to disturb your meal, but there is a matter I would like to discuss with you in private."

"It is no problem, I was finished anyway." He got up, leaving the remains of his breakfast on the table for the women to clean up.

Gátra led the way to his quarters, Thalaté following with every indication of subservience.

Once the door was closed, the leader said, "Is this about what we discussed earlier?"

"Indeed it is."

"Tell me."

"I spoke at length with Kallian Dorn. Uncomfortable as it was for me to lie about such things, I told him that I was planning to betray you, and could promise him freedom if he would tell me what his mission was."

"Did he believe you?"

"He did. Whatever else you might say about the young man, he is not deceitful. Wary, perhaps, as any man would be in his situation, but honest. Such men usually make the assumption that others are honest as well, many times to their own misfortune. And he told me that he trusted me."

"What did you find out about his intentions? What had his leaders tasked him with doing?"

Thalaté frowned, recalling. "He said he was sent by his leaders to the city in the south, as you suspected. What he was after, apparently, was information. He claims that the people in the city retain memory of the Before Time, and that it could be valuable to find out what they know."

"From before the flood and the plague?"

Thalaté nodded. "So he says."

"Why?" Gátra shook his head. "Whatever information they had has lain dead for over six hundred years."

"I found this surprising as well at first, but upon reconsideration, I came to the conclusion that however long the knowledge has been neglected, this does not mean it would be without profit to learn about it. You no doubt know the legends concerning what our distant ancestors could do."

The leader stared at his advisor for a moment, then gave a belly laugh. "You believe such children's tales? Of flying machines and weapons that could kill at any distance and medicines that gave people health, strength, and long life? Of devices that showed you pictures of what was happening hundreds of miles away?"

"It matters little whether I believe them, leader. The important thing is that *he* does."

Gátra considered this for a moment, his smile fading, fingers drumming on the arm of his chair.

"Wisely said. A belief can be a strong motivation to a man. It is unimportant if the belief is true or not. But he told you that was enough of a motivation for his leaders to send him to find out? Odd. You are convinced that he was telling the truth?"

"As I said, I do not believe it is in him to lie. To evade, perhaps, but once I told him that I was on his side and against yours, he became frank enough."

"I have to admit to curiosity about what exactly he hoped to learn."

"I am curious as well. He did not seem to know any specifics."

"So he undertook a long trek, alone, on the off chance that something of value might be learned from people he'd never seen or spoken with before."

"It does sound foolish, leader."

"Even if Kallian is a young fool, I doubt his leaders are. They must have some sense of how they could profit by this knowledge. Do you think it could be valuable to us as well?"

"Indeed, I have no way of knowing, leader."

"We should find out. Should we reconsider what to do with Kallian Dorn? Instead of making an example of him, let him go his way, but tell him to bring us news of anything he learns. We might have advantage of what he finds without risking any of our own people."

"Leader," Thalaté said, a frown creasing his brow, there and gone in a moment. He shook his head. "I do not want to be seen as contradicting your wishes."

"No, what is it? I do not keep you in my employ simply to tell me you agree with me whether you do or not."

"Thank you. I have no wish to usurp your role as the supreme leader of the Samada."

Sometimes the man's deference was more of an annoyance than anything, but Gátra said, trying to keep his voice patient, "You do not usurp my role by giving me advice." He paused. "Especially when I ask for it."

Thalaté bowed. "I wonder if sending Kallian out as a scout, as it were, is a wise plan. The risk is entirely his, as you have pointed out. But suppose he does learn something valuable—some powerful secret of the Before Time that has been kept alive in the city all these years. Do you think he will voluntarily come back here to tell you about it, or allow himself to be captured a second time? Wouldn't he evade us in whatever way possible, even if it meant going far out of his way? As you have said, the young man is clearly wary. Myself, I doubt that the knowledge of the Before Time still exists, in the city or anywhere else. Who would have remembered it and passed it down, through all the years of plague and famine and hardship? I believe that most of what is claimed about our ancestors is mere legend in any case. Anything known by the people in the city, therefore, would be no more than that."

"So you recommend killing him."

"I think it is wiser than letting him go, and being seen by the people as bowing to the wishes of a young outsider."

Gátra considered for a moment. "Perhaps you are right." He leaned back in his chair. "Very well. I will think on it further, and decide by tomorrow morning what is to be done. Whatever I decide—to release him or to kill him—it shall be done at nightfall tomorrow."

Thalaté bowed. "Whichever it is, I have no doubt whatsoever that it will be to the benefit of the Samada and to your own glory."

Well, that seemed satisfactory enough. Once again, he had the sudden sting of misgiving that his advisor was feigning his loyalty, laughing at Gátra while he wove other plans. But there was no trace of anything but respect in the man's face.

He dismissed the thought. For one thing, following up that suspicion would require him to press hard into Thalaté's secret thoughts and opinions. If he did so, and his advisor really *was* loyal, Gátra would look a fool for doubting him. And that was even assuming he *could* find out. Thalaté had a long history of keeping his own counsel. Determining if there was something more there would not be easy. He wondered if the man would even admit such a thing under torture.

Besides, he had other, more urgent things in the forefront of his mind. Despite having been with a woman the previous night, horniness had been building in him since he woke. He drove the heel of his hand into his groin and took a deep breath.

"One more thing. I feel myself in need of a woman. Go…" A slow smile spread across Gátra's face. "Go find Shisla and send her to me."

Shisla came in ten minutes later, her eyes cast downward respectfully. "You wished to see me, leader?"

Gátra frowned. Was there fear in her voice? What could she possibly be afraid of? She had been his lover on many occasions, but there was something new there, something he couldn't quite identify.

Gátra didn't answer, simply gave a jerk of his head toward the bed.

Shisla nodded, now with a resigned expression, and began to undress. That, at least, was more ordinary.

What he needed didn't take that long. Afterward, he lay on top of her for a few minutes, still coupled with her, feeling his pulse and breathing return to normal. He looked down at her, and she would not meet his eyes. That, too, was not unusual.

"What do you think of the young outsider?"

"In what way, leader?"

There it was again—that tone of subtle fear in her voice. His mind glanced across possible reasons for it, but once more he pushed the thoughts away as absurd.

"In any way you find worth noting. It seemed, at least, from the noises I heard coming from his cabin, that you served him well last night."

"I did so because you commanded it."

"Very good. Was there anything said between you that was unusual? I wish to know what he is thinking, and often a man in the throes of passion will say things he would not otherwise."

She gave a short, sharp shake of the head. "He said little to me, leader. Only telling me when he wanted me again, and afterward sleeping."

"He had you more than once, then?"

"Four times, leader."

Gátra chuckled. "Randy young buck. I wouldn't have predicted that." He pulled away from her and rolled aside to lie along the edge of the bed. Shisla didn't move, but lay there as if waiting for his permission. He propped his head up on one hand. "When he spoke to you, did he give you the impression that he mistrusted me, or that he believed my reassurances to him were false? That he recognized his danger?"

"None, leader. I doubt a man in fear for his life would be in the mood for lovemaking."

Another chuckle. Shisla was clever, for a woman.

"Probably true. In any case, I will offer you to him again tonight, and now I wish you to see if you can find out if he has any suspicions of my good intentions. Don't ask him outright, though. Don't place the idea in his mind. Talk to him freely, and see if you can bring him to the topic without it being obvious. Do it before you make love to him. A man is less wary when he feels desire. Afterward, when that need is satisfied, his mind is freer to think rationally."

"I will do as you ask, leader."

"Excellent. You may go."

She got up and dressed. Gátra, still naked, swung his legs over and moved up into a sitting position. He watched her until she gave a bow—eyes still downcast—and silently left the cabin.

He frowned, his gaze turned toward the floor but his eyes unfocused and distant. What was wrong with him? Everything was seeming out of joint lately. He'd begun having the vague sensation that he was not really in control perhaps six months ago. At first, those thoughts had been quick misgivings when he noticed where one man was looking, or that another was smiling when there was nothing to smile about. All were easy to dismiss. But lately, the thoughts had crystallized into something more serious, something that no distraction or self-reassurance could overcome.

What he'd told Shisla, that men thought more clearly when their aching balls had been taken care of, was true of him as well, but now his mind was swirling with anxious thoughts even more than before. All of them, on examination, foolishness. That a guileless young outsider was outsmarting him and had all of his plans figured out. That his most loyal advisor was secretly his enemy. That a woman he'd had more times than he could remember, and who didn't have the brains or the courage to betray him in any case, hid thoughts and ulterior motives behind her subservient voice and expression.

His frown turned to a scowl. Caution was one thing, but paranoia was another. He couldn't let his emotions control him. Now, sitting there in his silent cabin, his physical needs met for the time being, he forcibly dismissed his ill-founded worries. Neither Shisla nor Kallian were smart enough to scheme against him successfully. Thalaté might be smart enough, but he wouldn't do it. And even on the off chance that the one of the three was plotting rebellion, they wouldn't dare to act.

His furrowed brow relaxed. If he didn't get control of his errant thoughts, it would inevitably show in his behavior, and the other men would certainly see that self-doubt as weakness.

Then he *would* have a problem. It'd be ironic to create the very thing he feared by his own attention to it.

Gátra stood and pulled on his clothes. Now that he had both mind and body under control, he felt a great deal better. Plus, having commanded Shisla's aid, he had two people keeping an eye on Kallian Dorn. If the young pup really was planning on trying to escape, Gátra would find out about it in short order.

In any case, the outsider had only a day and a half left to live. Any plans he had would come to an end in a fight to the death the next evening. A fire, much like what he'd felt earlier, began to burn in his belly, but this time, it was nothing sexual. What he felt was pure bloodlust. It had been a while since he'd killed a man. Far too long, in fact.

He pictured himself battering Kallian's pretty face until it was unrecognizable. If there *were* any who were considering rebellion, let them watch that spectacle and realize the foolishness of their plans.

By the time he left his cabin, he walked with a swagger, once again confident that he was secure in his position and would be for a very long time.

thirteen

. . .

After leaving the leader's cabin, Shisla made her way to the women's quarters, where food preparation for lunch would already be starting. She, like all the other women of the Samada, was required to pitch in, but other than that tacit expectation, they weren't supervised very closely. The men mostly assumed that if there was a serious breach of protocol they'd find out about it regardless, and that in any case the women weren't intelligent enough to cause any real trouble.

Both of these perceptions were wrong.

Certainly there were likes and dislikes amongst the women. The Samada women had disagreements, jealousies, and rivalries, just as any group does. But none of them would have dreamed of asking for one of the men to intercede or to settle them. For one thing, doing so would have probably triggered a much worse punishment than was warranted, and might be meted out regardless of who was right and who was wrong. For another, the women had a long-standing habit of secrecy. Within the Samada they almost operated like their own miniature society, with their own rules and customs, acting independently—and largely without the knowledge—of the men.

And as far as intelligence, there were women whose understanding, wit, and knowledge would have been a match for any of the men. Not, of course, that the men would be likely to know that. One does not even attempt an intellectual conversation with a slave, especially a slave whose sole purpose is doing menial chores and being available for sex any time and with anyone, as demanded.

Stepping into the women's quarters was almost like walking into a different world. Shisla's face relaxed into a smile as she was greeted by a dozen different voices, from young women barely more than girls to grandmothers more than seven decades old. She responded in kind, then took her place at one of the long tables in the big central room, where women and girls were cutting up deer meat and foraged vegetables for that day's lunch.

"The leader had his fill of you already?" asked one of the nearest, Shisla's friend Lilan.

"Only once this time."

"Lucky," Lilan said with a shake of the head.

Several of the women nearby nodded.

"Maybe he won't be so twitchy now," said a young woman named Dovak. "He's been on edge ever since that outsider got here."

"I don't know why Gátra thinks the outsider is a threat," Lilan said. "He's hardly more than a boy."

"When you're a bully and a thug, everything new or different is a threat." Dovak turned to Shisla. "You were with the outsider last night, weren't you?"

Shisla nodded.

"How was he?"

"He's sweet. Kind. He was gentle with me. The women of his people are fortunate." She frowned. "I warned him of his danger."

"Didn't he know already?" Lilan sounded incredulous.

"No. Apparently the men of his people aren't violent. When he found out that Gátra was almost certain to kill him eventually, he was aghast. But perhaps since he knows now, he will be ready to escape when the time comes, or at least to fight back."

"What chance does he have? Gátra is twice his size, and has killed many times before."

There was a soft laugh from Saskia, an older woman who stood across the table from Shisla, methodically slicing venison thin and laying the strips in neat rows on a wooden platter. Shisla looked at her, raising one eyebrow.

"He may have a better chance than you realize," Saskia said.

"How do you mean?"

"This morning I was approached by Thalaté. Tomorrow night, far more will be decided than the fate of one young outsider."

"Oh." Shisla's eyes widened. It was no secret amongst the women that the senior advisor was looking for a way of overthrowing Gátra and becoming leader himself. The older man hadn't said anything—as far as Shisla knew, he didn't reveal his thoughts to anyone—but the contempt he felt when looking at Gátra was plain in his face, at least to someone who wasn't blinded by his own arrogant sense of invulnerability.

Saskia's motions with the knife never slowed, and she didn't look up from her work. "Thalaté sees this as an ideal opportunity to take what he's wanted for years. Perhaps the only opportunity he'll get. He's probably right."

Dovak goggled at her. "Why did he tell you?"

Saskia laughed again. "He's asked for my help. He will see to it that the fight Gátra is planning with the young outsider happens tomorrow after the evening meal. He has asked me to place some *adnéka* leaves, finely chopped, into Gátra's food."

The entire room fell dead silent except for the clicking of Saskia's knife against the table.

"He believes that will work?" Shisla spoke in a near whisper. "That it will disable him enough that the outsider stands a chance?"

Saskia shrugged. "Thalaté may only be hoping, but I know for certain. My mother knew about the uses of plants. She is the one who taught me how to use *kistas* root for women to rid themselves of it when they conceive after being raped. It is why Gátra has no children, you know?" She gave a mirthless laugh. "She also used *adnéka* to dull the pain of people who were mortally ill. It is a strong sedative. The amount has to be right, however. It is the difference between sedation, delirium, and death. He asked that I put enough in the leader's food to make his reflexes slow and sluggish, but not enough that it's obvious he's been poisoned. He is afraid that if Gátra shows clear signs of poison, the other men will denounce him as a traitor. On the other hand, if the outsider seems to win fairly, there will be no question of succession."

"And you're sure you can do that?"

"Of course I'm sure."

A wild hope rose in Shisla's heart, both because of the possibility of Kallian's deliverance and that Gátra's downfall might be imminent. Just about all of the men considered the women as servants, but there was no doubt that Gátra was by far the most brutal of them. The oldest women claimed that he was the worst leader in memory. Whoever took his place—whether it was the crafty, cunning senior advisor, or another—it would be an improvement for everyone.

"Gátra told me that I was to spend the night with Kallian again tonight."

Saskia gave her a worried frown. "You won't tell him, of course?"

"Of course not." She paused. "I would not betray women's knowledge to a man, however kind he is. But it does hearten me to know that he has a chance."

"I would hate to see such a handsome young man killed," Dovak said earnestly.

"As would I." Shisla took a deep breath. "But perhaps it might be best if any of you who are willing would bring knives with you when the time comes for the fight. Whatever happens to Kallian, I think we all agree that we cannot let Thalaté lose."

Murmurs of assent.

"What will the other men think if there is a fight between those who support Thalaté and those who support Gátra, and the women take part?" Lilan asked. "Nothing of the kind has ever happened before."

"I am hopeful of two things," Shisla said. "First, that the poison works well enough that Kallian can kill Gátra outright. That would be the best outcome. But if that doesn't happen, that there are enough people who hate Gátra that if he does survive, the Samada—men as well as women—will turn on him. I, for one, would not shy away from taking part in that, even if I die in the attempt."

Shisla spent the rest of the morning and afternoon in deep thought, going through her chores with only half of her attention. The weather was hot, sultry, heavy, promising rain later, but for now, it was oppressive, still as death.

But that was not the reason for her distraction.

As she was serving the midday meal she watched Gátra, Thalaté, and Kallian closely, looking for any sign of trouble, any indication that the fight to the death might happen earlier than planned. Gátra seemed in high spirits, laughing and joking with the other men, once again poking fun at Kallian about everything from his strength to his intelligence to his sexual prowess. When Kallian responded it was quietly and with few words, seeming uncomfortable but neither challenging the leader's taunts nor giving away that he knew what was planned for him.

Thalaté, as always, spoke only when spoken to, and showed no emotion at all.

It was after the remains of lunch were cleaned up and the preparations begun for the evening meal that Shisla mumbled some excuse and left the women's quarters. Her heart was pounding in her ribcage from fear for what she was about to do combined with certainty that there was no other choice to be made.

Her fondness for Kallian and hatred for Gátra were strong enough, but they were nothing compared to her fierce loyalty to the other mothers, sisters, daughters, and friends with whom she spent most of her waking hours. Saskia, she knew, would consider it a betrayal, but she hoped that once it was all over, she'd be forgiven for the breach of confidence.

She caught Thalaté as he was leaving a discussion with the leader and heading back to his own quarters, probably for a quick nap in the heat of the afternoon. He had one foot on the first step up into his cabin when Shisla said, "Sir, may I have a moment of your time? There is something I need to say to you."

Thalaté turned, and for once his face showed surprise. It was quickly hidden by his usual impassivity, but for a moment, there was shock in his eyes—shock and fear. It was more than the oddness of being approached by a woman.

It was a sudden fear that his plan was known to others.

But he said in a level voice, "Of course," and motioned her to follow him into his quarters.

He shut the door behind them. No need to ask him for privacy. Shisla smiled to herself. The wily senior advisor clearly knew how precarious his situation was.

After the door closed, she turned to him, at first with her eyes respectfully downcast.

"What is it, then?" he said, an impatient edge to his voice.

"I have a request, sir."

"Yes?"

Shisla forced herself to raise her chin, and—for one of the first times she could recall—her gaze locked on to a man's with a fierce intensity.

"I know what you've planned. Saskia told me. I wish to make a bargain with you."

Thalaté's face paled. "What plan?" he choked out. "And a… a bargain? What do you mean?"

Shisla didn't flinch. "I do not believe we have time to play games. Surely others saw me come in here. If we spend too long in conversation, there will be questions. Questions you do not want to answer."

There was a long pause, then Thalaté swallowed hard. "Very well. I am listening."

"When the fight happens tomorrow night, Kallian Dorn must win. At all costs, he must win."

"Let us assume that I know what you're talking about."

Shisla smiled. Even now, the old fox couldn't bring himself to admit that his secret plan was known to others. She forged ahead.

"I will help to make certain that Kallian wins, and that you take Gátra's place as leader. But only on two conditions. If you do not agree to them, I will go to Gátra with what I know."

His face showed outrage, but when he spoke, it was nearly a whisper. He was taking no chances of being overheard.

"He would slay you for even hinting at such an accusation!"

"You're so certain?" Shisla raised one eyebrow. "You believe your own position so safe that Gátra would never even consider the possibility that you would betray him? To me, Gátra does not seem the type of man whose faith in a person is ever really secure. I doubt it would take much to shake it, and what then? You've seen before how he deals with people whom he suspects of disloyalty." She tilted her head. "But perhaps I am wrong. You know him better than I do."

He licked his thin lips, a nervous, furtive gesture. "You are playing a dangerous game, my dear."

"As are you," she shot back. "But the difference is, I'm not the one who is right now in a cold sweat with fear."

Thalaté clenched his fists. "I should kill you where you stand."

"Are you armed? I doubt it." She pulled one of the long knives used in meat preparation from the deep pocket of her dress. "I am. You think I won't use it? I may have hazarded everything on one throw of the dice, but having gone this far, surely you must realize I would not hesitate to go the rest of the way. So I repeat myself—I have two conditions. You must swear to both or I will tell Gátra what I know, and afterwards I think I will not be the one facing execution."

Again, there was silence for a moment. That bolt evidently struck its target.

"Very well. What are your conditions?"

"First, that if Kallian lives, you allow him to go free."

Thalaté frowned, and gave a quick gesture with one hand. "I was already planning to do that. What is the other?"

Shisla inhaled deeply, and let the breath out slowly, trying to steady her voice. "My other condition is when you become leader, that you change how women are treated. I and my sisters were taught by our mothers and grandmothers that long ago, in the Before Time, men and women were equals, that neither took precedence. That every person had the right to their own will and their own body. I want you to assure me that you will see to it that this happens."

Thalaté gave a scoffing noise. "You overestimate what the leader is capable of. Even if I were to become leader and make that demand, you believe that the other men would agree to it?"

"There will be some who will fight it, and you. But a man such as yourself, skilled with words, will no doubt be able to convince others to see the benefits. I spoke at length to Kallian about the customs of his home place, where women are treated as equals. My eyes were opened. For many years, the Samada have been wasting half of our collective intelligence, courage, and abilities, because the men thought the women unworthy of anything but slave labor and the pleasures of the bed." She was silent for a moment, her gaze locked on his. He seemed to want to look away, but simply couldn't. "As far as our intelligence and courage," she added, a flicker of a smile touching her lips, "I hope this discussion has convinced you that I, at least, am any man's equal."

A long silence. "I will do what I can." It came out thin, strained, reluctant.

"No. That is not good enough." Her voice was low but intense, cutting through the heavy, humid air like a blade. "You will do more than that. Now that you know what mere women are capable of, you will not dare to break your word. Once Gátra is overthrown, and everyone knows our role in it, you think we would not turn against you if you prove to be false? What would we have to lose but our lives? Some men may resist, yes. But women are strong, and we will never again kneel to you, or offer up our bodies freely to assuage your lust. For my sisters and me, this is our chance to free ourselves from chattel slavery. Why would we ever accept that role again?"

Thalaté's dark eyes looked into hers. In them she saw anger, resentment—and fear. Crafty as he was, he knew he was cornered.

"You speak for many. Are you sure the other women will

back you? That if the men fight for what they've always had by birthright, the women will not simply crumple and resume the position they've always had? At least it is safe."

"Safe? If this is safety, I choose to fight."

"And the other women?"

"I have faith that they will not falter. Another mistake you men have made is to assume that because women don't speak to you about their hopes and dreams, they don't speak to each other. But you are right—I am one woman presuming to speak for many. So for myself and myself alone, I tell you this. I will never turn back, not on pain of death. I'm not afraid to die. And once you've lost death as a threat, where will you go?"

fourteen

. . .

After the evening meal, Kallian excused himself, saying he felt unwell, and went to his cabin. Thalaté had told him the fight might happen that evening, and when he said he was leaving the table he half expected Gátra to stand up and challenge him on the spot, but the leader simply watched him with an amused smile and said to have a pleasant sleep. There was an eruption of laughter from the men as soon as he was nearing his cabin door—another joke at his expense, he was certain of it—but he simply continued walking as if he hadn't heard.

All during both meals that day, Gátra had taunted him. It was impossible to tell whether it was simply to ridicule someone he looked down upon, or an attempt to goad Kallian into defending himself. He held his tongue through it all.

What Gátra thought or said was irrelevant. Let him brag about having more courage, stronger muscles, and a bigger dick. None of that mattered. All that would count was whether Thalaté's plan was going to work, and if Kallian could somehow win the fight against Gátra the next day—or escape beforehand.

Escape, though, seemed impossible. Whenever he was

outside his cabin, he was being watched. Guards, usually two but sometimes three, followed his movements, acting as if they were otherwise occupied, but clearly monitoring him for any sign of bolting. The men on guard were obviously chosen for strength and speed. Any attempt to run would be over quickly.

So there was nothing for it but to hope that Thalaté had not only told him the truth, but could follow through on his plan without Gátra finding out.

He sat down on the cot. It was still early evening, but truth be told, he was exhausted. Perpetual worry and wariness drain a man's energy. He yawned, kicked his shoes off, then pulled his shirt over his head and tossed it aside. May as well try to get some sleep.

Then there was a quiet knock on the door.

"Yes?"

The door opened, and Shisla's form was silhouetted, backlit by the light from the fire burning in the center of the camp, where everyone took their meals.

"May I come in?"

"Sure."

She stepped inside and closed the door.

"I would like to spend the night with you again, Kallian."

"You would like to? Or Gátra told you that you had to?"

She smiled. "It could be both, you know."

He nodded. Tiredness swept over him, a deep weariness coupled with a desire that this all be over, whatever was destined to happen tomorrow night. He wished momentarily that he had Syra's foresight. Knowing what would happen would have taken the sting out of it. Half of anxiety, he realized, was never being certain which way things would go.

"May I stay?"

He looked up at her, and as with the night before, saw nothing but kindness in her eyes.

"Yes. But I don't feel like making love right now."

"That's all right. There are other ways of finding comfort in someone else's presence."

She sat next to him on the bed, slipping one arm around his waist. After a moment, she drew him down next to her, holding him close.

"Are you afraid?"

"Of course. Only a fool would not be."

"At least you are forewarned."

"I don't know what good it will do me."

She stroked his hair. "All is not lost. Gátra is overconfident. When he asked me to come to you tonight, he told me I was to find out if you had any suspicions of him. Tomorrow, I will assure him that you do not, that you trust him completely and have no idea what is being planned."

He didn't respond. Should he tell her about Thalaté's plan to drug the leader before the fight? His tendency was always to keep his own counsel. He had been quiet and solitary since he was a small child. But even so, he knew that he often trusted people too much. He himself was straightforward and honest, and expected others would be the same. Now he was caught in a dangerous game of cat-and-mouse, with cross purposes and deceit and trickery on all sides. It was impossible to know what people's actual motives were, who was on whose side, or even who was telling the truth and who was lying.

In the end, he said nothing. Shisla continued to hold him and stroke the back of his head.

Finally she said, "There are many who want you to prevail tomorrow night."

He sighed. "Do all the Samada know what is planned, then?"

"I think that everyone is expecting it. Gátra's ways are known all too well. Probably few know exactly when it will happen, but most think a combat to the death is all but a certainty."

A tremor ran through his body. By this time tomorrow, would he be lying, battered and dying, on the forest floor?

It seemed the most likely outcome.

"Gátra does not have the support he thinks he has." Her voice was quiet and soothing. "He has wronged far too many people in his time as leader. If there is a possibility you might triumph over him, you will have every chance of going free."

"I have to kill him first."

"Take courage, Kallian. There are subtleties here you do not see."

He frowned. Did Shisla know of Thalaté's betrayal? The plan to poison Gátra's food involved one of the women, he'd said. Perhaps Shisla had overheard Thalaté and his accomplice talking?

Or was she referring to something else entirely?

The whole game was too intricate for his mind. He buried his face in Shisla's neck.

"I can't imagine how the Samada live like this, every day filled with such violence and fear and deceit."

"It is terrible, yes. But I am hopeful that it will not stay this way forever." She kissed his forehead. "You should try to sleep. Whatever happens tomorrow, it will not be helped by your worrying yourself into sleeplessness now." She ran her hand down his side, and kissed him again, this time on the mouth.

He gave a shuddering sigh. This might well be his last night alive. Would he ever again be held lovingly, laugh with a friend, kiss a woman? The weight of it dragged him downwards. Too much more talk of it, and he'd cry. Even though Shisla's concern for him was touching, he wasn't ready to be that vulnerable in front of her.

A sense of bleakness enveloped him. He would die here, and be forgotten, and that was that. What good was tenderness and kindness when it would all end in blood and pain?

Useless. Garlin Abraham had been right to question his desire to go on this fool's errand. If only he'd listened.

It seemed like sleep would be impossible. How could a man sleep the night before he was to be executed? Shisla drifted off—her breathing slowed and deepened, and even though her arm around his middle relaxed, it never moved away. But finally, despite himself, he slipped into an uneasy sleep.

Kallian woke in the middle of the night. Shisla was sound asleep, curled up next to him, one hand still on his belly. The air was warm and heavy, his skin damp with sweat. He still wore nothing but his lightweight pants, but even those felt uncomfortably hot. He got up, moving her hand gently—she didn't stir—and walked to the door, letting himself out as quietly as he could.

He was certain he was still being guarded. Gátra wasn't nearly fool enough not to watch for an escape during the cover of darkness.

He went to a nearby tree and peed against the trunk. There was a small view of the night sky above him, and the moon near full peeked through the arching branches of fir trees. It looked hazy, blurred, and there was a ring around it. The people in his home place thought it was a sign from the gods of coming misfortune when there was a ring around the moon. He doubted it, but what could its cause be if not that?

Perhaps that knowledge was somewhere in the vast collection of books Lanya had told him about, held by the people of the city in the south. Maybe the men and women of the Before Time had known such things. No one did now, it seemed, unless the knowledge had somehow survived and a scholar in the city had stumbled upon the explanation.

He finished up, readjusted his pants, and looked around.

He couldn't see who was watching him, but he felt the man's eyes following his every move. He turned back, walking the few feet to the cabin, his footsteps heavy with weariness. Once inside, even the dim, occluded light from the moon coming in through the little window left the interior of the cabin nearly pitch dark, but he found his way to the bed and climbed back in.

This time he slipped his arm around Shisla and gently pulled her close. The idea that such a kind, intelligent, articulate woman was trapped here, victim of a brutal tribal leader and his cronies, was heartbreaking, but at least he could keep her safe and comfortable for the rest of the night, even if he couldn't change her situation.

Only a minute later, he was asleep again.

When he awoke again, a gray light trickled in through the window. Morning, but dreary, and still dripping with humidity. He stretched and yawned, and his movements made Shisla stir.

She slid her hand over his chest, then down his belly, then down lower still. He felt her smile against his shoulder.

"You seem to be in the mood this morning."

"I frequently wake up this way," Kallian said, embarrassed. "It doesn't mean you're under any obligation to do anything about it."

"That is really an important thing to your people."

"What is?"

"Consent."

"It's the most important thing."

"Has it always been that way?"

"Yes. It is one of our most dearly held beliefs, because we know what happens when that rule is broken and people are allowed to use each other and take what is not theirs to take.

One of our founders, Blessed Mary—the tradition is that right before she died, six hundred years ago, she told everyone, 'The world has been dragged down by people who obey neither the rules of the gods nor the rules of men and women'…" He frowned. "I'm sorry, you don't want a history lesson."

"No." Shisla stroked his skin softly, but her touch was calming, not arousing. "I want to know. You have the memory of people from so long ago? The Samada barely recall what happened to our grandfathers and grandmothers. The past is considered irrelevant."

His frown turned into a smile. "Our cultures… they are so different. Our devotion to our heritage runs deep. There is a person in Klen who is the repository of our entire history, all our stories and music, and both of our languages, the common and the sacred. She…" His cheeks warmed. "I am her apprentice."

"So you are learning what she knows?"

"Yes. I am not very far along, yet. I've only been with her a year. It is a lot to learn. If I knew more, if I'd studied with her longer, the four oracles who are our leaders would probably have forbidden me to leave. There would be too much chance of losing our collective knowledge, if the Guardian of the Word were to die while I was gone, and then I… died too."

She must have caught the hesitation in his voice, because she again gently moved her hand against his skin. "I do not believe you are going to die today."

He didn't answer. Anything he could have said would have sounded either self-pitying or fatuous.

"Tell me some legend from the history you have learned."

"You really want to hear it?"

"Of course. The Samada have their stories and songs, of course, but nothing like what you have described. Of all that you know, which story is your favorite?"

He took a deep breath. She was trying to distract him from

his fear, but her interest seemed sincere. Of the hundreds of tales he'd learned, what should he tell her? He thought of the stories that inspired courage. Perhaps recounting one of them would draw on the strength of his forebears, lift him up from the helpless terror he felt. He tried to relax his mind, sinking into the lessons that Syra had taught him, remembering the histories they had recited over and over until he knew them flawlessly, down to the last word.

"In the Before Time, there was a man named Soren. He would one day become Blessed Soren, one of the nine founders, and take the mantle as the second oracle in the lineage of Blessed Mary of the Bridge. But before that, he was an ordinary man, a teacher, a man of great knowledge but not yet one of the chosen. On the last day, he was with the Blessed Quaice, who gave us the sacred language, all unawares of what was transpiring until the Blessed Quaice said, 'It has begun. Just as I foretold.' And at those words the Blessed Soren was deathly afraid, not only for himself but for his beloved, Finn, who was at the time far away, too far for Soren to find and take to safety."

"One of your people's heroes took another man as a lover?"

"Why should he not?"

Shisla gave a little shrug. "Such urges are considered unnatural by the Samada, as if a man is lowering himself to the status of a woman. Such a man would be driven out, not revered."

"To us, love is love, whatever form it comes in. Men and women have the same status, and they are free to express love and desire to whom they wish."

She didn't respond for a moment, then finally said, "It seems to me a much happier way to live. I find myself wishing that I lived with your people, not my own." She stroked his shoulder. "But please continue with your tale."

He took a deep breath.

"It was at this time that the terror started, led by She of the Unspeakable Name, who brought fire and misery and death to all she encountered. But despite Soren's fear, he knew he could not save only himself and leave Finn behind, and he swore an oath to the gods that he would not leave without his beloved, not if the sword was at his throat. He searched everywhere, and in each place the people said, 'We know no one named Finn. Perhaps he is dead.' But Soren would not believe them, and would not abandon his search.

"Along the way he was captured by She of the Unspeakable Name and beaten nearly to death, but at the last moment he tricked her with a clever ruse and escaped. Even then, bleeding and bruised, he still would not give up. He found twelve little children, whose parents had been slain, and swore an oath to save them as well, putting his own life and safety behind any of the children's, and especially, behind Finn's. His path reunited him with the other Founders, and finally his beloved Finn, and great was their joy when they were rejoined forever. But the Blessed Mary, whose foresight never failed her, said, 'We cannot tarry, for there is great peril. There will be time for you to embrace once the danger is past. For death follows on our very heels.'

"And the Blessed Soren said, 'I have faced death and he has not claimed me. Neither will he claim me now, not me nor any of these who are under my protection.' But Mary urged them with all speed to the Bridge, and when they were in the midst of it, she said, 'This is my time. You must go now.' And she turned to face their foe. But Soren and Finn would not let her face She of the Unspeakable Name all alone, so they were standing behind her when Mary saw their enemy coming up with her ranks, to slay them all. Mary raised her hand and said, 'I truly pity you. The world has been dragged down by people who obey neither the rules of the gods nor the rules of men and women, and now there is no appeal to the gods that will save you.' She held out her hands, and there was a great noise and tremor, and the Bridge collapsed into the cold waters, carrying She of the Unspeakable Name and all her men to their deaths. But Blessed Mary herself was standing too close to the breach, and she fell with her enemies, of all the Founders the only one who never saw the valley of Klen in this life.

"Finn himself was nearly taken, too, but Soren caught him before he fell, fulfilling his oath to live if his beloved lived and die if his beloved died. Then the waters rose, and Soren knew that there was little time left to get the people to safety, so he turned and fled, urging the children and the others to all speed. They fled to a hill, exhausted and unable to go any farther, and Soren turned back toward the rising waters, holding out one hand and saying, 'No. Not one of these. You shall not take a single one. They are under my protection.'

His throat tightened, and against his will a tear trickled from the corner of his eye. When he spoke again, his voice was strained and trembling.

"And the waters, as if they dared not disobey, turned back, not harming a single one of them. The children he saved have become our ancestors, so without the unswerving courage and great heart of Blessed Soren, and his oath to find his beloved Finn, Klen would never have been founded, and all of our long history, our tales and legends and songs and languages, would vanish like a mote of dust."

He stopped, and his breath caught in a helpless sob. "I can't do it, Shisla." Now the tears would not be stopped, and the words tumbled out of him like a torrent. "I can't. I'm not like the Blessed Soren. My heart is pitiful and feeble. I'm just a boy, one pathetic boy, not a hero like our Founders were. All I can think of is running away. I'm no fitting heir to the Guardian of the Word. She should never have chosen me as apprentice. I'm not the Blessed Soren. I'm nothing like him. He faced his enemies and his courage never flagged, never wavered. Me?" He spat the word out as if it tasted foul. "I haven't the strength to fight Gátra like a man, and tonight I will simply cower and let him strike me down. He will slay me tonight, and my story will end." He gasped out, "Like a mote of dust," and then he couldn't say anything more, but wept for his own cowardice and weakness, as Shisla held him, rocking him gently as if he were a small child.

fifteen

. . .

After breakfast, Gátra was still laughing with his men—all laughing except for Thalaté, who sat stony-faced as always, his expression unreadable, his food barely touched—when Shisla came up to him and stood, hands clasped in front of her, eyes respectfully downcast. She waited for him to speak, and he made a point of ignoring her long enough to remind her of her place.

"Yes?" he finally said, as if only then noticing her.

"A word with you, leader."

He nodded and stood, motioning her to come with him. The eyes of the men, and more than one of the women, followed them, all filled with some mixture of curiosity and puzzlement.

Once they were out of earshot, Gátra said, "What is it? Did you do as I asked?"

"Of course, leader. I spent the night with the outsider."

"Pleasured him well, I hope?" He smiled, but he intended it to be anything but cheerful. This smile felt more like a predator baring its fangs. The image pleased him.

"Yes, leader. He was clearly in need of what a woman could give him."

Gátra laughed. "Excellent. A man who is to be executed deserves one last night to revel in being alive. You pressed him on the matter we discussed?"

"Yes, leader. Without seeming to. As you said, when brought to the point cautiously, he was willing enough to talk. He seems to trust me completely. He gave no indication that he was aware of his plight, and in fact spoke with great confidence about being feasted with honors soon and then sent on his way."

"Did he?" Now he couldn't help a belly laugh. That much at least was genuine. This was shaping up to be better than he'd thought. He was already anticipating the look on the young fool's face when he realized what was in store for him.

"Yes, leader. He trusts you completely."

"Excellent. You have done well." Once again, he snorted laughter. "You are an accomplished liar."

"When you require it, leader."

"You may go. Tell Thalaté to meet me in my quarters. I would have a word with him about tonight. I want it to go exactly to plan."

"Yes, leader." She gave a little bow.

Gátra didn't acknowledge it, simply turned away and walked into his cabin.

Minutes later, his senior advisor gave a gentle knock and entered. "You wish to speak with me, leader?"

"The outsider is still unaware of what I have planned."

"As far as I know, leader."

"It was not a question. Shisla spent the night with him, and she told me."

"I see."

"I want the fight tonight to be a fine spectacle, to remind the Sámada that their lives are in my hands. He may simply be a worthless outsider—not even truly human—but if we make the lesson sharp enough, the point will be made. The fight will begin as tradition demands, with no weapons. But you will stand to one side, and you will bring with you the sacrificial knife. When I have knocked the young fool senseless, you will give me the knife. I plan to cut his heart from his chest as he lies there, still alive." He took a deep breath. "Let them watch and fear me."

"It shall be as you demand, leader."

Gátra looked at the senior advisor with one eyebrow cocked. Once again, there was that undertone of sly sarcasm he'd heard the previous day.

"You are not hiding sympathies for Kallian Dorn, are you?"

"Sympathies, leader? My concern is, as always, for the Samada, not for an outsider."

"You will not quail at the last moment? The sight of his heart in my hands will not turn your stomach?"

"Indeed, leader, I would be sorely disappointed were tonight not to end in blood spilled."

He did not answer for a moment, but regarded his advisor with one eyebrow raised. "Excellent. You may go. I have no doubt that all will go as planned."

"I am confident as well." Thalaté inclined his head slightly, and left the cabin.

Gátra sat for a time, drumming his fingertips on the arms of his chair. He had never been patient, but now, the thought of the fight to come felt like an internal itch. Until tonight, there was nothing in particular he needed to do, but sitting through the day in idleness bothered him. A hunting party had come in the previous evening with fresh meat, so tonight's feast was already well provisioned. Another hunt was unnecessary. Also, he didn't want anything to squander his stamina.

Being alone in his quarters, though, invited the evil thoughts to creep stealthily back into his mind. Thalaté was laughing at him. The senior advisor held him in disdain, and had for some time now. He was spinning his own plots and biding his time. But what of the others? If Thalaté was plotting, surely he wasn't acting alone. Shisla, for example, had acquiesced quickly enough when he had called her a skillful liar. Did that mean more than it seemed?

He scowled. Foolishness. It was all foolishness. There was no one more loyal to him than Thalaté. As for Shisla, he had *asked* her to lie. She was stupid enough to take being praised for it as a genuine compliment. All she had done—all any of them had done—was exactly what he required of them.

But the doubts still gnawed at him.

The heat didn't help. It was odd weather even for the end of summer—sultry, humid, not a breath of wind stirring the branches of the fir trees. Such weather made him uneasy, restless, irritable, but also robbed him of his energy. Staying in the cool dimness of his cabin during the height of day was unusual unless he was conducting business, but the heavy air left him listless. He'd had a flash of confidence when Shisla told him Kallian was ignorant of tonight's plans, and for a moment, had felt like his old self. But left alone to his thoughts for only a few minutes, and that pleasant self-assurance evaporated completely.

No matter. He would have spirit enough once the fight started. And if—ridiculous as it seemed to his rational mind—any of them, whether Thalaté, Shisla, or anyone else, were plotting treason, they would think differently when he cut the young outsider's chest open.

He shifted in his seat, unable to get comfortable. Even the mental image of his certain victory over Kallian Dorn provided little relief from the misgivings. When the ugly thoughts had begun six months ago they'd been mild and ephemeral, but now it seemed like every day they returned stronger than before.

If those voices become too intense for him to fight back, what then? At some point he would not be able to stop himself from acting. However, upon reflection, perhaps that wouldn't be a bad thing. Have Thalaté publicly tortured to death. Kill Shisla as well. For her, merciful and quick—she had been pleasant enough to have in bed. If they were innocent, so what? As with the outsider's death tonight, it would make everyone else doubly careful to honor his will and not even to have the slightest thought of betrayal. If all of the Samada felt uncertain of where they stood, not only would none dare plot against him, but potential conspirators would betray each other to save their own lives.

All in all, a good position for a leader to be in.

His thoughts were interrupted by a quiet knock, almost imperceptible, but it still jolted him. "Yes?" he snapped, not bothering to hide the annoyance in his voice.

The door opened to admit a young woman. Small, thin, pretty enough, with long brown hair and wide gray eyes. What was her name? He'd only had her in bed once or twice, and he had no doubt known it then, but now it would not come to him.

That irritated him further.

The woman stood, eyes downward, one hand twisted around the fabric of her dress in a grip so tight her knuckles were pale. She didn't speak.

Finally, he snapped impatiently, "Well, what is it?"

"Leader, I… I need to tell you something."

"That's obvious, since you're here. Don't waste my time, just tell me."

"But it's… I do not wish to anger you." Her voice shook. "I am only telling you about it, I do not have any part in it myself, I fear being blamed…"

"What is it?" he repeated, in growing fury. If he had to say it again, he'd strike her.

"It is a matter amongst the women. Something I heard about that concerns me. I thought if I told you, I might be rewarded."

Gátra sighed harshly. "What is your name?"

"My… my name, leader?"

"Yes, your name. You do know it, don't you?"

"Of course, leader. I'm Dovak."

Dovak. That was it. How had he forgotten that? He used to know every single Samada, man, woman, and child, not only by name, but their loves and hatreds and rivalries and fears. Knowledge was critical as a means for control. In the last six months, though, it seemed as if his knowledge was leaking away along with his confidence, like he had grabbed a handful of dry sand and was watching it trickle through his fingers. The harder he clenched, the more escaped.

Now, here was this girl, trying to drop her trivial worries into his lap.

"Why do you think I need to know about these… women's matters?" He could hear the anger and scorn in his own voice.

"But, leader…" she squeaked. "A woman… her name is Saskia. She is one of those who prepares the food for meals."

"Yes, yes, I know that."

"It is something she said yesterday that I… I didn't like."

This was the point that his temper boiled over.

"Then fight it out with her yourself."

"I thought it best to tell you…"

He slammed his fist down on the arm of the chair, and her voice was cut off instantly. "Women's gossip is no concern of mine. Saskia is Thalaté's lover. I don't know why he fancies her, unattractive as she is, but that too is irrelevant to me. Thalaté can fuck who he wants to. As far as what Saskia said to you, let the women solve their own squabbles." He gave her a tight, sardonic smile. "Unless Thalaté wishes to get involved. Go tell him about it, perhaps he will be more interested in backbiting amongst the women than I am. I have no doubt he'll reward you handsomely for this essential information."

Dovak's eyes widened, but her gaze was still angled to the

floor. For some reason, that suggestion only added to her fear. She looked terrified, her face ghostly pale in the dim light, her feet frozen to the spot. A rabbit cornered by a wolf.

Ordinarily, seeing this kind of abject helplessness in a woman would have turned him on, and he would have stood up and had her right then and there, perhaps simply pulled up her dress and taken her as she stood. His disordered thoughts and paranoia, though, left him as devoid of desire as he was of focus, energy, drive, confidence, everything. He knew with sickening certainty that right now he couldn't have gotten an erection if he wanted to. It felt like a final blow to his leadership. Despised by everyone, trusting no one, and finally, unmanned.

All that was left to him was a burning anger. At least he could exercise that on Kallian Dorn's body tonight, and perhaps afterward he would feel his vitality and virility return.

After several minutes of silence, he snapped out, "Leave me."

Dovak jerked as if she'd been struck, and without another word, she turned and went out of the cabin.

sixteen

. . .

Kallian went to the evening meal that day, at first trying to keep his anxiety out of his face, and then deciding that he didn't care if Gátra knew he was scared.

It wouldn't change the outcome.

By the time he got there, Gátra was already eating his dinner voraciously. Kallian glanced at the platter, looking for any sign that what he had been served was different than what everyone else had, but it looked identical. Of course. If Thalaté's accomplice was as smart about poisons as he'd said, she surely wouldn't have made it obvious the food had been tampered with.

Shisla was serving one of the long tables, and he looked in her direction. For an instant, their eyes met, then she looked away, her face unreadable. However sympathetic she was to his cause, there was no way she'd intervene tonight, so appealing to her was useless. He scanned the other women. Which of them was Thalaté's lover? No way to know, and probably irrelevant anyway.

As for Thalaté, he wouldn't even look in Kallian's direction.

Kallian had never felt so completely alone in his entire life.

The meal drew to its close as the men pushed aside their platters, leaving the remainder for the women's meal and for them to clean up afterward. The sun had set, and the bonfire lit in the center of the open space near the tables. Kallian looked over at Gátra, who for once seemed to be ignoring his presence entirely. Maybe the senior advisor had been wrong? Maybe the whole fight scenario had been invented to frighten a young, naive outsider. Maybe Gátra had been telling the truth about letting him go, allowing him to continue his quest. Maybe...

"Kallian!" Gátra shouted.

He jumped as if stung, snapping out of his reverie, and looked up at the leader with wide eyes.

"You've feasted at our table now for three nights. It is time that you provide us with some entertainment to repay our hospitality."

Everyone fell silent, staring at the two men, who had locked gazes along the table, as if there was a glowing bond connecting them.

"Entertainment?" Kallian faltered.

"Your people have no entertainment? No games, no contests of skill?"

"I... I don't know."

A number of the men laughed. They had undoubtedly seen this scenario played out before, and knew precisely what was about to happen.

"You don't know?" Gátra gave a loud laugh as well. "Then let me introduce you to our way of providing entertainment." He stood. "I challenge you to a fight. Bare-handed."

"I... I don't want to fight you."

More laughter.

"It was not a request." Gátra pulled his shirt over his head and tossed it aside. "Nothing but our two bodies against each other. A fight... to the death."

Kallian didn't move. He looked at the other man's broad torso, already glistening with a sheen of sweat.

"Come on. Strip down to your waist. It is too easy to hide a weapon in a shirt. Or, are you afraid that if I see your chest, I will be so intimidated by your muscles that I'll cry for mercy and give up immediately?"

Now the laughter was an uproar.

Slowly, Kallian stood, and he pulled his shirt off, hoping the others didn't see his hands trembling.

Gátra came up to him and slapped him on the upper arm.

"You look a formidable enemy. The rules are—no weapons, and the opponents must stay within the area lit by the fire. Anyone setting foot outside, or trying to escape, will be shot by the bowmen I have placed around the perimeter. Other than that—anything is allowed." Gátra grinned. "The fight continues until one of us is dead." He turned toward a stooped old man with rheumy eyes who had been sitting to Thalaté's left. "Banniso, anoint us and give the blessing."

The old man stood without saying anything, and from underneath the table he took a small wooden box. Had it been there all along, or had he brought it because he knew the fight was going to happen? Banniso hobbled over to Gátra, opened the box, and with his fingertips scooped out some greasy brown substance. He smeared it on Gátra's forehead, his upper chest, and across his navel, mumbling some words that Kallian didn't catch. Then he turned to Kallian and repeated the motions. The paste smelled sharp, bitter, the kind of odor that catches in the back of the throat.

He murmured in a monotone, "May the gods hold their hands over the stronger man. May the weaker die and be forgotten."

Then he stepped back, and Kallian and Gátra faced each other.

Kallian looked into the leader's eyes. Gátra's pupils were

dilated. Was that the dim light, or an effect of the poison? Or excitement at the blood sport that was about to happen?

He had little time to consider the question. Gátra lunged toward him, swinging one fist toward his face, a punch that would have knocked him down and ended the contest if he hadn't pulled back at the last moment. It missed him by less than an inch.

Gátra laughed again, circling him, swinging at him over and over. Some of the punches hit their target. One caught him right under the left armpit, and there was a sharp, agonizing jolt as one of his ribs cracked. But so far, all Kallian had done was try to dodge. The knowledge was like a blazing beacon in his mind. It wasn't enough to avoid being hit. That could only last so long, weaving around until his exhaustion gave Gátra the victory.

So all right, he was going to die. It was all but certain.

But the Blessed Soren wouldn't have ended his life like a coward, running and ducking until his luck ran out.

The Blessed Soren would have fought back.

With a suddenness that startled even himself, Kallian launched himself at Gátra, throwing three punches rapid-fire, right-left-right. The third one caught Gátra squarely in the jaw, rocking his head back. With a roar of anger, the leader charged Kallian. His eyes were insane with fury. He was done playing. Unless the gods or the Blessed Soren himself somehow intervened, Kallian was moments from death.

But the onslaught came to an end when Gátra threw a punch at Kallian far too early, as if somehow he had misjudged the distance between them. The momentum swung the bigger man around, and his expression of rage turned to confusion. Only then did Kallian become aware of the sounds of the onlookers. Some were laughing at Gátra's miss. Some cheered, hoping for blood, anyone's blood. A few urged Kallian on to use those few moments when Gátra had, strangely, lost sight of his opponent.

Kallian danced around him and rained blow after blow onto his exposed side, grunting with exertion and finally shouting as each punch struck its target. The pain seemed to wake Gátra up, and he pivoted toward his opponent, his teeth bared in a feral expression that looked barely human. His eyes were unfocused, the pupils so dilated they looked like glossy black pits.

This time, the leader was taking no chances. He lurched forward, reaching for Kallian's throat, waiting until his hands made contact to choke, strangle, kill. Despite his obvious clumsiness—almost certainly from Thalaté's poison—it still couldn't erase Gátra's weight and strength advantage. Kallian backed up, caught his heel on an exposed root, and fell flat on his back.

Screaming with triumph, Gátra jumped forward, ready to land on top of Kallian and end this fight once and for all.

Kallian tried to twist aside and keep Gátra from locking a death grip around his neck. He planted his left hand on the ground, and underneath was a fir branch, long dead. His fingers closed around it, and with a final desperate action, he swung it backhanded at Gátra's face.

Whether from skill, luck, or the guidance of the Blessed Soren himself, the jagged end of the branch swept across Gátra's eyes. Gátra's own momentum drove the rough edge of the wood home, tearing great rents in both of his eyelids. He screamed and fell to his knees, clutching his face with both hands as blood streamed down his cheeks.

Kallian scrambled to his feet, breathing hard, trying to ignore the pain in his side. He looked around him at the faces of the onlookers, glowing ruddy in the firelight. He saw, to his surprise, no dismay that their leader had been incapacitated. The main emotion seemed to be relief. A few even cheered.

Apparently Thalaté had been right about how many enemies the man had made.

Gátra, still on his knees, bellowed with pain and struggled

to get back on his feet. The blood made it impossible to tell how much damage the blow from the stick had done, if he could recover or if Kallian had actually blinded the man permanently. Kallian could not afford to take any chances.

He said, in a low, intense voice, "This is for all the people you have hurt or killed, all the women you have raped, all the damage you have done." And he cocked his right fist back, and giving a great shout, struck Gátra in the face as hard as he could.

He put his heart, soul, and entire body into that punch. It snapped Gátra's head back, and there was a crunch as the man's nose broke. The leader flopped backwards to the ground and lay there, stunned.

He stared down, his chest rising and falling spasmodically as he tried to catch his breath. Thalaté walked up to him, his expression as impassive as ever.

"Well? Finish him off."

He looked at Thalaté and then at his opponent, splayed out on the ground, barely conscious. What was Thalaté expecting? That he'd strangle Gátra with his bare hands?

"No," he said in a strained whisper.

"It is the way the game is played."

"I do not play games with other people's lives."

Thalaté gave him a long look. "He would have killed you without a second thought."

"I am not him." He looked at the helpless leader, only now coming back to himself, struggling weakly to stand. "What will become of him?"

"He has lost the fight. You damaged his eyes, probably beyond healing. No man with such a physical defect is fit to rule. He will be taken out into the wilderness and abandoned to the wild animals."

Shisla stepped forward, flanked with a dozen of the other women. Each of them held a knife, and each had an expression of ferocity, courage—and self-determination.

"Not yet. He has not lost enough to compensate what he has taken. He may survive the wild animals, but we shall make sure he never again uses his body to take from a woman what is not his to take." She gestured at four of the women. "Hold him down."

They knelt and held down Gátra's arms and legs. Whether the leader sensed what was happening or not was uncertain, but he began to struggle harder. The women's grips did not slacken.

Shisla dropped to her knees between Gátra's spread legs, and yanked down his pants. She looked up at Kallian.

"Go. Run. You do not want to watch this. I have placed your backpack and your other belongings by the biggest fir tree at the bottom of the path. Take them, cross the creek, and keep running until you cannot run farther. May your quest succeed and bring you home safely."

She looked down at Gátra, icy hatred in her eyes, lifted the knife with one hand, and reached down with the other.

Kallian turned and ran, pausing only long enough to snatch up his pack, shirt, and the other things Shisla had collected for him.

By the time he reached the creek, the shrieks of agony had already begun, and they followed him for what seemed like miles.

part three
the spiderweb

seventeen

. . .

Challis Acoca was the twenty-first and youngest child of his majesty the High King Sweyn Acoca VII, although as soon as she'd grown old enough to understand such things she had begun to doubt he was really her father.

Physically, they looked nothing alike. Sweyn had curly red hair and was monstrously fat, to the point that some days he could barely walk from his bedroom in the royal residence to the throne room. In fact, of late she'd heard the courtiers, servants, and even some of the slaves making snickering speculations about when the throne was going to collapse under him.

"I hear the legs of the chair crying for mercy every time he sits down," one of the cooks said under her breath when Challis was walking past the kitchen on the way to her own bedroom. If the woman had known she was there, she certainly wouldn't have spoken. Whatever Challis's actual parentage, she was considered to be royal blood, and therefore not to be trusted. If King Sweyn had gotten wind of the ridicule he was receiving, there would have been a line forming at the headsman's block the next morning.

Challis was fascinated with the Gallery Room, where the

paintings were hung of various nobles and members of the royal family. Her mother's portrait was there—Letha Desorla, or Letha Acoca as she became when she married and was forced to take her husband's name—a willowy blonde with a sad expression in her wide eyes, deep blue like a late summer evening. Anyone who saw the painting would have no doubt about Challis's relationship with her. Letha had been the king's tenth wife, and was executed on charges of witchcraft when Challis was only three, but there were rumors that the actual reason was adultery.

Truthfully, she was probably guilty of it. Challis had found a dusty portrait in the corner of the Gallery Room labeled *Tanil Mazerine, Twelfth Chamberlain of the Kingdom of Tecoa*, and his narrow face and quirky smile looked so much like what Challis saw in the mirror every morning that she had no real doubt he was her actual father. When she was fifteen she'd asked her history instructor, trying to make it sound offhand, what had happened to the previous chamberlains.

It would have sounded suspicious if she'd asked about Tanil Mazerine specifically, but fortunately, she didn't have to.

"Oh, a lot of them came to bad ends," the old man had said, warming to the topic immediately. "Power and money and influence, you know, can corrupt almost anyone, and the chamberlain is second only to the king in those respects. Several ended up being beheaded in the public square, usually for either thievery or conspiracy, or both."

"Which ones?" Challis asked.

"Several," he repeated. "The one before the current chamberlain—a woman named Aulia Kaudry—was part of a plot to overthrow your father King Sweyn, long may he live. And the one before her, Tanil Mazerine, was accused of extortion and accepting bribes. Same outcome, of course." He drew one finger across his throat and shrugged.

"When did that happen?"

The old man frowned, looking upward. "Well, let me see.

Mazerine was chamberlain for four years, and if I'm reckoning correctly, his fall from power was fourteen years ago. We could look it up in one of the histories during your next lesson."

Challis didn't press further. If the historian was correct, that would have been when Challis was four—so, shortly after her mother's execution.

All of this made her more certain than ever that Tanil Mazerine had been her actual father. Perhaps his dalliance with Challis's mother was discovered and that led to his downfall. It certainly didn't take any brilliance to see the similarity in features between Challis and Tanil. Odd, then, that the chamberlain wasn't accused of adultery with Sweyn's wife, which would also have been a capital offense.

Maybe that would have been too much of a blow to the king's pride. He was determined to present a façade of power and virility, as irresistible to women and terrifying to men, so admitting that the chamberlain had not only cuckolded him but fathered a child in the process would have been beyond his ability. Easier to trump up charges of witchcraft, extortion, and bribery and get rid of both of them without having to make it public that they'd been sharing a bed.

Challis found the whole thing sad, but also wonderfully reassuring. King Sweyn was grotesque, not to mention cruel. The idea that such a man was her father was repellent. In his presence she did her best to avoid meeting his small, piggy eyes, but that was hardly an uncommon attitude. Not being noticed by the king was the best way to avoid suspicion. In private, she thought of herself as Challis Mazerine, and wished she had grown up knowing her mother and her actual father. She wished even more that she'd been born to a family of commoners where she might have had to work for a living, but at least wouldn't be facing an arranged marriage and a lifetime of navigating palace intrigue.

Her history instructor, circumspect though he was, had

been unable to hide the fact that in the past two hundred years, the most common ways for members of the royal family to die were murder and execution. "Died of old age" was so rare that it seemed almost an aberration.

King Sweyn's senior wife was a woman named Pavona, who was tall, beautiful, and had a vicious temper almost matching her husband's. Despite being his third marriage, she'd become senior wife by outliving the first and second, something everyone knew had not been simple good fortune. The Queen Pavona had several doctors amongst her personal staff, not because she needed their medical knowledge but because they had other knowledge she could make use of. It was remarkable how often someone who crossed Queen Pavona would quietly die shortly thereafter.

Challis had been terrified of her when she was little—Pavona was quick with a slap or a pinch if she felt someone was being disrespectful, or even if they didn't answer quickly enough—and when she was older and heard about her stepmother's reputation she was fearful about every forkful of food, every swallow of drink. That Challis *hadn't* been poisoned was most likely because she was the youngest child of twenty-one, was female, and was the daughter of a wife who had been disgraced and executed. She was in no position to challenge the succession of Pavona's son, who would become King Sweyn VIII when his father died.

Or maybe she'd just been fortunate so far. Survival in the palace was often more a matter of luck than brains.

She looked into her mirror, once again reassuring herself that she looked like her mother and the Twelfth Chamberlain of Tecoa, not the corpulent king.

"Challis Mazerine," she whispered softly to her reflection. "That's who I am. That's who I'll always be."

The door to her bedroom opened to admit her personal servant. Nerys was a lanky, underfed-looking woman not a lot older than Challis, and singularly unattractive. Limp, thin hair of some indeterminate shade of brown, muddy eyes, and a receding chin. Challis would have reproved herself for her assessment of Nerys's appearance, which after all wasn't the poor girl's fault, if it hadn't been for two things.

First, Nerys had been chosen by Queen Pavona because she *wasn't* pretty. Pretty women in the palace entourage were inevitably coerced into becoming the king's mistresses. Pavona must have known the king would pursue any nice-looking female he cast his eyes on, and she seemed to have accepted that in exchange for her position of power, but decided it was better to remove temptation if possible. Her female hires were, one and all, unattractive.

The second reason was that Challis knew for a fact that Nerys was a spy and would have been all too happy to get Challis in trouble. She'd borne gossip back to Pavona before, always about other servants, resulting in three of them being fired, one of whom was flogged in the public square first. Apparently Nerys had the same approach to rising in the ranks that her employer did—keep your eyes open for any opportunity to eliminate the competition.

Challis, thus far, had been extremely careful about what she said and did in the servant's presence, and thus far, had been spared any conflict with her stepmother. She had trained herself to play the wide-eyed innocent in the presence of almost everyone, from the king all the way down to the slaves.

Better to trust no one than to trust the wrong person and find out when you're on the way to the headsman's axe.

Today, Nerys was all obsequious deference, and only someone with Challis's trained eye could see a hint of her potential treachery.

"Lady Challis," she said, eyes downcast, "I'm here to help you with your hair and clothing. Your father, long may he live, wishes to speak to you, and I thought you'd want to look your best."

"What about?"

Her gaze flickered upward for a moment, and just as quickly dropped. "Well, I couldn't say, I'm sure. I'm not privy to royal business. But it must be important. Queen Pavona, long may she live, said not to dawdle, that you're needed immediately. I asked if there would be time to help you dress, and she said, 'Of course, but hurry up about it.'"

As Nerys fussed about, brushing and braiding her hair, Challis pondered what this could mean. She considered various possibilities, and none of them were good. The most likely was that the king and her stepmother had finally come up with an arranged marriage for her. It was ultimately inevitable, but she held on to the forlorn hope that if she just kept quiet and unnoticed, they'd forget about it and her. Other, less likely scenarios flitted across her mind—had they somehow discovered her disdain for them? Did they finally realize she wasn't the biological daughter of either of them, and as such, they had no real reason to keep her around?

Or even alive?

It wouldn't be the first time someone with connections to the royal family faced elimination on trumped-up charges, or for no reason at all. King Sweyn had five full siblings and at least ten half-siblings, and just about all of them were dead, several publicly executed. The most notorious of the royal executions, though, was Sweyn's paternal aunt, Solina, who was accused of treason, specifically of trying to get her own son to rebel and claim the throne. The son died in battle, his followers slaughtered to the man.

When Solina was taken to the block, she refused to cooperate, telling the headsman that if he wanted her head, he'd have to fight her for it. She struggled so furiously, shouting obscenities and flailing around, it took three men to wrestle her into position. At that point, the headsman was so flustered that he only grazed her skull on the first stroke. At least that knocked her out and stopped her screaming.

The second one finished the job.

Solina had become something of a legend after that. Even if she'd ended up dead, there was no doubt she showed more spunk than most.

Challis thought back of her behavior in the past few weeks, as Nerys helped her into one of her nicest dresses, made of smooth, ivory-colored cloth decorated with tiny silver beads. Had she given any indication of her attitude? Said anything remotely critical to a servant? She finally concluded that she hadn't. If they were thinking of getting rid of her, it would be because they'd simply decided she wasn't serving any important purpose.

Wouldn't be the first time that happened, either.

Once she was dressed, her long, wavy blonde hair in a neat braid coiled into a loop and clipped into place, she stood.

"Well, I'd better go see why they want me."

Nerys nodded, a hint of a secret smile flickering across her lips. "Yes, Lady Challis."

She took a deep breath and walked out of her bedroom, then down the labyrinth of hallways leading to the throne room.

When she entered, there were about a dozen people seated around the perimeter, and they all turned in her direction, which was a little unsettling. She walked to the center of the room then dropped to her knees and touched her forehead to the floor.

"Rise, child." King Sweyn sounded positively jolly.

Whether this boded well or not was anyone's guess.

She stood, looking around cautiously, trying to find some hint of what was going on.

Queen Pavona, seated at the king's right hand, addressed a tall, heavyset man with a graying beard, who stared at Challis with an evaluative expression in his shrewd dark eyes.

"You can see she's not unattractive."

"Indeed not."

Oh, heavens above, were they marrying her off to an old man? He looked like he was at least fifty.

But Pavona turned toward a coltish young man with unruly brown hair and wary eyes.

"What think you, Eldrin?"

The young man jumped, as if he hadn't been expecting to be spoken to.

"I… she seems nice."

King Sweyn chortled, his entire body jostling.

"*Nice* may be premature, since you haven't spoken to her yet." He leered. "Besides, I doubt 'nice' is what a hot-blooded young man like you is looking for, right?"

Eldrin attempted a smile, failed, and blushed scarlet.

Challis fought down a feeling of nausea. Not because of Eldrin specifically. If five minutes' impression meant anything, he didn't seem particularly villainous. At least he had the decency to be embarrassed by the king's comment. But to be stood there, being evaluated as if she were in the slave market…

"Your majesty," Eldrin's father said, "I'm sure the two young people will learn to know each other and be satisfied. Might I suggest that they be dismissed to converse by themselves, while we discuss the details of the arrangement?"

"Oh, certainly." The king gave Challis another salacious grin. "Just don't rush things too fast. That goes double for you, my boy." He winked at Eldrin, whose blush deepened. "Don't take what isn't yours yet."

Challis turned on her heel and walked for the door, and only then realized she hadn't done obeisance toward the king when she was dismissed. She half turned, but he, Queen Pavona, Eldrin's father, and the other adults were already in deep, but apparently cheerful, conversation.

Eldrin followed her to the door, and as soon as it closed behind them, he said in a whisper, "I'm sorry about that."

"It's all right. I'm used to it."

"Do you want to go somewhere and talk for a while?" She relaxed as soon as the door closed. He, on the other hand, seemed even more nervous. He tried for a smile, and failed rather badly. "I mean, if you don't want to, that's fine…"

She shook her head. "No, that would be nice. I know a lovely place where we could sit."

She led him through the halls of the palace and out into a small sheltered garden, resplendent with multicolored flowers. It was one of her favorite places, and had been since she was little, not only for its beauty but because the other people in the palace, including her twenty half-brothers and half-sisters, seldom went there. As usual, it was empty, a place of tranquility and solitude, an escape from her precarious and tightly-controlled life.

She motioned him toward a stone bench next to a long bed of roses, and he sat. When she joined him, he edged away a little. Either King Sweyn's lewd comments had scared him—or maybe he just didn't want to appear too forward.

In other words, maybe he was simply nice. Too early to be sure, and it certainly wasn't worth trusting him too far and regretting it later. Her habit of secrecy was too ingrained, too automatic, to set aside easily.

"My name is Eldrin Kenzius." He met her gaze for a moment and then looked away. "My father is Nerick Kenzius. He's the governor of Galith Province, south of here. He holds allegiance to your father, though, and when he found out that the king was looking for a suitable husband for his daughter, he thought if I was chosen, it would bring benefits for the entire province."

Challis nodded silently, even though her first impulse was to say, "He's not my father."

"How do you feel about this?" Eldrin ventured.

Challis shrugged. "I knew it was going to happen."

"You knew I was coming?"

She shook her head. "Not you specifically. But I knew they were going to find a husband for me. It was only a matter of time."

"But…" He looked out across the lush gardens, then up at the blue sky, as if trying to find the words. "How do you *feel* about it? About being… being married to me."

She studied his face carefully. He certainly looked like he felt genuine concern for her. It would be easy to say too much. Challis always felt more at risk around people who were nice than those who were angry and threatening. Anger was obvious on the outside. You knew where it was and where you stood.

Nice, though, could mean anything.

She responded cautiously, "It's okay. Like I said, I knew it was coming."

Eldrin took a deep breath. "That's good, I guess." He looked at her straight on for the first time, and seemed to have come to a decision. "It's probably easier if you just accept your fate and don't question it. I wish I could do that."

"Well, you're here, aren't you?"

His forehead creased. "For now."

"What do you mean, for now?"

"Because I'm not going to go through with it. I'm sorry, because you seem like a really sweet person, and that you've resigned yourself to being married off, like a farmer selling a cow to another farmer. But I can't do that, not to you, and not to myself. I made up my mind once I heard we were going to travel here, and that I had a wife waiting for me." Their eyes locked. "I'm not sure how I'm going to do it. But I'm going to run as soon as I get a chance. I can't marry you, and if I tell them that, I'll be executed. If not here and now, then when I get back home, and my father won't lift a finger to stop it. So I really have nothing to lose."

eighteen

. . .

Kallian slept curled up in a little hollow lined with low vegetation. It wouldn't be easily visible to someone passing, even from quite close. He was exhausted both physically and mentally. His chest pained him, and there was a purpling bruise where Gátra's fist had made solid contact. Probably, he thought ruefully, not the only bruise he had. Still and all, he was lucky not to have gotten far worse.

Gátra, of course, had gotten the worst of all. He winced even thinking of the agony the leader of the Samada must have experienced. He deserved it, there was no doubt of that, but there wasn't a man alive who wouldn't cringe at the thought.

Over the silhouettes of the mountains in the east shone the pale gray light of morning. It had rained during the night—he'd slept so soundly he hadn't even been aware of it——and it seemed to have broken the oppressive humidity. It looked like it would be a pleasant day, warm and dry, with a cornflower-blue sky showing only a few puffy clouds.

He got to his feet, groaning with stiffness, and gathered up his things. After a little walk he found a clear, reed-lined pond, and after drinking deeply he stripped naked and dove in. The sweat and grime and residue of that horrible paste that had been smeared on his skin washed away, and he dove again and again, running his hands through his wet hair and simply relishing being comfortable and clean, and for now, safe.

Once he was done bathing he climbed out, rinsed his clothes, and set them over a log in the sun to dry. He lay back on a carpet of dry leaves, hands cupped behind his head. The warmth and comfort were soporific, and he dozed then slept deeply, waking only when the sun was approaching its zenith.

His skin was dry, his curly hair and his clothes barely damp. He dressed, with some difficulty donned his backpack —raising his left arm made his bruised ribs ache—and after a quick look around to get his bearings struck off as nearly due south as he could manage.

Kallian's encounter with the Samada had left him wary. A good lesson, but one that had nearly cost him his life. When he'd left Klen—could it really be only a week ago?—he'd blithely walked into the forest, aware of the danger only as some hypothetical race of spear-throwing savages. When he'd actually met the ones his people called the Border Runners, they'd turned out to be a far more formidable and complex foe than he ever would have guessed.

Now, the important thing was not to get caught unawares again. What kind of threat the people of the city in the south might pose was uncertain. But the fact that Lanya and her parents, and Syra's mother, had all been fleeing from some kind of danger there left the impression that he shouldn't anticipate being welcomed with open arms.

He expected the debilitating fatigue he'd felt since his capture by the Samada to return, and to tire of hiking quickly, but much of it had come from fear of Gátra and his cronies. Now, left to himself, he was content to walk in the dappled sunlight of the woods all day long. Not only did it get him closer to his goal of reaching the mysterious city, each step carried him farther away from the horrible place he'd been captive.

He hoped Shisla hadn't come to any harm from what she did. Thalaté, as cold and dispassionate as he was, had been instrumental in Gátra's fall, and it seemed unlikely he'd blame her for taking her horrific revenge at the end. The crafty senior advisor—was he the leader now? it seemed likely—had risked being tortured to death to see Gátra overthrown. For his own gain, certainly, but hopefully also to the gain of the rest of the Samada. And the women had played no small part in his success.

Perhaps he'd be a more merciful leader than Gátra had been. It was hard to imagine how he could be any worse.

By mid-afternoon of the first day, Kallian had descended from the low foothills of the mountains to the east into a rolling landscape of open forest, dominated by maples with their enormous, five-pointed leaves rather than the dark and somber firs that surrounded Klen. He passed squared-off pieces of gray stone, cracked and crumbling, that looked like the ruins of house foundations, but nothing else remained to show their original purpose for certain. Laden berry bushes abounded in the understory, and he ate his fill.

He'd been pleasantly surprised to find that Shisla had put some food into his backpack—dried, strongly-spiced meat and a hard circle of flatbread—but it wouldn't last very long. With luck, he'd find the city before the provisions ran out. Lanya had been told by her mother that the city was only two or three days' walk from the Samada encampment, so as long as he was generally walking in the right direction, he'd be in populated regions soon.

What kind of reception he'd get was another matter entirely.

The land dropped lower and lower, into a region of

wetlands and shallow ponds alive with the croaking of frogs and the furtive noises of small birds. Crossing dry-shod was, in some places, a challenge, but soon the land rose gently again into a long, low hill. When he crested it, he stopped, dumbstruck.

Lying in the distance was the largest body of water he'd ever seen, shimmering golden in the lowering sun of late afternoon. On the other side were shorelines dark with trees, and farther than that, snow-capped mountains. Evidently there were high peaks not only to the east, but to the west.

In between were the shattered ruins of an enormous city.

At the base of the hill where he stood were the remnants of a broad road. It had once been paved—it looked like the same gray stone as the foundation he'd seen earlier—but now was in pieces, cracks running throughout it from which grew bushes, vines, and in some places, mature trees that had heaved up and pushed aside great blocks as if they were nothing. To his right were the remnants of what had been a bridge. The pylons that had held up the span still stood, but the bridge itself had collapsed. It was uncertain what its purpose had been. It did not cross a river, or even a gorge, but a road. Why the people who built it took the trouble to raise the entire surface onto a bridge merely to arch over another road, when they could simply have intersected, he could not imagine.

He continued his descent down the hillside, passing more building foundations, and in some places, standing walls. He saw none with surviving roofs. The whole place looked immeasurably ancient. Here, he was certain, were the shattered remnants of the Before Time.

Who had lived here, and where had they gone? Had they perished in the flood that nearly killed the ancestors of the people of Klen, during the years of plague that followed, or from some other peril? There was no way to tell.

What was certain, though, was that the entire place had been abandoned. He shaded his eyes and looked out across the wasteland and saw not a hint of movement. There could be people hiding amongst those ruined walls, but at the same time he was sure he was alone.

Well, perhaps *alone* wasn't the right word. There was a wary watchfulness about the devastated city, not from any living human guarding it, but from the place itself. The phrase *there is no one here but ghosts* came, unbidden, to his mind. He'd never really believed in ghosts or the afterlife, although they figured into the legends he'd learned while studying with Syra. So many of the tales of spirits of the dead speaking to the living seemed like myths invented to scare children or give hope to elderly adults facing death. It was hard to have much confidence in their truth. But here, he felt the presence of throngs of specters, insubstantial creatures who envied his warmth and vitality and the blood coursing through his veins. Not hostile, exactly, but certainly not friendly.

You may cross through here safely, they seemed to say. *But do not stay long. This is not a place for a living man.*

He entered the city itself just before nightfall, and found a place to sleep tucked in the corner of two standing walls. The floor was broken and uneven, but a thick drift of leaves made it comfortable enough to lie on. It had evidently been part of a large complex of buildings. As he crossed toward it, he saw the remnants of a stone block that had letters impressed into the surface. Some of it was damaged and unreadable, but from his reading lessons with Lanya he was able to sound out what was left.

...NTWOOD
HIGH SCHO...

Beneath that was written, in a smaller, loopy script that was difficult to read.

Home of the Con...

But try as he might, he couldn't make sense of what it said.

His earlier impressions of the ghostly inhabitants made him wonder if his sleep would be troubled by dreams, or if the apparitions he'd felt would become frighteningly visible once darkness fell. But he ate a little bit of Shisla's food, and afterward was sleepy and relaxed. It was a warm night, and he pulled his shirt off, balled it up, and put it behind his head as a pillow. The summer stars wheeled overhead, and he lay back, taking a deep breath and lacing his hands across his belly.

In minutes he had sunk into a deep, dreamless sleep.

He hardly stirred till the sun rose over the mountains in the east. He got up, stretched and yawned, then went outside and peed against the outside wall. He came back to where he'd slept, and after eating some more of his provisions he peered under his left arm at the bruise on his chest. The purple had spread, but the pain seemed less. It might take a while, but he'd heal. He pulled his shirt on, slipped his arms through the straps of his backpack, and prepared for another day's walk.

By midday he'd left most of the ruins behind, although there were still numerous remains of foundations and roads. The terrain flattened, and there were signs of current habitation—a field that looked recently tilled, ground with wheel ruts, and in one place, a fence that reminded him of the double line of barriers around Klen. Not long after he saw an intact house, not made of stone like the ruins in the city, but of cedar logs. Near it was a man pushing a plow through a small field, grimacing and grunting with effort.

Kallian immediately wondered if he should give the man a wide berth, but there was something about his appearance that suggested he was not a danger. When he got closer, he called out to the man, who startled, then turned toward him, wiping sweat from his forehead then raising one hand in greeting.

"Where did you come from?" His tone was friendly. He spoke the common speech. Although his accent was strange, it was perfectly understandable. "I thought I lived the farthest out."

Kallian laughed. "From a lot farther than you might think. My home is four days' march to the north."

Now the man looked flatly astonished. "Four *days*? What would bring you on such a long journey, all alone?"

"I'm trying to find the city in the south."

"Tecoa?"

"I don't know its name."

This elicited a frown. "You're going to a place and you don't know what it's called?"

The question sounded more like curiosity than suspicion, so Kallian said, "I've heard its reputation, but never its name."

"Oh." He shrugged. "I try to avoid the place as much as possible. I only go near it when I have produce to sell."

"Why? Is it dangerous?"

"Nah. I mean, no more dangerous than any crowded place would be. There are people who'll knock you down and rob you, but most folks are just wanting to take care of their own business and be left alone."

"And visitors?"

"Mostly get ignored as long as they mind themselves.

People come and go all the time. Ordinary people, like I said. It's crowded and dirty, but most people are decent even to strangers. It's different for the nobles, though. I'd rather push this damn plow every day of my life than be part of the nobility."

"The nobility?"

He nodded. "Well, they call themselves that. Mostly seems to me what they do is try to outsmart each other and get rich at everyone's expense. But it's a risky position to put yourself in. The nobles, and especially King Sweyn and his relatives, are constantly trying to move their game piece ahead and knock everyone else's off the board. Thing is, no one stays ahead for long, and if they're not careful, they'll find themselves in the middle of the town square, tied to the whipping post, if they're not publicly beheaded."

"They do that?"

"So I've heard. I've never seen it. Never want to, either. Like I said, when I have to go to the city, I make it quick and get back here as fast as possible. But honestly, the common people aren't usually in any real danger. You just don't want to get yourself tangled with the higher-ups."

More jockeying for power. It sounded like the Samada, only on a much bigger scale. But there was no obvious reason he'd have to interact with the people who ran the place, and crowded enough that one lone stranger would barely be noticed.

"What's your business there?" The man paused. "If you don't mind my asking. I don't see other people often, so having a chat is a nice diversion."

Kallian didn't answer for a moment, but again, his intuition suggested the man was trustworthy, at least that far.

"I've heard there's a great repository for books, including some from the Before Time."

The man's eyes widened a little. "A scholar, are you?"

"Hardly that." Kallian smiled. "But interested in learning."

"Huh. I didn't know how I expected you to answer, but it wasn't that. Anyway, yes, you're talking about the Library. I've never been there, but I've heard about it. Thousands of books, some of them really old. Scholars visit it from other places farther south. There are more cities down there, people say, but you're the first one I've ever heard of coming from the north. I'd always heard that after the flood and the plagues, there wasn't a soul left alive in the north lands, and people never went back because it's haunted by all the poor souls who perished."

Kallian recalled his feeling about the ruined city, and shuddered.

"So there would be no reason I couldn't visit the Library?"

Another shrug. "None I know of. There might be rules about who can visit, but I've never heard of any and don't see why there would be. Like I said, other scholars come, and write out copies of the texts from the books, then bring the copies back to their home places. Myself, I can't see what might be in a book that'd be important enough to spend hours copying out by hand, but that's just me. I learned to read a little—my mother taught me—but honestly, I've not had much use for it since."

"I'm interested in any knowledge I can acquire. My name is Kallian Dorn, by the way."

The man reached out one sweaty arm and clasped Kallian's.

"Audris Galvan. It's a pleasure talking with you, young scholar." He frowned. "While there, you'll want lodging. A woman named Bara runs an inn not so far from the Library. Ask just about anyone to give you directions to Bara's inn, they'll tell you. She'll feed you and house you for a fair price."

"What price?"

"For five copper pennies a night, you can stay as long as you want."

"I have no copper pennies."

"You're heading to the city with no money in hand?"

"I didn't know I'd need any."

"How on earth do they do business in your home place?"

Kallian blushed, feeling his naïveté on full display. "We simply trade one thing for another, and make sure none go without."

"Huh. Nice idea, I guess. In a place as big as the city, though, it'd never work. I'm not sure how you'll manage without money." Audris glanced at his half-plowed field. "I'll tell you what. I need to get back to the plow, and if you'll help me, I'll pay you enough to stay there at least a few nights. I just brought a harvest to the city, I've got enough coin to spare. And perhaps if you tell Bara I sent you, she'll give you a discount."

"I'm happy to help. But I was injured two days ago, so I'm not sure what kind of work I'll be good for." He lifted his shirt to show Audris the broad purple bruise under his left armpit.

"Heavens above, young man." The farmer squinted at the injury and reached out a gentle finger to touch it. "How did you acquire that?"

"A fight with a man intent on killing me. A day and a half's march north of here." Kallian recalled Gátra's fate, and shuddered. "But he got far worse than I did."

"So the tales are true, then, of the savages that live north of here?"

"True up to a point. The man who gave me this was a savage, no doubt. But the people he ruled over were just... people. Some good, some bad. In fact, if it hadn't been for the help of three of them, I'd have been beaten to death, not just have a hurt I'll soon recover from."

"It's a big, strange world."

There was no arguing that.

"What would you like me to do?"

"I doubt you'll be able to push the plow, not with your injured ribs. You could go behind me and pull up any rocks the plow turns up. No matter how many I rid the field of, the plow always brings up more. I wonder if they grow in the ground like potatoes."

Kallian laughed, and followed Audris over to where he'd left the plow.

The older man shook his head. "That's one thing I did learn from a book. Did you know that in the Before Time, they had machines that ran themselves and plowed the field for you?"

"So I've heard. I've never been able to make out if those were just children's tales, or if there was any truth in them."

"There's no doubt they were clever, those folks. Every so often I still plow up artifacts from back then. Coins are the most common. Beautifully-made things, with stamped designs. I found a strange square container made of some sort of clear flexible stuff—cracked on one edge, but still usable. I keep eggs in it."

"Hard to believe it survived so long."

"It is that. It even had a sort of inscription on the bottom, barely readable. I think it says *Rubbermaid*. I don't know what that means, and it doesn't make sense. Every so often I find pieces of the same kind of stuff, everything from thin scraps to big chunks, but that container is the only thing I've found intact or useful. Whatever it is, it doesn't look natural and I've no idea how it was made. So they had skills of all sorts that we've lost."

"But self-running plowing machines?" Kallian gave another chuckle.

"That's a stretch, I'll admit. What I've heard is that the people who weren't rich enough to own one of those machines, they had animals to pull the plows. But then the

Black Years came, and no one knew how to make the machines, and all the plow animals died of the plague, along with most of the people. Bad times, those were." He brightened. "Hey, maybe if you learn how to make a plowing machine from one of those books, you can come back by on your return trip and teach me how to make one."

Kallian laughed. "I'll do that."

nineteen

. . .

Eldrin Kenzius, eldest child and only son of Nerick Kenzius, governor of Galith Province, looked up at his father warily. Nerick was wolfing down his dinner, while Eldrin's lay in front of him, barely touched.

"Not hungry?" Nerick said around a mouthful of roast chicken. "The king's feeding us well. Take advantage of it, boy."

Eldrin took a small bite, chewed, and swallowed, trying to fight the queasiness he'd been feeling ever since they'd passed the city gates late the previous evening. The stone walls of the little room where they dined were damp and gray, as cheerless as Eldrin felt.

Nerick, however, seemed positively ebullient.

"What do you think of your young woman?" He stabbed a piece of tomato with his fork.

"She's kind."

"That's all? Kind?" His father snorted laughter. "The king said it this morning. You must be thinking about more than her personality. Gods know I would have been, at your age. Beautiful girl like that? You're lucky. Think of what you have to look forward to on your wedding night."

Eldrin tried for a smile, but it didn't really matter. His father was still giving more attention to his food than his son.

"True." He kept his voice carefully level.

Finally Nerick looked up, and gave his son a grin. "It's too soon to get nervous, son. Trust me, the time comes, you'll know what to do. Hell, if you want to practice, when we get home I can send you a slave girl for a night or two."

"All right." It didn't matter if he acquiesced or not to his father's offer, a suggestion he found repellent. By the time Nerick Kenzius got home, Eldrin would either be escaped and out of reach, or else dead.

At that point, Nerick seemed satisfied that he'd given his son sufficient advice for one evening, and returned his attention to his dinner. As he finished, a servant came in to collect the dishes, and Nerick leaned back in his chair and belched loudly.

"Excellent dinner. Tell the cook so. Bring a flagon of wine to my room. I'll be retiring early. Negotiating with royalty is tiring work."

Nerick stood, leaving Eldrin alone at the table.

"Will you be eating more, young master?" The servant's voice was cautious, quiet.

"No, thank you."

The servant nodded and picked up Eldrin's barely-touched plate. If he hoped to carry off his plans for tonight, he shouldn't be fainting with hunger. But his anxiety made even the thought of food nauseating.

He had to find a way to calm down. He stood, and went to the only window in the room, a small, square opening that overlooked one of the palace's many courtyards, now sunk deep in shadow. He had tried to keep track of the layout of the palace when they were shown around the place earlier, but the corridors were a maze. They all looked the same. Finding an unguarded exit would be a matter of pure luck, and more still to find a way out of the city gates without being recognized and stopped.

He took a deep breath. It didn't matter if he succeeded. He'd made his decision. It would be better to be caught and executed than to be forced into a marriage he didn't want with an unfortunate girl who somehow had resigned herself to being treated as chattel.

A pang of heartache struck him when he thought about his farewell to Leos, two days earlier. Whatever happened, he'd never see Leos again. Better that way, hard as that was. Their relationship was doomed no matter what. Putting himself in danger was one thing. Taking the chance that their love would be discovered, and Leos tortured and killed as a result, was another. Protecting Leos was worth any risk. He pictured his lover's beautiful face, and for the hundredth time felt a fire of pure rage rising inside him that they could never be together. It was impossible. Eldrin was nobility, and Leos was a commoner.

Worse still, Leos was male.

Eldrin knew that some men took male slaves as lovers, often while simultaneously maintaining a marriage with a woman. As long as it was hushed up, and the semblance of a straight relationship kept intact, people looked the other way. But to do what Eldrin wanted—to live openly with Leos, declare his love publicly without shame or fear—was unimaginable. There were still laws on the books that prescribed the death penalty for sex between two men. The laws had not been enforced for many years, but Eldrin had no doubt that if he shouted his love for Leos from the rooftop of the governor's house, in very short order both he and Leos would be kneeling in front of the headsman's block in the center of the city square. His father did not tolerate being disgraced, and he'd stand there and watch them die rather than intervene.

His quietly having a dalliance on the side was one thing.

He might have gotten away with that. Overtly breaking the law, and showing no remorse—his father would make an example of them.

And not shed a single tear as his only son's headless body was dragged away.

He knew it had to be this way, but his last meeting with Leos had been like a knife in his heart.

"Is there no way you can take me with you?" Leos was already openly weeping.

Eldrin looked around them, at the shadowed tree trunks in the little grove where they'd arranged to meet. It was near midnight, and there was no reason anyone would be there, but his habit of caution was too well established.

"How?" he whispered. "My father knows we're acquainted, but he doesn't dream of what we actually are. He still thinks you're just the friendly grocer's boy who I chat with when I pass. I can't ask him for you to accompany us. What could I say that wouldn't make it immediately obvious what you are to me?"

Leos nodded, his face twisting with grief. "So this is it. This is goodbye, forever."

He was right, but to say so seemed to make it an inevitability, and that was simply too painful. In the end, he leaned in and kissed him.

He'd meant it to be a quick kiss, but Leos slipped his arms around him and pulled him close. The kiss deepened, and a thrill of pleasure coursed down his backbone as the tips of their tongues brushed each other.

When it finally broke, Leos said quietly, "There." He swiped his tears away with the back of his hand. "Now I have a memory of you to keep me alive."

"Don't say that. Once I'm gone, you won't be in danger any more. Every time we've made love, we've risked being discovered and killed."

"It was worth it, to be with you. Even knowing it couldn't last."

Eldrin reached out one hand and caressed the beloved contours of Leos's face—his strong, high cheekbones, the straight line of his jaw rough with stubble, his full lips. He reached around and ran his fingers through his lover's silky blond curls, and gave him another kiss on the mouth, a quick one this time.

"Maybe…" He faltered.

"Maybe what?"

"Maybe… I don't know, perhaps if I do escape, someday I'll find a way to come back and rescue you. If there's any way, you know I would. In a heartbeat, I would."

"I know." Leos touched Eldrin's face. "But I think… I think we shouldn't hope too hard for that."

Eldrin nodded, tears streaming down his face.

"Don't feel guilty, my love. You're right that this is your chance. You'll be away from home, with only a few of your father's servants and guards watching. And after… you'd be trapped in a marriage that wouldn't be easy to escape."

"I know."

"You should get back to your house. If one of the servants notices your bedroom is empty, the alarm will be raised."

Another nod. Then, one last kiss.

"I love you," Leos whispered into his ear. "Remember that. No matter what happens. Even if we never see each other again. I love you, and I will never stop loving you."

By the time Eldrin got back to his father's house, and successfully made his way to his bedroom without being seen, he had stopped himself from crying. But it was a temporary respite. Once the door was closed behind him, he flopped down on his bed fully clothed, and wept so hard his body shook with it, until at some unknown time later he fell into an exhausted sleep.

Now, staring out of a little window in the High King's

palace up into the night sky, he let his mind drift. What was Leos doing right now? Maybe he was looking up at the same stars, reliving the same painful memories, feeling the same anguish.

He took a deep breath and turned away. It was better this way. Leos was safe now. He could in time take over his father's grocer shop, live a quiet life, and content himself with remembering a happy year during which he'd loved and been loved.

It was enough. It would have to be.

The distant tolling of a bell. Midnight. Eldrin sat in his bedroom, sleepless, waiting for the signal. He'd made the decision when the servant who'd shown him to his room told him about the bell ringing at midnight.

"Your room faces away from the steeple, young master." The servant grinned. "You'll be glad of that when they ring the midnight bell. I've no idea why they do it, but every night, and they've done it for years. You live nearby, you get used to it and sleep right through it, but visitors are often startled by it. Thought you might want some warning ahead of time."

Eldrin thanked him, but his mind was already racing ahead. That would be the sign. Wait for the bell, and then go, see if he could get out of the palace without being seen, or at worst, without being challenged and stopped.

When the low clang of the bell sounded, he rose, picked up his satchel with shaking hands, and walked silently toward the door. It opened soundlessly, and he peered up and down the hallway, lit only with flickering oil lamps.

Empty.

Closing the door behind him felt final. He knew rationally that at any time he could turn, go back to his room, and allow the elaborate plan for his wedding to go forward. He pictured Leos's face if he returned with his new bride. Was it better to stay alive, return to Galith and pretend enthusiasm over a marriage he didn't want, or to make a run for it? Either way, his dreams of being with Leos were over. It hardly mattered which way he chose.

But then he thought about Challis. He had not been lying when he told his father that Challis was kind. She'd seemed genuinely concerned when he told her that he was planning to flee, but she hadn't tried to talk him out of it. All of her talk afterward was about him—how he'd evade capture, where he'd go if he succeeded, how he'd survive in the wilderness. He got the impression that behind her innocent, guileless façade was a fine brain, and that the conversation had started her mind rolling along a different path, but she said nothing of what she was thinking. Whenever he tried to steer it toward what she was feeling, she skillfully brought it back to him and his plans.

Apparently she had as long-standing a habit of caution as he did. He wondered what she had to be afraid of—daughter of the king, wealth and comfort without having to work for it, the best clothes and food to be had anywhere. But to ask directly seemed an invasion of her privacy, breaching a fence that she had erected around her heart.

It seemed Challis was no more enthusiastic about the marriage than he was. He was glad. At least it meant that by running, he wasn't going to be dashing any dearly-held hopes.

Down the hall, down a set of stairs, his feet making no sounds on the smooth stones. Every time he reached a corner, he stopped, peered around cautiously, and then moved on when he saw no one. Surely they must have some night watch in the palace. Or was King Sweyn so secure that he felt no need?

He descended a second set of stairs into a long, broad

hallway that led to a pair of double doors made of heavy, dark wood. There was no other egress, so the doors were unlikely to lead into someone's bedroom. More likely an exterior exit, or so he hoped. He came up to the doors, closed his eyes for a moment, swallowed hard, then grasped the ornate wrought-iron handle and pulled.

As soon as the door opened a crack, he knew he'd made the right choice. Cool, damp air brushed his face, carrying with it the scent of green and growing things. Either it was an entrance to an enclosed garden, like the one where he and Challis had talked, or it was the way out to escape and freedom.

He stepped through and pulled the door quietly shut behind him. He was standing in a portico, open at one end and lined on both sides with stone columns. It wasn't the entrance he and his father had been brought through the previous evening, but it clearly led to outside. He let out a breath he hadn't been aware he was holding, and started to walk toward the short staircase at the end that led out down the empty, night-covered streets of Tecoa.

His face broke into a grin, and he realized it was the first time he'd smiled in… how long? Certainly since he'd found out about the arranged marriage. Probably before that. It was unfamiliar but welcome.

He was going to make it after all. Getting out of the palace had been the hard part. Once out in the city, he'd just be another young man out walking, recognized by no one.

It wasn't until he put his foot down on the first step that he heard a noise behind him. A deep, angry masculine voice.

"Hey! Who are you and where are you going?"

His reaction was no different than a rabbit suddenly spotting a fox. He took off at a run down the stairs, the guard who'd challenged him clattering behind him, right on his heels. It was only once he was at a dead sprint that he thought, *Maybe I should have challenged the guard? I'm the son of a visiting dignitary. I could have probably told him that I'd go where I damn well wanted, and he'd have backed down.*

Too late now. His panicked flight had given away the game. There was nothing for it but to keep running.

He'd only gone a little way when he heard the sound of a horn raising the alarm.

twenty

. . .

When Challis saw her personal servant the next morning, she went on instantaneous high alert. Nerys had a gleeful smirk, the kind she only wore when she knew some salacious gossip. Preferably gossip that included information that she could later turn to her advantage.

"Good morning, Nerys." She hoped her wariness didn't come through in her voice.

"Good morning, Lady Challis." Nerys gave a little curtsey. "I'm here to help you dress for breakfast with your royal father, long may he live."

"Father wants to dine with me?"

"Oh, yes, Lady Challis. He asked specifically." The smirk flashed out again, and she covered it up with one hand and pretended to cough.

"Do you know why, Nerys?"

"I'm sure I don't, ma'am. But I will say that your father and your stepmother are both in a right state this morning. I don't think I've ever seen Queen Pavona so angry."

Well, that wasn't good. "About what, do you know?"

"Didn't you hear the hue and cry last night?"

"I didn't, no."

"Probably because your bedroom is on the opposite side of the palace," she said in a musing sort of way that indicated she'd already thought of that but wanted to make it appear offhand. "The young man—Eldrin, is that his name? The son of the governor—he fled during the night."

He did it. The boy actually did it. There was no need to feign her surprise. She had half believed he'd never have the guts to go through with his plan. He seemed to be reserved and shy by temperament. It was hard to imagine him doing something that bold. He hadn't told her his reason for opposing his marriage so vehemently, but it must be something powerful. Perhaps in love with another girl back home? But when she'd obliquely come at the question of his motivation, he'd avoided the topic, and in fact, seemed to regret telling her any of it. The rest of their conversation had been polite trivia.

His caution was understandable, given the danger he'd be in if he went through with it. Why would he trust someone he just met, and who obviously had a serious stake in the game, with a secret plan to thwart his powerful father, not to mention the High King himself, and undo the entire thing?

In a level voice, trying to sound as if she were only showing interest to be polite, she said, "Did they pursue him?"

Nerys stepped behind her and began to pull a comb through her long hair.

"Oh, yes, my lady. Most of the night through. But the guards who were chasing him lost him in the maze of streets on the north end of the city. They went house to house, pounding on doors, to see where he'd gone to ground, but couldn't find him. Your father, long may he live, was beside himself with anger."

Challis could only imagine. Not only had Eldrin deliberately disobeyed, he'd done something to shame both the High King and his own father. Being publicly shamed was one thing King Sweyn could not tolerate. He almost never had to face it, because everyone was so afraid of him. Challis had often thought that before she died, she wanted just once to see him make one of his conceited comments about his looks or his intelligence or his sexual prowess and have an entire room full of people burst into helpless laughter.

It'd never happen, but it was an amusing daydream.

"They're still searching for him, then?"

"I'd imagine so." The servant's nimble fingers twisted Challis's hair into a complex braid. "I don't know for certain, of course, but I can't imagine they've given up. He wasn't sighted at any of the gates, so he's bound to still be hiding in the city somewhere. It's only a matter of time before they find him."

A sad thought, but Nerys was probably correct in her assessment of Eldrin's chances. And when caught, his punishment would be quick and severe.

"You're disappointed, of course, my lady." Nerys smirked again, until she saw Challis watching her in the mirror.

"Of course I am." No need to explain further. It was the truth—she was disappointed that Eldrin hadn't escaped outright. Even the short meeting they'd had the previous day gave her the impression that he was kind and gentle. Certainly she could do worse in a husband. But she didn't want to be married to someone who didn't want it himself, and truth be told, she was just as happy that the wedding plans were in ruins. Now, if he could just get out of the city safely so she wouldn't have to feel guilty that her own continuing independence had cost someone his freedom, or maybe even his life.

Nerys helped her into her dress—not the fancy thing she'd worn yesterday, something simple but nice, for everyday wear—and when she stood, the servant looked at her from one angle and then the other.

"Very nice, my lady. Perhaps if you look your best, your

father, long may he live, and your stepmother won't aim their anger at you."

"At me?" Once again, she didn't need to feign surprise. Why would they be angry at her?

Nerys seemed to realize she'd overstepped her role, and cast her eyes downward.

"Forgive my being forward, my lady. I'm merely worried, as they seemed so overwrought. I wouldn't want them to think it was anything you'd said to the young man that spurred him to flee."

Oh, of course. She should have realized it. When King Sweyn was angry, he always cast around for someone nearby to blame, fairly or not. That person usually bore the brunt of it until he was distracted by other concerns or maneuvered in a different direction by his wife or his handlers. He'd never think that perhaps Eldrin had reasons of his own not to want the marriage, so it had to be Challis's fault somehow.

Well, there was nothing for it but to face their anger and try to convince them she'd had nothing to do with Eldrin's flight. Which indeed she hadn't. Not that this made it any easier. With the King, the actual truth mattered far less than his ideas about what *should* be the truth.

At least she was forewarned. For once, Nerys's fondness for gossip had worked in her favor.

Challis sighed, took one more quick glance in the mirror, and said in a resigned voice, "Well, I'd better go join them."

Nerys curtseyed again. "Very good, my lady. Shall I see to cleaning your room while you're gone?"

"Yes, that would be lovely."

Another curtsey.

Challis followed the wandering halls down to the royal dining room, trying to calm her nerves and decide what approach would be best. She finally concluded that pretending to be shocked was the best idea. It wasn't strictly true that they couldn't blame her if she hadn't known, but it was at least less likely she'd be punished for it. King Sweyn had a jackrabbit temper and tended to lash out at whoever was around. Queen Pavona was more cruel and calculating, not to mention a great deal smarter, but she wouldn't want to waste her time shouting at someone who honestly had nothing to do with what had happened. Sweyn might continue to rage at Challis because she was handy, but Pavona would turn her venom out toward Eldrin.

And the gods save the poor boy if he *was* caught. People who truly angered Queen Pavona generally had a remaining life expectancy measured in hours.

The king and his wife were the only ones dining when she arrived. Bad sign, but nothing she could do about it. As she knelt and touched her forehead to the floor, the two servants who were in attendance beat a hasty retreat to the kitchen.

"Rise, girl," Sweyn snarled.

She did. Both her father and stepmother were glaring at her in undisguised fury.

"Sit," he commanded.

"Yes, father."

Sweyn looked at Pavona, his face suffused with a dull red flush. She gave him a sharp little nod.

"You no doubt have heard the news," Pavona said, in a tight voice.

"What news, my lady?" Challis looked from one of them to the other in what she hoped was a plausible semblance of confused ignorance.

"Your young man fled from the palace last night."

"He did?" She swallowed. "Why?"

The king snorted, and Pavona said, "We were hoping you might tell us that."

"I truly have no idea, my lady."

"He gave you no sense that he was planning on running away?"

"None, my lady."

The king's anger boiled over. "What did you say to him that repulsed him enough he'd flee from marriage to the daughter of the king?"

"Nothing, father." She gave him a wide-eyed stare. "We talked about nothing but pleasantries. How beautiful the palace and the gardens are, what happened during his travel here, and what it's like in his home city. Nothing of any import. Mostly what I did was listen attentively. I can think of nothing whatsoever that might have offended him."

The king and his wife exchanged glances again. The irritation on Sweyn's round face seemed to indicate he dearly wished to find some way to blame her, but she wasn't making it easy for him.

"Was there no one in attendance—a servant, perhaps—that might corroborate what you are saying?" Queen Pavona's eyes glittered at her coldly. "Because you can see with the young man gone, we have only your word for what went between you."

"No, my lady, I fear not. We went to one of the little gardens in the south wing of the palace, where there are benches. No one was there, unless they were well hidden."

Pavona's mouth curled in a sneer. "And this hidden witness, should he exist—you are quite certain that he would agree that your conversation with Eldrin gave no indication of his plans to flee?"

Her heart gave a stutter. That sounded like there *had* been a witness, and Pavona knew perfectly well she was lying. But no—if that'd been the case, there'd have been no reason for the subterfuge. The king, especially, wouldn't have been able to stop himself from blurting it out.

"I'm quite certain, my lady. Should such a witness be found, he would tell you exactly what I have." She gave a shrug she hoped looked nonchalant. "Perhaps someone was listening at the door. Shall I inquire amongst the servants?"

King Sweyn snorted, and Queen Pavona gave a stiff wave

of the hand. "No, girl, you needn't trouble yourself. I've already made my own inquiries."

Challis had to stop herself from saying, *Then why did you bother asking me?* "Very good, my lady."

Sweyn squinted at her. "You don't look very upset that your future husband has fled."

Challis put on her wide-eyed expression again. It seemed to have a fair history of convincing people she was innocent.

"Indeed, father, I am quite concerned for him. He seems a nice young man, and handsome. I fear that something ill has befallen him."

"If it hasn't already, it will soon," Sweyn growled.

"I beseech you, husband, not to let your anger overmaster you," Pavona said, modulating her voice. "If your daughter truly had no foreknowledge of the young man's rash actions, instead of discussing the matter with her, we should put our efforts into determining where he has gone. And to find out if he had help from anyone, either in his father's employ or in our own."

As predicted, once Pavona was convinced Challis had nothing to do with Eldrin's flight, the girl effectively ceased to exist.

Sweyn made an inarticulate grumbling noise.

Queen Pavona turned toward Challis, looking down her long nose, and said, "Very well, then. You may go."

"But… breakfast?" Challis blurted out.

A quick frown crossed Pavona's face. "I will tell one of the kitchen servants to bring it to you in your room."

Challis stood, and gave her stepmother a curtsey. "My lady, might I ask… if there is further news of Eldrin, might I be kept informed of it? As I said, although I only met him yesterday, he seems like a fine young man and I am worried about him."

Pavona gave her an evaluative look, as if trying to figure out whether the words meant more than they said explicitly.

"Very well, that is reasonable. When we gain news of him, or better still, actually find him, I will have your servant Nerys bring you word. I am glad to see you are disappointed that your marriage may have to be delayed."

The older woman's eyes seemed to bore into her, as if looking for any evidence she hadn't told the truth. Or, worse still, that she'd somehow helped Eldrin escape. Challis blinked at her, keeping her face completely still.

Pavona turned away from her, a momentary frown giving away that she hadn't found what she was looking for.

Challis walked to the door and let herself out, once again only realizing she hadn't done her father obeisance until the door had closed behind her and it was too late to do so. And just like yesterday, neither her father nor her stepmother appeared to notice. As she walked down the hall, she could hear the strident voice of the king and the patient, quiet voice of Queen Pavona, but not clearly enough to catch what they were saying.

She didn't need to. They would be making plans for how to catch Eldrin Kenzius. Poor boy. Challis offered up a quick prayer to the gods that he be safe, and stay safe, and somehow find his way out of the city without getting caught.

Then the thought occurred to her that maybe it was time to do more than pray. If he'd gone to ground somewhere in the north end of the city, it shouldn't be that hard to do some inquiries of her own. She'd spoken the truth when she told her father and stepmother that she hadn't helped Eldrin escape, but that didn't mean she couldn't try to help him now.

And perhaps, if she could figure out how to get him out of the city and away to safety, he would be so grateful that he'd take her with him. Not as a wife. It was clear neither of them wanted that.

But even if he didn't want a wife, perhaps he wouldn't say no to an accomplice.

twenty-one

. . .

Bara the innkeeper turned out to be an imposing figure, as tall as Kallian but twice his girth, with a towering pile of graying curls partially tamed by a bright red hair band. Her inn was crowded, boisterous, and noisy, full of the evening crowd in for food, drink, and socializing. The place looked like it must be hundreds of years old, with heavy cedar beams across the roof and rough-hewn planks paneling the walls, darkened by smoke from the fireplace and the passage of time. The air was redolent with the smells of cooking, beer, wood fire, and sweat, but on this cool late summer night was kept from being oppressive with open windows and doors.

Audris Galvan had been right that anyone he asked would know where the inn was. It evidently had a reputation for being one of the best places in the city to meet friends for a pint. Kallian had expected suspicion if he approached strangers, but the first man he asked simply smiled and given him directions. The city, unlike Klen or the home of the Samada, was so big that visitors were met with an unconcerned shrug, and running into someone you didn't know an everyday occurrence.

The man's directions were flawless, and upon entering Kallian was greeted by a pretty barmaid, with the same light hair and blue eyes that Syra had. She gave him an appreciative up-and-down look and asked what she could get for him.

"I'd like to speak to Bara, please." He had to shout to be heard over the din of conversation.

"She's over there." She pointed toward where the innkeeper stood, towering over most of the people around her, men and women alike. "When you need food or drink, just find me. My name is Mira."

Kallian assured her that he would, and maneuvered his way through the crowd toward Bara, in earnest conversation with a fat elderly man with a red face, who was evidently already cheerfully and volubly drunk. Bara glanced at Kallian —also gave him a once-over—patted the elderly man on the shoulder and said, "Excuse me for a moment, Landin." She turned back to Kallian with a smile. "What can I do for you, young master?"

He explained that he was new to the city, looking for food and lodging, and how he'd found the place. When she heard he'd been sent her way by Audris Galvan, her face lit up.

"How is that rascal? I haven't seen him in months."

"He's well. He sends his greetings. I can't say when he'll come visit, though. I think other than seeing you and a few friends, he's just as happy spending as little time in the city as possible."

She gave a loud laugh. "He does seem twitchy as a rabbit while he's here. Comes from living all by himself out on the edge of nowhere. But you come from farther still, sounds like."

He nodded. "A lot farther."

"And what brings you all this way?"

"I heard about the Library. I thought it sounded like a place worth visiting, somewhere I could learn a great deal."

Her eyebrows rose on her broad forehead. "A scholar, then?"

He smiled and gave a little shake of the head. "That's what Audris called me. I don't think I'm a scholar, really. Merely curious."

"Modestly said. In any case, the Library isn't far from here. A bit south, closer to the city center. I don't think many people go there these days. I hear that years ago, it used to be visited by scholars from all over, come to read the books and whatnot. But the city's developed a reputation for being unsafe, and I think that's kept people away." She frowned thoughtfully. "It's safe enough for common folk, I daresay. I mean, you hear about people being robbed sometimes, but there are ruffians wherever you go. But the squabbling between the nobles spread to the provinces, and there've been more than one battle between rivals that caused bloodshed, not only amongst the nobles themselves but the ordinary people who just want to be let alone to live their lives in peace. That kind of thing makes people think twice about leaving home, you know? If there's a war going on in the land lying between some scholar's home place and the city, my guess is he'd stay put, however curious he was."

"That's pretty much what Audris told me."

"But in any case, you got here safely."

That was hardly true, but he didn't feel like telling the story of his captivity and narrow escape, so he simply smiled and nodded.

They did some quick negotiation for a fair price for lodging and meals, and as Audris had predicted, Bara gave him a discount.

"As long as you deliver a message back to him on your return voyage. Tell him next time he's in the city, he'd better pay a visit. If he doesn't, the next friend of his who mentions his name to me will get charged double."

He laughed. "Do you know if anyone can visit the Library, or do you need permission?"

"Don't imagine you'd need permission. In any case, permission from who? The Librarian and his assistants are the only ones there most days, and I don't even know that the assistants show up sometimes. No need, you know? Silent room after silent room of old, dusty books, and no one to read them. He'd probably be delighted to show you around. Has to be boring for him, day after day, all by himself with no one for company." She tilted her head. "Are you looking to learn anything in particular?"

"Not really. Just seeing what I can find out."

"Huh." She shrugged. "Funny you came all this way without any particular goal in mind. But that's your business, and in any case, you're welcome to stay as long as your quest lasts. I expect you're hungry."

"Famished."

"We have a nice chicken stew for supper, and Yani the brewer just delivered two new casks of brown ale. If that sounds acceptable?"

"More than acceptable."

"That's fine, then. I'll have Mira show you to your room, and whenever you're ready, you can come back down and I'll see you're fed and your thirst quenched."

After a better meal, happier company, and a more comfortable night's sleep than he'd had since leaving Klen, Kallian woke early. He breakfasted in the pub, now hosting only a few patrons talking quietly amongst each other.

"Off to your scholarly pursuits this morning?" Bara asked as she served him a plate of fried eggs, rashers of bacon, and a pint of light ale.

"That's my plan."

She smiled. "I learned some reading when I was a child, but haven't used it since. I have to admit, though, I'm curious to find out what you'll discover. Some of the books there come from before the flood, so I'm told. Few these days are interested in ancient history, so I've no doubt you'll see books there that haven't been touched in hundreds of years."

His heart beat a little faster. His captivity in the Samada's home place had been a frightening ordeal that had almost stopped him permanently, but now that he was here in the city, it looked very much like there would be no further impediment to achieving his goal. Today he would walk into the Library and have at his fingertips the knowledge of the old world, of people from the Blessed Soren's time and even earlier. Could it really be this easy?

The day was clear, sunny, and cool, and on the walk to the Library—barely a mile and a half from Bara's inn—he was given nothing but friendly greetings as he passed grocers and butchers and bakers. The city was still in the quiet of early morning, and his fears of crowds of scurrilous and dangerous ruffians looked like nothing more than wild imaginings.

He'd pictured many times what the Library might look like, but as he turned a corner by a large open-air market and caught his first glimpse, he realized his mental image had far underestimated its grandeur.

It was by far the largest building he'd ever seen. Bara had told him it was the second-biggest in the city, only exceeded by the palace of the king, but Kallian's benchmark for impressive structures was the Hall of Images in Klen. By comparison to the Library, the Hall of Images looked like a woodsman's hovel. The building consisted of tan and gray stone, with broad stairs leading upward from the street to the entryway. It was at least three stories high, although the roof had angles and insets that made it difficult to judge. There were rows of windows with curved tops, and a cupola sat on the roof like an odd, bowl-shaped hat. From the brief glimpse of the

Library's side as he passed the market, it looked as if it extended back a full block's length. In the shade of the entryway was a trio of double doors, and above them, deeply incised letters in the stone spelling out simply, *LIBRARY*.

In awe, his steps slowed as he ascended the stairs. When he crossed the portico and reached out to grasp the ornate metal door handle, his hand trembled.

The door swung open smoothly, and he stepped in, allowing it to close silently behind him. He was in a wide foyer, also paved with the same marbled stone, its surface worn by the passage of time and thousands of feet. He crossed the foyer toward a wooden desk, behind which sat an old man with thinning white hair and very pale gray eyes, eyeing him with a nearsighted squint.

"Can I help you?" The man's voice creaked. It sounded as if he didn't get much opportunity to use it.

"I'm a visiting scholar." The word came out before he could stop himself, and he blushed a little at the conceit. "I would like to have the opportunity to learn from the books here."

The old man's eyes lit up. It looked as if Bara had been right, and there were few enough visitors that any would be appreciated.

"Oh, that's lovely. I'm Kasprit Seely. I'm the Librarian. I'd be glad to assist you."

"Kallian Dorn." He reached out and they clasped forearms. Kallian's long fingers wrapped all the way around the skinny limb of the Librarian.

"Where do you hail from, Kallian Dorn?"

"From the settlement of Klen, about six days' march north from here."

The Librarian's pale eyes opened wide. "Indeed? I thought the only ones north from here were the barbarians. And you haven't the look of a barbarian."

"No, I'm from farther away still. But I was captured and

nearly killed by the barbarians on the way here, so your information is correct as far as it goes. My home place is another two or three days march farther, so I'm not surprised you haven't heard of it."

"My word. What knowledge are you seeking that is worth such risks and such a long voyage?"

Kallian laughed. "I've been asked that before. The truth is, I'm not sure. I merely had heard of the rich trove of books housed here, and wanted to see it with my own eyes and learn from it what I can."

"Heard? From whom?"

For the first time that day, Kallian hesitated. The openness and kindness of the people he'd met thus far had made him lower his guard. But he recalled how he'd found out about the Library in the first place—from a girl whose parents had fled the city, presumably in peril of their lives. Lanya's flight had only been six years earlier. If he mentioned her name, surely someone would recognize it, and this could put his own safety in jeopardy. Also, what of the people who had threatened Lanya's parents? What would they do if they found out the girl was still alive? She herself hadn't known what danger they were fleeing from. Perhaps that danger was still present, somewhere in the city. He didn't want to put himself at risk, but he also didn't want to bring any risk back home to Lanya.

In the end, he said in an offhand voice, "I learned of it from the legends of our people. I believe that some time, perhaps long ago, some of my kin came here, or possibly some of the city folk came to us. Whichever way it was, we learned that the Library still stood here, and that the knowledge it contained has persisted to this day. I felt driven to see it for myself."

He expected to be pressed further, but the Librarian merely gave him a mild smile.

"Lovely. I wish more people would come. Books are made

to be read, and sadly, many books here have sat on their shelves for decades. Possibly for centuries. There are so many rooms, all filled floor-to-ceiling—even I don't have a good idea of what is here."

"And they all came from so long ago?"

"Most of them, yes. People still write books, of course, and keep records, but they're precious things and take time to copy. Most of what's here was written long, long ago, by some technique we've lost."

"So much has been lost." Kallian could hear the pang of sadness in his own voice.

"That's the truth." Kasprit gestured with both hands and looked upward. "This collection may be the only one of its kind left. Tecoa was fortunate that the flood damaged only the buildings close by the water. Most of the city was spared." The librarian shook his head. "We didn't escape the plagues and famines that followed, of course. No one did. But at least the Library survived."

"It's a remarkable place."

"It is indeed. The story is that before the flood, they had a magical way of keeping track, and amazing machines that could tell you the exact location of a book at the touch of a finger. But if such devices ever existed, we don't have them now. The books are arranged more or less by topic, but you still have to know where to look or you could spend days searching." He laughed. "And if you don't know the floor plan, days more trying to find your way out. It's a labyrinth. Besides the three above-ground floors, there are two subfloors below-ground. I've no idea how they were built—it's hard to imagine all of this stonework and excavation being done by hand, but I don't know how else one would do it." Another chuckle. "Perhaps they had help from the gods."

"Would you show me around?"

"I would be delighted." Kasprit rose stiffly, and gave a gesture with one hand. "This floor has fictional stories. It's the floor I know best, mostly because I don't have to manage the stairs with my old knees giving me the pain they do. I often pass my time reading the tales I've found here. It's fascinating to have a window into the creativity and imagination of men and women long dead. It makes one feel like they're not quite gone, that a piece of them lives on."

He followed the Librarian through room after room whose dusty floors often bore only a single line of footprints in and out, presumably the Librarian's own on his trips to find reading material. A couple of the rooms didn't even have that, just an undisturbed layer of dust that had been collecting, probably for years.

The Librarian let his fingertips brush the nearest row of books. "You can see the titles of the stories, and the names of the women and men who wrote them, on the spines of the books. All of those people, and all that's left of them are their names and the tales they told."

Kallian's eyes grew wider and wider as he took it all in, a collection of thousands of stories grander than anything he could have imagined, faded pages bearing the tales of authors from a bygone age. Who were these people, and what stories did these books contain? It was more than anyone could read in a hundred lifetimes. He let his eyes wander over the mysterious-sounding titles, his mind creating pictures of what they might mean, what legends and lore were trapped within those closed covers.

Foucault's Pendulum by Umberto Eco. *Known Order Girls* by Andrew Butters. *Spree* by Gil Miller. *The Wind-Up Bird Chronicle* by Haruki Murakami. *Epilogue* by K. D. McCrite. *Too Like the Lightning* by Travis Beaudoin. *Heartstopper* by Alice Oseman. *The Lathe of Heaven* by Ursula LeGuin.

Seeing the reality that he had so underestimated, he felt lower than a provincial, that the accumulated knowledge of Klen and its history he'd now spent a year studying was no more than the vague meanderings of some second-rate storyteller. Here—with the written word—you could capture the minds and hearts of people permanently, with no painstaking memorization and risk that the Guardian of the Word would remember incompletely or incorrectly, or worse, would die before transmitting all the knowledge she had to her apprentice. Here, knowledge was permanent, if care was taken to keep the books safe. Permanent, complete, and available to all.

"Non-fiction is on the second and third floors." Kasprit gestured toward a staircase. "The subfloors seem to be mainly archives, although I must admit I haven't explored them fully myself. There are no windows, obviously, and carrying around an oil lamp in rooms filled with paper is a risk. Besides, a lot of them are hand-written, not printed, and my eyesight isn't so good any more. So mostly I stay here above ground, where there are windows and the books are easier to read."

Upon reaching the second floor there was a sign on the wall saying *Science* with an arrow pointing to a long hallway with rooms on both sides.

"Science?" Kallian said, sounding the word out. It was neither a word in the common speech of Klen, nor was it one Lanya had taught him.

"The study of how things work. When I was younger I spent some time in those rooms, but I must say, much of it is beyond my ken. There is a great deal of mathematics—the process of handling numbers—involved, and my training in that area is rudimentary at best. But I've no doubt that if you had the mind for it and the time, you could learn a tremendous amount on this floor alone."

"Do these books come from the Before Time?"

Kasprit nodded, looking around them at the shadowed shelves, laden with dust-covered books.

"Before the flood, you mean? I've no doubt that many of them do. During the Black Years, with the floods and the plagues, people were trying their hardest just to survive. A lot of them didn't, of course. From what I've read, in the time before, there were a thousandfold more people than there are now, and they had ample food and living space and comfort and could spend their time reading and writing books. But when a hundred years passes with deprivation and famine and death on your doorstep every day, a lot is forgotten. You'll see in some books there are numbers that I believe were some sort of system of keeping track of the passage of years. But I've not been able to decipher how it's to be read, nor how it relates to the present day. Nowadays we simply track time by the year of the reign of the current king. So this is the twenty-first year of the reign of High King Sweyn VII, long may he live." Kasprit pulled a book off a shelf in the room they'd entered—the cover said *The Diversity of Life* by E. O. Wilson, and was adorned with a design of a brightly-colored beetle with long antennae. He blew the dust off the top and opened the cover, flipped a couple of pages in, and rested the tip of his long index finger on a line that said, *Copyright 1992*.

"I think *1992* refers to the year it was written," he said. "But how long ago that was, I have no idea. I doubt anyone knows." He sat on a stone bench against the wall. "I'm sorry, but I must rest for a moment. I'm getting to the age that my knees ache and my lungs rebel if I take things too quickly."

"Please don't overdo it. I can explore the rest on my own, if that's all right with you. I'll come back to your desk if I have questions. You have my word I won't damage anything."

"No, I'm sure you won't, young man. I know an inquisitive mind when I meet one, and in my experience inquisitive minds don't want to destroy what they're fascinated with."

Kallian smiled at him. "Thank you for showing me the place. I'm sure I'll be spending many days studying here."

Kasprit smiled back and stood, groaning a little. "I've no doubt that's true. Very well, if you don't mind, I'll leave you to your exploration. I was only joking about getting lost.

Should you lose your way, there are maps on the walls in the hallways, and they'll direct you to where you need to go. The third floor is mainly devoted to history. Some of the books are written in other tongues, however, so if you see odd scripts or indecipherable text, be aware of that. Like the timekeeping system, I fear that the knowledge of those languages has been lost over the years. Sad thing, that, but I suppose we're fortunate to have what we do."

"Indeed."

Kasprit patted him on the shoulder. "You know where to find me should you need me. Until then, the entire Library is yours to explore."

He limped his way out into the corridor, and his slow footsteps receded toward the staircase leading back to the first floor.

Silence fell again.

Kallian looked around at the laden shelves, once again overwhelmed with the wealth of knowledge contained in this single building. It was both tremendously exciting and terribly frustrating. Even Kasprit Seely, who spent every day in the Library, had only touched the barest minimum of what was here.

How would Kallian find a way to begin? And what could he learn from a week's study, or two, or three? Even a year? He never desired to stay in the city permanently. But now, he was weighed down with the thought of how he would bring home with him enough of the information the Library contained to justify the time and risk. He was glad he hadn't known how big the Library was ahead of time. He would have recognized it as a ridiculous enterprise and never would have come.

But for now, he was here. May as well use what time he had. He pulled another book off the shelf—*The Origin of Species*, by Charles Darwin—sat down crosslegged on the floor, and began to read.

twenty-two

. . .

Eldrin peered out from around the corner of the dirty alleyway in which he'd taken refuge. Empty. The last people he'd seen pass by the gap where the alley intersected the street had been fifteen minutes earlier, but they'd looked like ordinary citizens ambling toward their homes and beds. There was an oil lamp on a hook at the corner, and in its fitful yellow glow there was no movement other than a furtive scuttling that was probably a rat foraging in the pile of trash against the far wall.

He'd been in hiding for three days. In that time, there were several near misses, the most recent that morning when a frustrated and footsore group of soldiers came clumping their way down the street, and paused when they saw the narrow alley entrance.

Eldrin ducked into the shadows behind the trash pile and held his breath.

"We should check down there," said one of them in a gruff voice.

"We can't search every damn alley in the city." Footsteps approaching. "I don't see anyone, and it only goes a little way back before there's a wall. He wouldn't hide in there, there's no place to run if he's spotted."

This wasn't true. There was an even narrower gap at the end that twisted around between two buildings and finally exited one block to the north, but it was nearly impossible to see until you were looking straight at it.

"Pretty little pampered nobleman's son wouldn't go in there in any case," another voice sneered. "Get his fine shoes dirty. If he's still in the city, mark my words, he won't be caught in some passageway through a slum. He's found an ally to take him in, someone of his own kind who's sheltering him. I've no doubt he's had his plans for ages, and they don't include foraging in garbage for food and drinking from puddles."

There were a couple of snorts of laughter.

Finally the first voice said, "Nah, you're probably right, Savin. Besides, I'm sick of looking for him. Rumor is, he did a bunk when his daddy tried to marry him off to the king's daughter, and I can't say I blame him. You couldn't pay me enough to marry into that family. Good way to lose your head, that is. One day, you give the king or one of his wives a squint 'cuz something's in your eye, next thing you know you're accused of treason."

"You'd best keep your voice down with that kind of talk, Varick."

A derisive chuckle, and he spat on the ground. "They wouldn't waste their time with the likes of me. They're too busy plotting against each other even to pay attention to us common folk. And that's just fine." He paused. "Very well, boys, you go on ahead. I need to take a piss."

Footsteps, then the sound of Varick peeing against the wall. A brief rustle as he readjusted his pants, then his steps as well receded and vanished as well.

Eldrin let out his breath slowly, peered around the pile of trash to make certain they'd gone, and cautiously stood.

He looked over to the wet mark on the wall. The soldier had been standing only three strides from where he sat, trembling in the shadows.

Once his panic at his near escape subsided, he laughed quietly to himself. The soldiers had misjudged his desperation, and also overestimated his ability to plan. Not only did he have no accomplices to take him in, he *had* been foraging in garbage and drinking from puddles. There had been a couple of beggars he'd run into who seemed sympathetic to another homeless person, but he hadn't told them his story for fear they'd be tempted if there was a reward for his capture. And they were penniless themselves. As much as they might have empathized, there was little they could do.

There was little enough he could do to help himself, honestly. He could only scavenge for food for so long before he'd starve. Plus, the kind weather of late summer would be drawing to a close all too soon. He had to get out of the city to somewhere safe before the rains and chill of fall started, or he'd die of exposure and illness. How he'd do that, though, was anyone's guess. The only glimpse he'd had of the main gates, east of the city, showed them to be closely watched. Due north—the direction he wanted to go—were long, narrow inlets of water, impossible to swim, crossed by bridges that also had soldiers keeping guard.

He thought about his statement to Leos, that he'd rather die than be forced into marriage. Now that the former was looking a great deal more likely, he had to stiffen his resolve. If he'd stayed in Galith, probably even if he'd married Challis and returned there, he wouldn't have been able to stop himself from having trysts with Leos. Eventually, they'd get caught. Even if somehow Eldrin was able to talk his way into its being a quick dalliance and to save his own head, as a commoner Leos would suffer for it. Eldrin's proud father wouldn't stand for his family being humiliated that way. There's no doubt that the following day, Leos would be stripped to the waist, his wrists tied to the post in the middle of the city center, and whipped until he was unconscious.

Eldrin shuddered at the ugly image in his mind. No, his own death was worth preventing that. The idea that anyone could touch Leos's beautiful body in anything but love and kindness made his heart rage.

He looked around. The street that intersected the alleyway looked empty. By this time night had fallen. The safest time to be out, when some shadowed figure walking down the road, hood drawn up, would be likely to be ignored as just another ordinary soul heading home from a long day's labor. Late enough for darkness, but not so late that he'd be stopped and questioned as to why he was out and about in the middle of the night.

There were a few pubs along the street that were often busy, and the trash heaps behind them frequently good sources of food scraps. One of them especially seemed popular, and was filled with the noise of conversation and merriment.

He made his furtive way down the street, trying not to look *too* furtive. Skulking was automatically suspicious. Best to lope along looking unconcerned, as if he had every right to be there, but getting out of sight as soon as possible.

He had reached the corner of the pub when he caught a glimpse of movement ahead. Someone on the same side of the road, moving toward him. He ducked around the corner and flattened himself against the wall, breathing hard. In his quick glimpse, though, it was clear the person was no soldier. He was a tall, slender man, in travel-worn clothes, but walked with a cheerful swagger. About Eldrin's age, with copper skin, untidy curls of black hair, and finely-cut features. His eyes, dark as his hair, caught the light of an oil lamp hung by the inn door as he glanced in Eldrin's direction. Had he seen him duck behind the wall? He waited, breathlessly, wondering if he'd be challenged.

But either the man hadn't noticed him, or didn't care if he chose to hide. The door at the front of the pub opened, and a female voice said, "Well, it's the young scholar! Did you enjoy being hunched over a bunch of old books all day?"

There was a burst of friendly laughter at this, and anything further said was drowned out by the general noise of the crowd.

Eldrin let out a long breath, then slunk along the wall toward the back of the inn. He was in luck—evidently the trash had just been dumped, and there were ample leftovers and scraps that the rats hadn't had time to get.

He had just finished—well, if not filling his stomach, at least blunting the edge of his hunger—and was wondering where he might be able to sleep, when there was another noise from the front of the inn. Two voices—both female—one of whom he recognized as the person who had spoken to the newcomer earlier. The other sounded younger, and was familiar, but he couldn't place where he'd heard it.

"You wanted to see me, your ladyship?" This from the woman who'd spoken to the young man a half-hour ago.

"Yes, thank you for coming out to speak with me," said the familiar young voice. "I'd have gone in, but..."

"Not a fitting place for someone of your rank."

A laugh. "I was going to say it was too loud for us to hear each other."

The other woman laughed as well, and seemed to relax a little. "As you say, your ladyship. It does get raucous. How can I help you this evening?"

"I'm looking for someone. His name is Eldrin Kenzius."

Eldrin froze, eyes wide, and suddenly he realized who was speaking. It was Challis Acoca, the daughter of the High King. But... why was she searching for him? When they'd spoken, only a few days ago, it had sounded very much like she was no more interested in marrying than he was. What earthly reason would she have for hunting him down?

Maybe she was doing it simply for her own gain. He suppressed a chill at the thought. If she turned him in to his father, she'd at least look to the High King like she was playing by the rules, and could make her own status more secure. But something about that didn't ring true. She didn't seem like the ruthless, grasping type—more sad, wary, patient, as if she herself had a secret life she dared not show.

So what could possibly be motivating her to search for him?

"What does this Eldrin Kenzius look like?"

"He's perhaps twenty years old. Tall, about a hand's span taller than I am. Slender, with wavy, light brown hair, gray eyes. Bit of a long nose, but otherwise nice features."

Eldrin frowned and reached up to run his finger down the length of his nose.

"No, your ladyship, I'm sorry, I haven't seen anyone like that. The only newcomer I've had here in three weeks is about twenty, but the resemblance stops there. Dark skin, curly black hair, brown eyes. He's been here six days now. A visiting scholar from somewhere up north. Amicable young man, but I doubt very much that he's the one you're looking for."

That sounded like the young man the innkeeper had greeted earlier. No, they looked nothing alike, fortunately for both of them.

"No." Challis's voice was quiet, disappointed. "I'm afraid no one's seen him. I'm becoming quite worried." She paused, and went on in stronger tones, "Bara, would you do me a favor? This young man—Eldrin—he's in a great deal of trouble. But he's a good, kind person, and doesn't deserve what will happen to him if others find him before I do. I've heard a great deal about you. You've got a well-deserved reputation throughout the city for wisdom and kindness. I know you talk to hundreds of people every day, and I've heard that you know who in the city to trust and who not to. People seek you out."

"I'm not sure about the wisdom part." Bara laughed. "But other than that, your ladyship. the rest is true enough. I'm kind of a fat old spider sitting in the middle of a spiderweb, and the flies come to me."

"At least you mean the flies no harm. Eldrin and me, we're in the middle of a much worse spiderweb, and I fear very much that if we don't extricate ourselves, we'll both end up entangled to our own destruction. I don't confide in people easily, so my saying this to you doesn't come easily."

"I'm honored by your trust, your ladyship."

"I hope it's well placed. Meaning no offense, but I don't exaggerate when I say that we both depend on your keeping your word to honor my confidence. I don't know what kind of reward I can offer you, if any, nothing but the knowledge that you may be saving two lives by doing what I ask. Can you talk to the people you trust—quietly—and find out if they've seen Eldrin or know where he's hiding?"

"You're so sure he's still in the city?"

"Virtually certain, yes. The gates to the east are being guarded, and there's no way he'd head south. To go north he'd have to cross the Waterway, and that'd be a challenge even for a strong swimmer. No, he's still here somewhere. And I need to talk to him, quickly. Because I know how to get him to safety. But I have to find him first."

Eldrin's heart gave a sudden leap. She wanted to get him out of Tecoa? Why?

He was on the verge of stepping out of the shadows, announcing his presence to her, when a sudden misgiving seized him.

This could well be a trap. Challis had seemed trustworthy —not to mention disgruntled with her scheming family—but was she ready to put her own safety on the line to help him?

Why would she do that for someone who was, honestly, a total stranger?

In the end, he held back.

"If I see him, or talk to someone who knows where he is, what message do you want me to give him?" Bara said.

Challis thought for a moment. "Tell him that I know a place that would be safe from the people searching for him, at least for a few days. It's seldom visited, and has a huge number of rooms and alcoves where someone could stay hidden for weeks if need be. But I hope it won't be for that long. If I can find him—well, I know how to get him across the Waterway. From there, we'll be outside the easy reach of the guards."

"We, your ladyship?"

Challis laughed quietly. "I'm becoming unwary. If I succeed in getting him to safety, I'm going with him."

"I see," Bara said knowingly.

"No, it's nothing like that. I'm not a lover, merely a friend. But I also need to get out of Tecoa myself. It would take too long to explain why, and I've been away from the palace long enough as it is. If my servant notices my absence, it will arouse suspicion. If you find Eldrin, just tell him… tell him to meet me at the north side of the Library."

"How will he know when to meet you, your ladyship?"

"Because when you talk to him you'll tell him to go that evening, after nightfall, and wait for me, then you will immediately afterward send your servant to the palace with a message for me that he'll be there. Tell your servant the message is to be delivered directly to me, not to anyone else, and if that's impossible for some reason, it's better to leave it undelivered than to tell anyone else."

"I'll do as you say." There was a pause. "The Library, then? Odd, but the young newcomer I was telling you about —he is also interested in the Library. For other reasons than hiding, though. Bit of a coincidence, that."

"That's all it is, I'm quite sure. And in any case, if everything goes well, we won't be hiding there long."

"Very well, your ladyship."

"Thank you. Bara, you can't imagine what this means to me, and what a risk I'm taking telling you. I don't know how I could ever repay you."

"No need to repay." She continued, a smile in her voice, "I'm delighted to help out a pair of young lovers in difficulties."

"We're not lovers."

"Of course not, your ladyship."

It was only after Challis turned and disappeared back down the street, and Bara went back into the noise and bustle of the pub, that Eldrin chided himself for hesitating, for staying hidden. When he thought about it, how likely was it really that the princess would wander around Tecoa at night, enlisting the aid of innkeepers, in order to set a trap for him? The more he thought about it, the more ludicrous it seemed.

Besides, what other opportunity for help would he get?

But perhaps he hadn't missed his chance altogether. Challis apparently trusted Bara enough to confide in her, and had specifically asked her to facilitate a meeting. This meant that she believed the innkeeper was unlikely to give away the game to the royal guard.

It was a gamble. A gamble with his life as the stakes. But there didn't seem to be any other choices at hand.

He sat down in the alleyway, his back against the wall, waiting for the pub to close and the guests to disperse—and to find out if Challis's trust in Bara was well-placed.

twenty-three

· · ·

Challis had been cautious all her life, playing the not very intelligent innocent any time she interacted with someone she didn't trust. Which was almost everyone. She was well aware that her blonde curls and blue eyes made it easier. It took little convincing for most people to believe she was high in beauty but low in brains. Also working in her favor was the fact that once people think they have you figured out, they forthwith dismiss anything to the contrary, if they even notice it. The few times she'd slipped and said something acerbic, or even perceptive, in the hearing of her elders, it'd caused no more than a quick flicker of a frown before being forgotten.

Of course, until now, she'd never done anything that actually *was* treasonous. Any resentment she had against her father and stepmother and their cronies had gone no further than angry thoughts. Sometimes the frustration bubbled over and she spoke aloud her conviction that she was actually the daughter of the Twelfth Chamberlain, not the High King, but even then she'd spoken the words *I am Challis Mazerine* to the mirror in her bedroom when there was no one, not even Nerys, within earshot.

Now, however, she was playing a dangerous game. And she realized there was only so long she could keep the entire plan a secret. She'd already hazarded her own life and security by searching for Eldrin Kenzius—a search that necessitated talking to others about the fugitive—and telling Bara the innkeeper to help her find and hide Eldrin was a worse risk still. She was nearly certain she could trust Bara. But to do what Challis had asked, Bara would have to talk to others. There was no guarantee the people Bara would choose were reliable, nor whom *they* might choose to talk to.

And the secret was rapidly leaking out, like water from a cracked bucket.

So it meant her only real hope for success was her message reaching Eldrin quickly. All it took was one wrong person getting a hint of what she was doing, and she'd find herself being questioned about what she was up to. Knowing her stepmother, it would probably involve torture.

She took a deep breath. There was no point in worrying about that now. She'd finally acted, knowing the consequences if she was caught. She'd done all she could—now there was nothing more but to hope Eldrin got the message.

Waiting to find out, though, kept her in a constant state of high fear. Every sly, sidelong glance from Nerys, every slight raise of the eyebrow from Queen Pavona, every scowl from King Sweyn, made her wonder if they knew precisely what she was doing and were playing her like a fish on a line. She reassured herself over and over that she'd seen such expressions from all three hundreds of times before, and it almost never had anything to do with her specifically. It was all part of the perpetual suspicion of everything and everyone that came from being part of the royal family and their retinue.

This time, of course, she was actually guilty of something.

"Girl, where is your brain this morning?" Queen Pavona snarled at her at breakfast, the day after her nighttime excursion into the city to talk to Bara the innkeeper.

Challis jumped as if stung. "I… I beg your pardon, my lady?"

Pavona rolled her eyes. "I asked you three times to pass the water pitcher, and there you sit, looking stunned." She gave a frowning glance to the king, who was stuffing a forkful of eggs and potatoes into his mouth. "I do not comprehend, your highness, how a man of your intelligence sired such a foolish slip of a girl."

"Blame her mother," Sweyn said, chewing noisily. "She was the same type. Pretty and idiotic."

Anger rose in Challis, along with the phrase, *Don't you dare insult my mother, you pig*, but she held her tongue. With luck, her days of having to put up with such slander would be few in number.

A shudder ran through her. If she and Eldrin got caught, her days would probably be even fewer than she anticipated.

She forced a simpering smile, and said, "My apologies, your ladyship," and handed the water pitcher to Pavona, who snorted angrily and filled her glass.

Sweyn returned his attention to his meal, and Challis— fortunately—was once more forgotten.

After being dismissed from the table, Challis retired to her room, where Nerys attended to her in her usual fussy manner.

"You must be ever so upset about the young man," Nerys said, while brushing her hair. "He's a handsome fellow, if you'll forgive my impertinence in saying so."

"He is that."

"They've not had any word of where he's gone then?"

"None that I've heard, no."

"Such a pity. Whatever can have possessed him to run away like that?"

Challis caught a glimpse of her servant's eager, hungry eyes in the mirror. Desperate for gossip as usual.

"I've no idea at all," Challis said.

"He gave no sign of it when you spoke with him?"

"None whatsoever. We only exchanged pleasantries, and he gave me no impression he was unhappy."

This, of course, was a lie. But Nerys's questions were suspiciously similar to the ones she'd been asked by King Sweyn and Queen Pavona. There was little doubt in Challis's mind that Nerys had been prompted by them to ask, perhaps thinking Challis might be more likely to let an incautious word slip to her personal servant than she would to her father and stepmother. The truth was that of the long list of palace staff Challis didn't trust, Nerys was near the top.

"The poor young man." Nerys drew the brush through Challis's hair one last time and worked it into a braid. "It's just sad, is what I think. I do hope they find him quickly."

I'll bet you do, thought Challis bitterly. *You'd love seeing him in trouble. You'd want a front-row seat to watch him dragged back to the palace in chains.*

But she just sighed and said, "So do I."

Nerys offered to help her get dressed, but Challis dismissed her. If a message was to come from Bara, it wouldn't do to have Nerys there—or to tell her to leave, and then worry that she'd hover around the door hoping to overhear.

"I'm exhausted with worry." It was nothing more than the plain truth. "After getting dressed, I think I'll spend some time reading. Perhaps you could ask Queen Pavona if there's anything she requires of you. If not, you may spend some time relaxing, until it's time to dress for dinner."

Nerys's forehead creased in a quick frown, as if she weren't quite sure what was behind this sudden good fortune.

"Why, thank you, your ladyship."

Challis forced a smile. "Enjoy your day."

She did an awkward curtsey. "You as well, my lady."

But once Nerys was dismissed, she was unable to focus on

any of the books she'd borrowed from the Library, and the time crept by. Nerys returned as requested, before dinner time, but this time Challis dined alone—the King and her stepmother never showed up, and a casual question to one of the servants about where they were elicited nothing more than a nervous shrug and, "I'm not sure, my lady."

Afterward, there were the usual nighttime rituals of preparing for bed, more attempts at conversation from Nerys about her fugitive erstwhile husband-to-be, and another early dismissal of her servant in the hopes that news would come from Bara.

None did. Another day had passed without Eldrin Kenzius being found.

Challis had not realized how much she detested inactivity, but having cast the dice, there wasn't much she could do but wait and see what numbers would come up. She spent another interminable day of waiting, hoping the anxiety wouldn't show in her face and lead to questions. It wasn't until after dinner that word finally came from Bara.

A young man who couldn't have been much more than fifteen, and who clearly had never set foot in the palace before, was accompanied to Challis's quarters by a stone-faced soldier who looked, fortunately, like the obey-without-question type. Once she opened the door to admit the lad, and said, "That is all, you may go," the soldier silently retreated down the hall. She watched him until he turned the corner and the sound of his footsteps on the flagstones disappeared.

"You have a message for me?"

The boy gave her a look in which awe and terror competed, and finally gulped out, "Yes, your ladyship."

"Very well, what is it?"

"It's... it's from Bara. Bara the innkeeper, you know, my lady. She said to tell you that what you talked about... it's tonight. That's all she said, I hope you understand, because she wouldn't explain to me any further."

He looked a little put out at not being in on the secret, but it was reassuring that Bara was being as circumspect as possible.

"It's not a problem, young man, tell her I understand completely. And here's some payment for your time."

She went to her writing desk, opened the drawer, and from it handed him three silver pennies. From the way his eyes widened, she guessed that it was more money than he'd seen in a long while, perhaps ever.

"Thank you... thank you so much, my lady." He gave her an awkward bow. "Is there... is there any other message you want delivered?"

She laughed softly. "Not right now, thank you. But if there is, I will ask for you specifically. What is your name?"

"Armin, my lady."

"Very well, Armin, you go on. Remember, this was a secret message, and you shouldn't speak to anyone except Bara and me about it."

"I won't, my lady, you can trust me."

"Thank you. Let Bara know you did well and I understand her message."

He gave another bow.

"Can you find your way out of the palace? It's a bit of a maze if you're unfamiliar with it. I could call one of the servants..."

"No, no thank you, my lady, I can find the way."

Just as well. One less person to ask questions about why a commoner was in Challis's quarters.

"Then run along, and thank you again."

He bowed one last time, then turned back down the hall,

his hand jingling the silver coins in his pocket as if he couldn't quite believe they were there.

As soon as Armin was well away, she closed her door, and quickly changed into clothes that she hoped would not be too conspicuous on the streets of Tecoa. She tucked her long curls underneath a simple linen cap, and quietly slipped out of the palace.

No one challenged her, and her confidence rose as she made her way across the shadowed courtyard and out into the lane beyond the gate. A light rain fell, and she pulled her shawl closer around her shoulders. She knew the way to the Library well—it had been one of her favorite haunts since she was little—and she met only a few people, all obviously hurrying home to get out of the weather and paying her little attention. She saw the looming edifice of the Library from a block away, lit at the front by guttering oil lamps hanging from poles in front. Instead of going up the front steps, she slipped around the back, feeling her way in the darkness with one hand against the stone wall on her right.

When she reached the back corner, she stopped. The only sounds were the hissing drizzle and the rustle of a night breeze in the leaves of the trees.

She listened for a moment, then whispered, "Eldrin?"

There was no answer but a soft movement somewhere ahead of her and to the right.

"Eldrin? It's me. It's Challis. I'm alone."

"Over here," came a quiet voice. A tall figure stepped out of the shadows. "I got your message."

"Obviously, since we're both here," Challis whispered. "We need to get you inside, where you'll be less likely to be caught."

"Inside the Library? But isn't it locked?"

"Of course it is. But I have a key."

"Why do you have a key to the Library?"

"Maybe we should discuss this once we're inside, rather than standing in the rain."

With a gesture from Challis, he followed her to a door in the rear wall that was nearly invisible in the darkness. She pulled a key from her pocket, deftly fit it into the lock, and moments later, the two stood in the pitch dark of a room filled with the dry smell of dust and old books.

"Now." She turned toward where she presumed Eldrin was standing. "In answer to your question, I've had a key to the Library for five years. My teacher is a close friend of the Head Librarian, and when it became obvious that I loved books, he persuaded the Librarian to lend me a key. The Librarian insisted it be a key to the door into the Archives rather than the front door—he said it wouldn't do for people to see me letting myself into the main entrance at all hours. The Librarian never asked for the key back, so that's why I still have it. For your purposes, the Archives are better than the main floor anyway, because what you really need is shelter and a warm, dry place away from prying eyes."

"And food," Eldrin said, a little desperately.

"And food. I'll see to that. But I didn't want to carry dinner here and find out the message had miscarried, and you weren't here. I'll make sure you get food this evening."

"Thank you. I've been living off scraps."

"Why did you run away? You could be eating at the king's table. You never told me why you were so determined to leave."

There was a long pause. "Because… because I can't marry you."

Understanding dawned in Challis's mind. "Ah. There's someone else."

"Yes."

"And you have already pledged your word to marry her."

Another long pause. "We… we're not betrothed. Just in love."

Something in his tone sounded hesitant, more than would be explained by his simply having another lover back home.

"What aren't you telling me?"

Silence. Finally, his voice reluctant, "Can I trust you not to abandon me?"

Challis snorted. "I've already got my head on the block if I get caught. I'm not going to abandon you now. What is it?"

"My lover… is a man."

"Ah."

"You probably find that repellent." Eldrin's voice sounded defeated. "Everyone else does."

"Repellent? No. My opinion is that the important thing isn't *who* you love, it's *that* you love. No one in my family loves anyone. They're all too busy stepping on each other to gain power and then hang onto it. If any of them really loved someone, maybe Tecoa wouldn't be such a miserable place. So I'm glad for you that you have someone you truly love. I hope you'll be reunited with him."

"Not likely." He still sounded dismal. "But why are you helping me? It sounds like you're not much like the rest of your family."

"I hope not," Challis said, with some fervor. "But I'm not helping you out of pure charity. I have ulterior motives." She smiled. "I'm going to get you out of Tecoa, and to safety, on one condition."

"I… I have no way to pay you."

She made a scoffing noise. "I don't want payment. I want to go with you."

"Go with me? Why?"

"For the same reasons you have, I'd think. Wanting to escape this awful spiderweb without being eaten alive."

"You want to come with me even if we won't ever marry?"

"Even if? *Especially* if. I'm no keener to be handed off like a piece of livestock than you are. If I ever take a lover, it will be *my* choice, not my father's." She almost added, *And he's not my father anyway*, but decided that part of the story could wait for later.

"But how will you get us away from Tecoa safely?"

"They know you're still in the city. The gates are all guarded, and they know you won't be fleeing back south. So there's only one way—across the Waterway. When I was little there was a kind man who used to work as the palace gardener but had retired. He lived right on the Waterway, and on nice days he used to bring me out in a rowboat. Some days we'd go right to the other side and land and have a picnic lunch. If we can get down to the south shore of the Waterway, I know where he keeps his rowboats—they're never locked up."

"Steal one, you mean? There'd be no way to get it back across."

"If he knew why I needed it, he'd *give* me one. But I can't risk telling him and getting him in trouble. We'll leave it right there on the shore in plain sight, so he can row across in one of his other boats, hitch the two together, and bring it back whenever he wants to. I think of it as a loan."

"Like the key to the Library."

"I'm not going to turn down something that's to my advantage," she said haughtily. "In any case, if you're too honorable to use what's given to you, you can go back to living in rainy alleyways and eating scraps and wondering how you're going to find your way out of the city."

Eldrin laughed. "No, that's all right."

"Good. I'm not prepared to get out of the city tonight— like I said, I didn't know if you'd really be here. But I think we should plan on it tomorrow. I'll find you some food—I'll get word to Bara to bring you something to eat here—and pack what I can manage to bring along. So after the sun sets tomorrow evening, be ready to run."

"I will."

"Good. I had better get back to the palace before someone notices I'm missing. For now, just wait, and rest. I'll be back tomorrow."

"Challis?"

"Yes?"

"Thank you."

"I'm glad to help. Honestly, I'm doing this as much for me as for you." She went on, in kinder tones, "And for your lover. This horrid place has far too little love in it. I'll do what I can to help what love I find."

She exited back into the cool damp of the evening. The rain was falling harder, and after a quick stop at Bara's inn to request food for Eldrin and let her know he was safe, she headed back to the palace at a trot. Once again, she wasn't stopped or questioned—even though she entered by a little-used door near the palace kitchens, the ease with which she'd gotten in and out seemed almost uncanny. Doubly fortunate on a rainy night. It would be impossible to explain her wandering as a simple desire for a long walk with the weather as it was.

She made it back to her bedroom without meeting anyone but a guard who seemed inclined to act as if she was invisible, studiously looking the other way as she slipped past. She shut the door, pulled the dripping wet linen cap from her head and tossed it to the floor, and took a deep breath of relief.

It wasn't until she turned around that she realized she wasn't alone in the room. Nerys, her lanky frame also clad in clothing soaked with rainwater, her thin hair plastered to her scalp, was sitting in a chair near the window, looking at Challis with a superior smile.

"Nerys?" Challis squeaked out.

"My lady," her servant replied.

twenty-four

· · ·

God thunders wondrously with his voice; he does great things that we cannot comprehend. For to the snow he says, "Fall on the Earth," likewise to the downpour, his mighty downpour. He seals up the hand of every man, that all men whom he made may know it. Then the beasts go into their lairs, and remain in their dens. From its chamber comes the whirlwind, and cold from the scattering winds. By the breath of God ice is given, and the broad waters are frozen fast. He loads the thick cloud with moisture; the clouds scatter his lightning.

Kallian re-read the passage several times. He had stumbled on a book of lore bearing the title *Holy Bible*—seemingly much older than any of the other books he'd yet found in the Library—two days earlier. Although he'd worked his way through many other books, and some he put aside because he lacked the skill at reading to understand, this one he kept coming back to. Finding out what the people were like in the Before Time, who they were and what stories *they* told, was quickly becoming an obsession.

After spending a great deal of time in a large room with the sign *History*, he was struck by the staggering realization that a great many of the tales he'd heard of the years before the floods and plagues seemed to be substantially true. They'd had machines to do virtually everything they'd needed. From the sound of it, they'd lived lives of great leisure, as their cars and factories and computers—whatever they were, he still didn't have a clear picture—had taken care of most of the work people now either toiled over. Some of what they did in the Before Time, of course, had been lost entirely, and references to professions like *air traffic controller* and *software developer* and *machinist* left him without the slightest idea what those might have been.

But what struck him most was how much bigger the world had been then. There were huge lands accessible only by long travel, over water or—amazing as it sounded—through the air, and thousands of people went back and forth from them daily. Did anyone still live there, or had the calamities that nearly destroyed his home place and the lands around wiped them clean, turning them into a barren and empty wasteland? Was there anyone left in the entire Earth but the inhabitants of Klen, the Samada, and the Kingdom of Tecoa and its dominions?

What was clear was that this had once been a crowded world. He'd known that in the Before Time there'd been more people, but what he hadn't understood was how many more. The Librarian had told him that before the earthquakes, floods, and plagues, there had been a thousand times more people than there were now, but even that seemed like an underestimate. One book he'd seen, which carried the latest of the mysterious date-numbers of any he could find—2033— said the population of the world at the time was something over ten billion.

He couldn't even wrap his brain around a number that immense.

So the catastrophes that had ended the former world had

been even more terrible than he'd realized. He looked back at the page he'd been reading in the *Holy Bible*. The God of those times had indeed blasted the world, and his scattering winds had not only driven the animals into their dens and unleashed the storm, it had very nearly destroyed humanity completely.

He yawned and stretched. Once again, he'd been at it all day, only taking a break to wolf down a quick lunch. How much longer could he keep working like this? His mind had been trained during his apprenticeship to remember details, down to specific words and phrases, but the amount of information contained in the Library was many times too great for him to read through, much less commit to memory. Like the population of the Earth in the Before Time, he had so vastly underestimated what he'd learn here that he was boggled almost to incomprehension.

At some point, he was going to have to figure out how much more time he wanted to spend in Tecoa. Living in Bara's inn was pleasant enough, and he was guaranteed of good food and company in the evenings. The pay he'd gotten from Audris Galvan would last a while yet, although he was certain that was mostly because Bara was kindly charging him far less than she ordinarily would.

But before long the weather would turn cold and rainy, and travel back home would be a great deal more unpleasant. Today had been a taste of what was to come, cool and showery, and the thought of a four-day march in icy drizzle was unappealing to say the least. But that meant either leaving soon—or committing to staying till next spring.

The thought of the latter made him somewhere beyond homesick.

Perhaps the task of memorizing the entire contents of the Library was impossible, but even if he left today, what he'd already learned had changed him forever. He looked back down at the *Holy Bible*, and flipped to a passage he had book-marked earlier, this from a section called the Gospel of Matthew. He read, *Take therefore no thought for the morrow: for the morrow shall take thought for the things of itself. Sufficient unto the day is the evil thereof.* When he'd first read that, he'd thought his heart was going to leap out of his chest.

They were the exact words he had learned as the teachings of the Blessed Julia. He recalled learning them from Syra on one stormy evening last winter and repeating them until he had them exact. Coming across them now turned upside down how he saw the world and his place in it.

Information had a genealogy just like people did. What he'd thought of as the collected knowledge of Klen, repre-sented by Syra as Guardian of the Word, predated not only her and her own mentor Leda Banfield, but Klen itself. Each story he'd learned from Syra, and now each thread he picked up in the Library, tied him to the immeasurable depths of time. Those threads were made of durable stuff, tougher than the weak flesh that made up his body. They had lasted through countless centuries, and would endure through countless more. Only if every copy of that thread was destroyed, and everyone who knew of it had died, was the knowledge truly gone.

And even then, it could be rediscovered, reinvented, recre-ated. As long as there were human minds curious enough and persistent enough, everything known was still out there, still accessible. Human individuals came and went, but the universe of information persisted forever.

He stood, wincing as he forced his muscles to straighten. Before he returned to Bara's inn this evening, he wanted to spend his last couple of hours going down into the Archives. The Librarian said it housed the oldest documents in the Library, and the old man had confessed that even he had no idea what all it contained. If it had books that antedated the ones in the upper floors of the Library, they would be old indeed. He still didn't have a good idea of how the odd date-numbers he found on every book he looked at could be used to determine how old they were, but the traditions he'd learned during his apprenticeship were that Klen had been founded about six hundred years ago. Using the latest dates he'd been able to find, he'd come to the conclusion that by the calendar of the Before Time it would now be about the year 2600, perhaps a bit more.

In the Archives, maybe he could find something that would help him to pin down the timeline a little more accurately.

He exited the History room and went two flights down the staircase to the first floor. He left the quill and ink bottle the Librarian had lent him on a little table, but took with him the books he'd been perusing along with the notes he'd jotted down regarding information he'd found and was afraid he wouldn't remember accurately. The Librarian was walking back to his station carrying three books, and catching his eye, gave him a friendly wave. He returned the gesture, then turned down the hall toward the back of the main room. He passed through a door into a dark, narrow staircase, taking an oil lamp from a hook on the wall before descending into the shadows.

The Archives were largely below ground, although the Librarian had explained that the Library had been built into a hill and at the very back was a door that led out into a grove of trees. But there were no windows, so any exploration he did would have to be with artificial light. The whole place smelled of dust and trapped air. It likely hadn't been disturbed for years.

He went into the first room he encountered. It was labeled "Maps." Holding the lamp aloft, he passed into a room filled with odd cabinets, most of which had very wide, shallow drawers. The nearest one said, *North America*, and he set the lamp down to open the top drawer.

Sitting on top was a yellowed piece of paper, about an arm's length wide and tall, with a drawing of… what was it? He peered closer, and read the inscription at the top, written in an ornate, curly script he could barely decipher. It said, *United States of America, The Year of Our Lord 1882*. There were names written in smaller, but equally frilly, lettering, and gave him enough information to conclude that it was a drawing of a land, as if seen from above. The faded blue bits were bodies of water: *Lake Ontario. The Caribbean Sea. The Atlantic Ocean.* The green parts—well, they were only green in splotches, mostly they had faded to a yellowish-brown—were land. There were features like *Appalachian Mountains* and *Great Plains* and *Mississippi Delta.* The land was divided by oddly artificial-looking black lines, some dead straight, others following natural features such as the course of rivers. Each of the blocks thus delineated had a strange and unfamiliar *name: Massachusetts. New York. Georgia. Kentucky.*

Had these been kingdoms of the Before Time?

1882—if he was correct about what the date-numbers signified, this would have been about a century and a half before the collapse, before the floods and plagues that had ended the old world. And a full 750 years before now.

But where was this United States of America, with its bizarrely-named mountains and lakes and kingdoms? Without a referent, without having an arrow on the map saying "You are here," he had no way to know if it was a day's march away or on the other side of the world.

He flipped through the maps in those and other cabinets, handling them carefully to keep the age-worn paper from crumbling in his hands. His mind was overwhelmed with how many different lands there were—whole cabinets devoted to maps from places called Europe, Africa, Asia, Australia. But even looking at them, as fascinating as it was,

was not like reading the books he'd found, where meaning provided an anchor to keep him fastened to reality as he knew it. Without a key, the maps gave him no way to tell scale or location of anything. Learning to read had unlocked one type of cipher. Here was an entirely different kind, one where even though he could read the words, they didn't make sense.

He left the map room, and went farther back into the Archives. One whole room was devoted to *Governmental Records of the State of Washington*, but that turned out to be dense and not very interesting writing delineating what was and was not legal, and why, and what happened to people who flouted the rules. Still, the fact that there was such a room for the State of Washington, but not for any other state, made him wonder if Tecoa—and possibly Klen—lay in what had once been called Washington. He recalled seeing that name on one of the maps, and resolved to go back and find it, and see if perhaps he might be able to figure out where he was.

His stomach growled. Before long it would be time to ascend back into the daylight, get his notes and belongings together, and return to Bara's inn for dinner and rest. But when he went back out into the long hallway that stretched into the depths of the Library building, he saw something he hadn't noticed before.

There were footprints on the floor.

Recent ones, too, given their sharp edges in the thick layer of dust that had accumulated over the years. They weren't the Librarian's—the farthest they came into the Archives was a room labeled *Family Histories and Genealogies of Pierce County*. He turned and looked. Nearer to the staircase that led to the upper levels was only one set of footprints—his own. Whoever made these prints had come in through the small door at the end of the hall, and had evidently never gotten farther in than the rear third of the Archives.

And he had the sudden certainty that whoever it was, was still here.

His immediate thought was to turn and quietly retreat to the upper floors. If there was another person down here, silently watching and listening, there was a reason he wasn't interacting. He was very likely hiding, probably frightened, and whatever his story, it had nothing to do with Kallian.

But then he had the sudden realization that he had to talk to the person in the shadows. Whether it was from the same certain foreknowledge Syra had, where the past and the future were identical, known, and fixed, he couldn't tell. All he knew was that this was a fork in the road. If he turned and silently ascended the stairs, his life would take an entirely different, and darker, path.

He swallowed hard, then took a deep breath.

"I'm… I know you're there." His voice sounded dull and echoless in the dead air. "I don't mean you any harm."

No response.

"I don't know why you're here, or how you got into the Library, and it's none of my business. I just don't want to stumble into you or startle you." And possibly provoke an attack, if the person was scared, but he didn't say that.

Still nothing but silence.

"I'd like to look in the remaining rooms, but I don't have to. I'm just visiting from the north, so whatever or whoever you're hiding from has nothing to do with me. Soon I'll be leaving for home, and I just…" His words trailed off.

If this person really was afraid, perhaps on the run, why would he believe Kallian? Maybe his own curiosity about the last two rooms in the Archives would have to be pushed aside. Someone who was a fugitive might well resort to violence if cornered. It just wasn't worth it to indulge some bizarre desire that he had to talk to him, and his conviction that he couldn't simply leave without seeing him face-to-face.

His stomach growled again. He wasn't a seer like Syra, at

least not yet. Whatever idea he had about the necessity of drawing this person out of hiding was just a fancy. He scowled. He'd spent too long studying ancient books of lore and dreaming about the past. Time to re-enter the present, and stop pretending he had the gift of foresight.

He heaved a sigh. "Look, I'm leaving, you have nothing to fear…"

Kallian started to back away down the hall toward the staircase, but stopped when there was a soft noise, and a tall, slender figure stepped out of the last room in the hallway. He was indistinct in the flickering light of the oil lamp, but at least he simply stood there, looking at Kallian, not showing any sign of attacking.

He was a young man, about Kallian's age. A bit taller, with light brown hair and wary gray eyes that gleamed in the dim light. He had finely-cut features, a narrow face with a long, straight nose, and there was an elegant grace in his stance that made Kallian wonder if he was a member of the royal family. Certainly he had that bearing.

"Hello." Kallian kept his voice low, gentle. The sense of this moment being a pivot point was back full force. But what he had to do next, he wasn't certain.

"You're staying at Bara's inn. I saw you."

"Yes, I am. I'm Kallian Dorn. I come from a place called Klen. I'm here studying for a while."

"I know. You seem young for a scholar."

Kallian laughed, and a little of the tension in his body relaxed.

"I'm not one, not really. Just someone trying to learn."

"Well, that's what a scholar does. So I guess they were right."

"They?"

"The people in the inn. When you went in, they said, 'The young scholar is back.'"

"Ah. You overheard that? I think it's more or less a joke. I don't know."

The young man shrugged.

"Why did you come out?" Kallian said. "I told you I was leaving."

He didn't respond for a moment, and fear flickered across his eyes. "I don't know. I felt like I had to."

"Why?"

Another shrug. "I recognized your face, so I knew you weren't from Tecoa. I and… and a friend, we're going to be leaving Tecoa tonight, heading north. But neither of us really knows the way, or knows where we're going. I thought if you're from there, you could guide us."

"I hadn't planned on leaving tonight."

He frowned. "I've got to get out of here as soon as possible. Every bump or creak I hear, I think it's the soldiers come to arrest me."

"I'm not a soldier."

He smiled. "I know. That's why I came out." The smile disappeared as quickly as it had come. "But I can't leave without my friend."

"Are you expecting him to come back?"

"Her. And yes. She said she's coming this evening, then we'll leave."

"Ah."

"We're not lovers."

"I didn't say you were."

"I thought that's what 'ah' meant. That's what it usually means."

"Well, it didn't. In any case, it's no business of mine who you travel with."

"Do you think you might be willing to leave tonight? I'm not sure how we'll find our way without someone who knows the land north of here."

Kallian took a deep breath. He'd had his thoughts on home earlier, but didn't expect them to manifest so quickly.

"What are you fleeing from?"

The stranger's gray eyes held Kallian's steadily.

"I'll be killed if I'm caught. I don't have any choice. So I have to run, one way or the other. Even if… even if my friend doesn't show up tonight. I have to find a way, with or without her. I think I've pushed my luck about as far as it will go."

twenty-five

. . .

Nerys had never been so enraged in her entire life.

She was furious at Challis, of course, but a large part of her anger was directed at herself. Having spent her entire life as a palace servant, navigating the wiles, trickery, lies, and outright treachery that was a part of everyday existence had become almost second nature to her. She trusted absolutely no one. Even the person with whom she'd chosen to ally herself, Queen Pavona, was only a means to an end, mostly involving the money and gifts Pavona showered lavishly on her cronies.

But she had no false conviction that Pavona actually cared about her. Loyalty effectively didn't exist within the walls of the palace. To Pavona, Nerys was a tool, to be used as long as it was needed, and tossed aside or replaced as soon as it wasn't.

She knew this, and it didn't bother her in the least as long as she was still in Pavona's favor. So she made sure she did whatever it took to keep the queen under the impression she was indispensable.

She had been certain for some time that Challis was plotting against her father and stepmother, and had hinted as much to the Queen, although avoiding any specifics. Indeed, even if Nerys was right, she had no idea what the specifics might be. The girl was good at camouflaging her feelings, and even better at playing dumb, but Nerys was far too skilled at parsing the secret thoughts of others to be fooled completely.

Whether Challis's intentions were something grandiose—overthrowing King Sweyn, perhaps, or killing Queen Pavona, whom it was obvious she hated—wasn't certain. She gave no indication of putting together the kind of conspiracy it would take to succeed at a coup that massive. It was more likely to be a minor act of rebellion. Running away, perhaps secretly marrying a lover, something like that.

When Eldrin Kenzius disappeared, Nerys's suspicions went on high alert. Challis played innocent, but there was a smugness in her expression signaling she wasn't at all disappointed it had happened—and her wide-eyed declaration that she knew nothing about why Eldrin had vanished, nor where he'd gone, was a blatant lie. Nerys's second sense was absolutely certain of that much. She went to Pavona with her doubts, and Pavona agreed entirely.

"Keep an eye on her, Nerys," Queen Pavona said, her thin lips drawn into a frosty smile. "I think you're right about our dear Challis. It's uncertain whether she actually induced Eldrin to run and is hiding him somewhere, or if she merely found out he intended to flee and is pretending ignorance to the King and me for her own reasons, but I am sure she knows more than she's saying. And I am quite sure that she knows precisely where he is. Eventually, she'll lead us right to him, mark my words." She tapped her chin with one long forefinger. "If you can help us find him, and especially if you can catch her at her game, I'll see to it that you're richly rewarded."

Nerys had been watching the previous evening from a shadowed niche in the hall near Challis's bedroom when she saw her leave, dressed in simple, drab clothing, more befitting an ordinary citizen of Tecoa than the daughter of the king. Challis was obviously nervous; she looked up and down the hallway before slipping past, but even so didn't see Nerys in her hiding place, nor notice as the servant edged out into the hall and followed, keeping far enough back to be invisible in the shadows.

Sure enough, Challis had led her through the wet, dismal evening to the back of the Library, and straight to the governor's errant son. She stood in the rain underneath the trees long enough to listen to a bit of their conversation, and watch Challis unlock the door to let Eldrin in, before trotting back to the Palace, all the while trying to stifle an excited giggle at how easy it had all been.

She waited for Challis to return, secure in the fact that the girl was inextricably trapped in the spiderweb Nerys and Pavona had fashioned. But this is when Nerys made three mistakes in rapid succession.

The first one was deciding to gloat over Challis's dismay first, instead of going to Pavona straightaway. If she went to Pavona, she'd be rewarded, but she couldn't bear the idea of giving Pavona the gratification of confronting Challis and being the first one to see the girl's dismay when she realized her plan had disintegrated. She wanted to reserve that little pleasure for herself.

And that part, at least, had been enjoyable enough. Challis's pretty face had crumpled when Nerys told her what she knew and what she'd seen. But that's when the servant had made her second mistake.

Nerys struggled against the strips of cloth binding her wrists and ankles. If she had room to turn, she might have had a possibility of working her way free. She made a strangled noise of fury, muffled by the gag stuffed into her mouth, as she remembered what had happened after their meeting in Challis's bedroom.

Stupid, stupid, stupid. And above all, greedy. When

Challis had begun to babble that if she kept Eldrin's secret, and helped them both to get away, the two of them would make sure Nerys would receive rewards beyond anything she'd dreamed of, she'd *believed* it.

Looking back, she realized that the likelihood of the young princess being able to give her more than the queen would have was blatantly idiotic. Even if she could have extorted enough money from Challis to make it worth it, the girl was headed for disgrace at best, more likely execution. Far more important was the approbation and boost in status Nerys would receive from the Queen for seeing that fate realized. But a wild thought had passed through Nerys's head—maybe she could get paid by Challis *and* Eldrin, and once she collected, she could double-cross them and bring the information to Queen Pavona—reaping three rewards instead of one.

So she'd agreed to give Challis a day to get together the money she'd promised—three hundred silver coins. Nerys had no real idea how much money the members of the royal family had access to, so no way of knowing if that was even possible. But she'd been blinded by the dreams of wealth, and maybe gaining enough in power and stature that she could move on to being Pavona's personal servant—once Challis ended her days in prison, or more likely, on the headsman's block.

They'd agreed to meet at around sunset the next day, at which time Challis promised to have the money ready. Nerys had chuckled to herself the entire way on the walk to the agreed-upon meeting place. Maybe Challis really *was* stupid. How could she not have realized that once Nerys had the three hundred silver coins in her hands, there was nothing stopping her from betraying the princess and the governor's son to Queen Pavona and the king anyway?

The glee, perhaps, was what prevented her from recognizing that she'd made her third, and worst, mistake—going to the meeting place, the old Gallery Room where the portraits of past kings, queens, and their retinue were kept, alone—and without telling anyone where she'd gone.

The room was dimly-lit, especially as dusk closed in and the small patch of sky visible through a high window faded to slate-gray. A single oil lamp was burning, hung on a hook by the door. Other than the faces of long-dead nobility, the room appeared to be empty.

"My lady?" She spoke quietly, stepping forward, sticking her head out like a long, skinny turtle. "It's Nerys, my lady."

That was when she was seized from behind, her arms pinned behind her, and a dirty piece of cloth stuffed into her mouth.

Challis was far stronger than she looked, Nerys had to credit her that much. The servant was no weakling, having been brought up since childhood to do manual labor, but her service of the princess had by and large been easy, and in the last years she'd gotten a little soft. Whether Challis got her strength from desperation, or from some unknown source of athleticism, Nerys had no idea, but she was rapidly overpowered, her wrists and ankles bound, and was dragged into a tall, narrow wooden closet standing in the corner of the room.

"That's what you get, you nasty little sneak." Challis glared down at her in triumph. "I know you were planning on turning Eldrin and me over to Pavona. Don't worry. I'm sure someone will find you eventually. I hope for your sake it's before you've starved to death, although that's what you deserve given what would have happened to us if you'd succeeded."

Nerys bit down on the gag and glared up at Challis, wild rage making her heart hammer in her chest, and thrashed against the wooden walls.

"Maybe instead of flailing about, you should give some thought to how you'll explain to my stepmother how you ended up tied up in a closet. I don't expect she'll be quick to see your side of things, and you know what happens to people who've failed her. Myself, I would work on coming up with a good story." She smiled. "Take care, Nerys. I hope I never see you again."

Challis shut the closet door. There was the sound of a key turning in the lock, then a light *tink* as she tossed the key away into some shadowed corner of the room.

The exterior door closed softly. Then there was silence.

She spent much of the next hour screaming ineffectively into the gag, and pounding her bound feet against the side of the closet. She quit only once she'd exhausted herself. Her anger at this point was significantly tempered by fear. Challis's barb about what she could expect from Pavona when the Queen found out she'd been hoodwinked was like a dash of ice water down her back. Nerys could leave out the part about having waited a whole day because of her own greed and her belief in Challis's promises, but harder to explain was how she'd trusted the girl enough to meet her alone—without letting Pavona know first what was going on.

Rage and frustration bubbled over in her again, and she kicked at the side of the closet three times as hard as she could.

On the third kick, there was the sound of wood splintering.

Her eyes opened wide, and galvanized into action by the noise, she kicked the panel again and again. She couldn't see anything—it was dark as midnight—but she could feel the side of the closet gradually giving way. Then she had an idea, and worked to swivel her body around so that her hands were nearer the cracked panel. This took a huge effort, as there was little room to maneuver, and with each aching bump and twist of her skinny body, she cursed Challis—as well as she could with the gag still firmly in her mouth. But eventually she was able to turn so that her cloth-bound wrists were near the sharp edges of the cracked wood, sharp enough that she'd cut her arm getting them into position.

Once there, she pressed the knotted band against an edge, and sawed back and forth. It only took about ten minutes, but it seemed like hours, and her shoulders throbbed with the odd and awkward movement, but she couldn't stop a muffled cry of triumph when the last threads of the cloth parted and her hands were free.

With frantic movements she pulled the gag out of her mouth and picked at the knots that tied her ankles until finally those came loose as well. She didn't waste any more time crying out. Her earlier screams had been pure frustration, as the Gallery Room wasn't close to anywhere frequented, and her chance of being overheard was slim. Instead, she began to work at breaking open the cracked wooden panel.

It was a well-built closet. The panels were far tougher than expected, given how thin they were. She gained several more cuts and scrapes, and a large tear in the sleeve of her dress, but eventually she pushed and kicked a hole through the side large enough for her to squeeze through. A few minutes later she emerged, disheveled and sweaty, into the shadowed Gallery Room, breathing hard, her face pinched with rage.

"You'll pay, you simpering little brat. See if you don't."

She pulled the door open—fortunately, Challis had not thought to lock the exterior door—and immediately set off in search of Queen Pavona.

The Queen looked up as Nerys burst in on her and the king at their meal. Nerys had considered various approaches, and decided in this situation *panicked* would have a better effect than *quietly deferential*.

"My lady." She panted dramatically. "Challis... the Lady Challis, she's run away!"

"What?" Pavona's usually pale face whitened even more,

and she set down her fork with a controlled, deliberate movement. "What do you mean, she's run away?"

"I… I tried to stop her. But she overpowered me and tied me up. I've just now gotten free, and came to you right away!"

The Queen's lips tightened. "I knew it. I knew she was lying to me."

King Sweyn's face turned crimson. "She's run away? To where?"

"She's gone and joined Eldrin. The young man. And I know where they are!"

"Where?" the King and Queen said simultaneously.

"The Library. That's where he's been hiding. She… she told me."

The King snorted with anger, but Queen Pavona's eyes narrowed. "She *told* you? Why in the gods' names would she *tell* you that?"

"I don't know. She was… gloating, like."

"How long ago was this?"

"I don't know, not for sure. Maybe two hours ago."

Pavona frowned, and she turned her head a little to the side. Nerys recognized that look, and shuddered. It was the expression Pavona had when she knew she was being lied to.

"Was it?" She tapped one finger on her chin. "Well, we can speak of that later. For now, go find the guardsman who is on duty, and tell him to let the captain of the guard know that our fugitive has been located. Hurry, now, waste no more time."

Nerys gave an awkward curtsey, and turned toward the door.

"Oh, and Nerys?"

The servant turned back toward the Queen.

"If I find you've lied to me, and you're helping Challis and Eldrin, I will see to it that you regret that decision deeply."

She gasped. "Oh, no, my lady, you must believe me, I would never..."

"I sincerely hope you would not." Pavona gave a little shooing motion with one hand. "But I also believe I told you to waste no more time."

Nerys gave another curtsey and scurried out of the door to find the nearest guardsman.

twenty-six

. . .

Eldrin looked at the young scholar's earnest face, wondering at the same time why he'd trusted him enough to come out from hiding, and then explain his dire situation. It came from what he could only call a compulsion, from a certainty that if he'd stayed in hiding, he and the stranger would pass each other like two leaves in a windstorm, and they'd both be carried off to their separate ruin.

"You said your name is Kallian? Mine's Eldrin. Eldrin Kenzius."

Kallian frowned. "You're being sought? Why? Are you a criminal?"

"The King thinks so. So does my father, who is the governor of Galith province. They wanted to marry me to the King's daughter."

"And you refused."

He nodded and waited for Kallian to ask him why, but the question never came.

"You're trying to get out of Tecoa."

"Yes."

"If they're trying to find you, they'll have all the gates and bridges guarded."

"I know. My friend said she knew how to get across the Waterway, and from there, we could head north without going through any of the main guard points. Northward from there, it's farmland, and after that, wilderness." He paused. "Or at least so I hear."

"No, that's accurate. I've been there. But how will we get across if your friend doesn't come?"

"I don't know." Eldrin bit his lip. "I hoped you might have an idea."

"No. I just came in across the bridge, and then through the main city gate. But then, no one was looking for me at the time."

There was a sudden commotion near the back door, and it flung open hard enough to bounce off the wall with a resounding bang. Challis, wearing a drab, rain-streaked linen dress, her hair tucked beneath a shapeless cloth cap, held aloft an oil lamp, then ran inside and slammed the door shut. She turned around, and gaped at the two men.

"Who… who the hell are you?" she said to Kallian.

"Kallian Dorn."

"Are you here to arrest Eldrin?" Her eyes glittered with a fierce intensity. "Because I've already dealt with one person who wanted to turn us over to the king today. If you mean to stop us, expect a fight."

Kallian patted the air. "Relax. I'm not a soldier."

She raised an eyebrow. "I didn't think you were. You're too skinny."

"This is my friend," Eldrin said to Kallian, rather unnecessarily.

"I figured."

"Her name is Challis."

She snorted. "Eldrin, we should finish the introductions later. We've got to get out of here."

"What took you so long?"

"You're right, I should have been here two hours ago. My

servant Nerys found out where you are, and I think I put her out of commission, at least for a while, but we can't count on it. Then I got delayed because my stepmother was looking for her, and had the idea I knew where she was. Which I did, of course, but I had to convince her of that." She nodded toward Kallian. "Why is he here?"

"Challis, Kallian comes from the north. I asked him if he could be our guide."

She was about to respond when Kallian said, a little desperately, "Look… I can go with you, but tonight? I don't even have any of my belongings. They're back at the inn. Isn't there time for me to…"

All three jumped as a volley of fists pounded against the door, and the handle jiggled. An angry voice said, "Eldrin. Eldrin Kenzius. We know you're in there. Come out and surrender yourself, or we'll break this door down. You're wanted dead or alive, so don't put up any resistance!"

"They made up the 'dead or alive' part," Challis whispered. "They want you and me both alive. So they can kill us publicly on their own schedule."

"That's reassuring," Eldrin said.

She looked over at Kallian. "Of course, anyone caught helping us, they probably wouldn't hesitate to kill on the spot."

Kallian swallowed. "On second thought, there's really nothing at the inn that I can't live without."

There was an earsplitting crash as something large was rammed against the door.

Simultaneously there was the noise of shouts and running footsteps from upstairs. The soldiers had stormed the front door as well.

"We're trapped," Eldrin said in a thin, breathless voice.

"Not yet." Challis gave a motion with one hand, leading them toward the staircase to the upper floors.

"They're waiting for us up there." Kallian sounded terrified.

"We're not going up there."

"How will we get out? They'll have every exit watched."

"They don't know every exit."

She grabbed Eldrin by the sleeve and pulled him toward the staircase, but instead of going up, she turned aside and pushed open a door. Beyond it was another set of stairs, this one going downward and disappearing into shadow.

"The Librarian said there were two subfloors." Kallian said.

Challis nodded. "I'm surprised he remembers. No one goes down there."

She stepped inside, and the two men followed.

The flickering light of the two lamps—Challis's and Kallian's—illuminated a wall that had probably once been white but was now a mildew-streaked gray. She trotted down the narrow, slick stairs, and Eldrin's sensitive nose was struck with the odor of mold and perpetual damp. From the smell of age and decay, whatever was down here hadn't fared as well as the upper archives. And in fact, when his foot reached the bottom stair, it made a sodden splash. There was a thumb's breadth of stagnant water pooled on the floor.

Hopefully there wouldn't be more farther on.

"Come on," Challis urged again.

"We'll be cornered here," Eldrin whispered. "It's underground."

"*Underground* doesn't mean *no exit*. I told you I spent a good portion of my childhood in the Library. You think I didn't explore every corner?"

An echoing crash came from the floor above, followed by the rushing noise of booted feet. The soldiers had broken through the door and were in the archives. Eldrin stopped to listen, waiting for some of them to head downward, but after a moment, all of the footsteps seemed to recede upward toward the first floor.

"Maybe they don't know about the lower floor."

"I doubt they do. The king's soldiers aren't hired for their brains. This is probably the first time any of them have actually been *inside* the Library. Even if they do know about the lower archives, I doubt it's where they'd expect us to go."

"So you have a plan?" Kallian said.

She rolled her eyes. "Of course I have a plan. I don't know how they do things where you come from, um... I've forgotten your name. But in Tecoa, if you don't have a plan you get chopped up and fed to the pigs."

Kallian's eyes widened.

"She's joking," Eldrin said.

Challis didn't respond, but continued to lead the way deeper into the halls of the lower subfloor. "What are those books you're carrying?" she asked Kallian, in a conversational tone. "They must be important if you're lugging them around with you. Oh, and what *is* your name? I can't keep referring to you as 'whoever you are, I've forgotten.'"

"I'm Kallian. And they're some books I was studying, and notes I've taken on these and others. One is a book of lore called *The Holy Bible*. I'd also picked up a couple earlier that I thought might be interesting. *Annotated History of the World, The Discoverers*, and *The History of the Scientific Endeavor*."

"Ambitious of you."

Eldrin brushed the wall and his fingertips came away wet.

"What's down here, anyway? Besides puddles, spiderwebs, and mildew?"

"I'm not sure. I think this once was like the next floor up —old records, maps, documents, that sort of thing. But this floor is all below ground, so it was inevitable that water got in and spoiled things. When I was little I came down here a few times, mostly when I was supposed to be studying and didn't want my teacher to find me. I tried to look at a few of the books in the lower archives, but the pages were all damp and swollen and the ink had faded. They fell apart if you moved them. But one thing I did find"—she gestured ahead with the hand holding the lamp—"is that there's a way out."

At the end of the hall was a door, and above it a sign, broken and tilted but still legible, that said *Exit*.

"Where will this bring us out?"

"There's a small building north of the Library—the direction we want to go—that's mostly empty. The roof was damaged in a storm, years ago, and no one ever repaired it, so it's been let go to ruin." She opened the door onto another narrow staircase, stepped inside, and gestured for them to follow her. "This staircase goes up two flights, and ends inside the building. We can either hide there for a while until the soldiers have given up, or find a way to get out on the north side of the building, where we're less likely to be seen."

"We shouldn't wait till they give up," Eldrin said. "We should go now, while they're occupied with searching the Library. If they figure out we're not there, they're sure to start looking in buildings nearby."

"That's good thinking," Kallian said.

They ascended into drier if not substantially better-smelling air. Challis reached the top first. The door at the head of the upper staircase was already partially ajar, and when she carefully pushed it open, it gave an alarming grinding sound as it dragged on a layer of dirt, stone, and debris. She lifted her lamp, slipped her upper body into the gap, and peered around. Eldrin got a glimpse of the broken remnants of old desks, chairs, and other furniture, laden with dust and strewn with cobwebs.

"I think we're clear," she said.

That was when an arrow came whizzing out of the darkness and struck Challis's lamp. The reservoir shattered. The cascade of shards of glass and flaming drops of oil fortunately sprayed away from Challis, but it splattered the nearest of the broken piles of ancient furniture.

It was as if time and neglect had prepared a bonfire, just waiting for the spark to set it alight. The dry, damaged wood burst aflame.

Eldrin backed up, ready to turn and flee back down into the depths of the Library archives, but Challis caught his sleeve.

"No! There's no way out down there!"

In under a minute the flames had turned into a conflagration. The three of them edged their way along the wall, trying to keep away from where the heat was the worst. Kallian, probably recognizing that the remaining lamp would be a target for bowmen, tossed it onto the burgeoning fire. The shadowy figures of soldiers showed themselves, alternately hidden and revealed as the plumes of smoke moved. At least the fire was between them, but it wouldn't be long before the soldiers circled the building and once more had them trapped.

And then what? Would the soldiers let them burn? Even Kallian, whose only crime had been being in the Library archives at the wrong time?

Eldrin coughed, and wiped his streaming eyes with one sleeve. Could it really be about to end, here, in the smoke and heat and stench of a burning building?

But Challis had once again grabbed his sleeve, and pulled him toward a dark space in the corner of a wall. He shook his head, ready to argue with her that there was no hiding from fire, but the words caught in his throat with another paroxysm of coughing.

Then Challis ducked down and disappeared.

What appeared to be a solid wall had a gap in it, just wide enough to fit through, where the stones that made up the outer shell of the building had fallen away.

As he stared, Challis poked her head back in.

"Come *on*."

He didn't need any further encouragement. First he, then Kallian, wriggled their way through, and found themselves in the cool, rainy night air, standing in a clump of dripping trees next to a building that roared as it burned.

"Which way?" Kallian whispered.

"Any way that takes us away from here." Challis turned and ran uphill, northward and away from the center of the city.

Once they'd gotten three blocks away, they slowed to a walk, alternately panting and coughing. Kallian's clothes were singed, but he still clutched his precious notes and books. Challis, in the lead as always, looked around to get her bearings, then struck off down a side street that fortunately seemed to be deserted.

"What if the fire spreads to the rest of the Library?" Kallian's voice was quiet, defeated.

"There's nothing we can do about it," Eldrin said.

"But all that knowledge." He held up the handful of books he'd taken. "And this is all that's left of it?"

"We'll have to hope it doesn't spread."

Challis turned around, a scowl on her face.

"Ssh."

Both men subsided into silence and followed her into the twisting streets of the north end of Tecoa, toward the Waterway and freedom.

twenty-seven

. . .

The rain hissed down steadily, the water swirling and bubbling its way along the gutters. Kallian, Eldrin, and Challis made their way past a row of darkened houses, keeping to the shadows, trying to be stealthy enough to avoid attention, but nonchalant enough not to look like the fugitives they were. After rising for a short way, the terrain began to descend steeply. In the distance Kallian heard the sound of waves, and his nose picked up the briny smell of seaweed and salt water.

He had seen the Waterway—a broad inlet of the sea—as he crossed the bridge on the way into the city three weeks ago. He hadn't given it much thought. All his attention was focused on the vastness of Tecoa, the crowds, the noise and bustle and commotion.

Is this what the Before Time had been like everywhere? Nothing but houses upon houses, buildings upon buildings, streets between them like rivers of stone running through steep-walled canyons, and people, people everywhere?

It was remarkable how fast he'd adjusted. The first couple of days he'd been fretful and unable to sleep, the never-ending tumult so different from the deep forest quiet of his home place that there seemed no solitude even when he was in his room in Bara's inn with the door closed.

But within that first week, he'd settled into his daily walks through the crowded streets to the Library, meals in the friendly chaos of the pub, and the constant undercurrent of noise. He had even contemplated staying in Tecoa over the winter, as homesick as that made him.

Now, here he was, fleeing without even taking his meager possessions, toward a blank expanse of water with two people he'd known for only a couple of hours.

Eldrin seemed nice enough, but Challis had been nothing short of abrasive, barking out orders when she said anything at all. Despite her plain clothes she had the bearing of a noble-woman, someone who was used to servants obeying orders and unused to having her wishes questioned. Some of her tension no doubt was because they were fleeing from mortal danger.

He looked back—no sign of pursuit, but there was a ruddy glow against the underside of the clouds. The fire still raged. He sent up another plea to the gods that it hadn't spread to the Library—the idea of all of that wealth of knowledge being reduced to ash was like a knife in his heart.

But there was nothing he could do about that. If the books and notes in his hands, and the knowledge he'd entrusted to his mind, were all that was left, at least *something* remained. He gave thanks for his training with Syra, brief as it was—his facility for exact recall meant that if he could get himself bodily back to Klen, he would still have what he'd learned left intact.

The obstacle was how to get there without getting caught and killed.

The three of them slunk past a small house right on the water's edge. Its windows were completely dark. Challis nodded toward it.

"Andrine's house. His boats are over there."

She gave a vague gesture with one hand toward a little grove of trees whose silhouettes were barely visible in the dark.

Downhill to the water's edge, through calf-high wet grass. A rowboat lay upside-down, and a set of wooden paddles leaned against the nearest tree.

"Good. He's only got one down here." She took a deep breath. "If he'd had more, I'm afraid we'd have had to break holes in the bottoms of the others. The soldiers haven't given up, and if we left boats here, we could be followed too easily. I'd hate to do that to my friend's property, but we'd have had no choice."

Together they lifted the rowboat, flipped it, and slid it out onto the surface of the water. Kallian stepped out into the shallows and icy cold bit right through the worn leather of his shoes. He clambered into the boat—unfamiliar movements to someone who had never been in one before—and clumsily sat down near the stern. Eldrin and Challis, with more grace, climbed in afterward. She handed him a paddle and kept one for herself, and together they maneuvered the little craft out into the gently rocking waves of the Waterway.

"This was easier than I thought it'd be," Challis said.

That was when an arrow embedded itself in the side of the boat, missing Kallian's left hand by inches.

"Will you stop saying optimistic things?" Eldrin said in a harsh whisper. "Every time you do, someone shoots arrows at us."

Challis and Kallian began to paddle crazily, and even though Kallian had never held a paddle in his life, he was able to help her guide the boat farther out onto the water. By this time soldiers had clustered on the shore and they heard, rather than saw, volley after volley of arrows aimed their way. Only one found its mark—a sharp arrowhead sliced Eldrin's upper arm, and he gave a cry of pain.

"Are you all right?" Challis and Kallian said together, still paddling frantically.

"Just got grazed." Eldrin's voice was thin. "Hurts, but I'll live."

There was a clamor of voices—orders being given. The noises faded away.

Evidently the soldiers had given up on wasting arrows shooting at them into the dark.

"Can they get across another way, circle around, and catch us on the other side?" Kallian said.

"Yes, but it will take a long time. The bridge is five miles east of here, and then it'd be another five miles back to where we're going to land. That's a half-day's march even at a near run. They may try it, but we'll be long gone by then."

"Don't say anything more about how easy this has been," Eldrin said.

"I wasn't going to."

The rain finally stopped, shortly before they reached the opposite shore. The breeze had picked up, the temperature dropping, but the wind at least was shredding the omnipresent clouds and letting in the fitful light of a half moon. They dragged the boat up onto the gravelly bank and headed uphill away from the Waterway. The only houses nearby seemed to be derelicts. If this part of the north shore had ever been settled, it was long since abandoned.

"Do you know your way from here?" Challis asked.

"I haven't been here before."

"I thought you told Eldrin you knew this region."

He gave a harsh sigh. "I'm not a professional guide. I live far north of here, and I came near here once, on my way to Tecoa. I can tell you generally which direction to go, but that's about it." He snorted. "And allow me to remind you that it wasn't my idea to lead you *anywhere*. If you and your friend hadn't attracted a mob of soldiers to the place I was quietly studying, I wouldn't be here and you'd be on your own."

She gave him a frowning glance, then looked down. "I'm sorry. I'm just wound to the breaking point. Ever since I met Eldrin, a week ago, I've been ready to burst."

It was the most conciliatory thing she'd said yet.

"I want to hear the story," he said, in kinder tones. "But we should get somewhere less open to being spotted from a distance. And we need to see to Eldrin's injury."

"I'm okay," Eldrin said.

"Small wounds can turn evil fast. I've seen it happen. I learned some ways of preventing that, but we need to get to a place where we can build a fire without it being like a signal beacon."

After another fifteen minutes' walk they found an old house foundation that still had a piece of overhanging roof. The corner was dry and had accumulated years of blown leaves and twigs. Kallian scooped the debris together until he had a small pile, then searched until he found a straight branch.

"I don't have my knife. It's back at the inn. But I think I can make this work even so. Fortunately the floor is dry stone. That'll help."

"What are you doing?" Challis asked.

"Building a fire."

"How?"

"Watch."

He snapped pieces off the branch until it was about the length of his forearm, then scraped the end into a blunt point. Taking some of the crumbled bits of leaves and bark from the pile, he placed the branch point down against the stone and began to spin it rapidly back and forth between his palms. Before long it began to smoke, and after a bit of blowing and puffing, he had a little flame going. It rapidly grew as he added bits of fuel, and soon he had a nice blaze.

"That's a good skill to know." Eldrin was clearly impressed.

Kallian nodded. "Fire is odd. It can warm or it can destroy. It can heal or it can kill."

"You're still thinking about the Library, aren't you?" Challis said.

"Yes."

She touched his arm. "I'm sorry. It meant a lot to you, I know."

He met her eyes across the flickering of the flame. "I hope it still stands. But getting you away was more important."

"Why do you say that?" Her mouth quirked in a smile. "I mean, I'm thankful you feel that way. But we're total strangers to you."

"Human lives are always more important than knowledge. Knowledge can be rediscovered, reinvented, rekindled, just like I could start this fire again if it went out. But once a life is destroyed…" He shrugged. "Gone forever."

"I'd heard there were people living in the north. You're not what I'd have expected."

He grinned at her. "You thought we were all half-naked barbarians?"

"More or less."

"We've only just discovered written language exists. That's why I'm here. Until now, all of our people's knowledge has been entrusted to the mind of one person, the Guardian of the Word. I'm her apprentice."

"Isn't that risky? What if she died? I mean, before you could learn everything?"

"There's always that danger, I suppose. But that's one thing that comes with being the Guardian—she knows her own future. So if she were going to die soon, she'd have told the other three Oracles. Then they would have time to make sure the knowledge wasn't lost."

"How does she know the future?" Eldrin asked.

"No one really knows. It's a gift that's been passed down from Oracle to Oracle, starting with the first, Blessed Mary of the Bridge. It's a gift and a burden, though. An honor to be the Guardian, but also an enormous responsibility. Your life is no longer truly your own."

"And you're learning everything she knows?" Challis asked.

"I'm trying. I've only been her apprentice for a year. But when we found out that there were other ways of keeping knowledge alive—I asked to be sent out to see what I could learn. That's why I came to Tecoa."

"How did you learn that?"

By this time, dawn was lightening the eastern horizon, still gray with the receding rainclouds.

"I'll tell you," Kallian said, "but we need to see to Eldrin's wound first. Do either of you have something we could heat water in?"

Challis nodded. "I have a metal cup in my pack. I thought it might be useful."

She retrieved a drinking cup from her pack, which she'd tossed on the ground once they found a dry place to sit, and handed it to him. After a short walk, Kallian came upon a little stream where he filled the cup with water, and added a few twigs from a shrub growing nearby.

"Alder." He knelt next to the little fire. "Steeped in hot water, it makes a wash that can keep wounds from going septic. It always grows near running water."

Within a few minutes, he'd heated the water and broken twigs to boiling, then left the mixture to cool.

By that time the light had improved enough for Kallian to examine Eldrin's arm.

"You'll need to pull your shirt off."

Eldrin obliged, wincing as he worked his injured arm out of the sleeve. The arrow had cut a deep slice into the muscle of his upper arm, but it looked like it hadn't torn the flesh too badly. "You're lucky. Aimed little bit to the left, and it'd have embedded itself into your arm. This should heal completely. You'll have a scar, but no worse."

He tore a strip from Eldrin's already-damaged shirt, and used the warm alder-water to clean away the dried blood. He rinsed the piece of cloth, soaked it in the water, then bound it to the wound with another strip tied snugly around his arm.

"Thank you," Eldrin said. "Where did you learn to do that?"

"Same place as I learned to make fire. Have your people forgotten about all that sort of thing?"

"Where I'm from, there are doctors who have an understanding of healing. As far as fire, our fires are never allowed to go out, so if you live in the city, you have no need to know how to make new ones." He looked thoughtful. "I guess each of our peoples kept some pieces of knowledge and forgot others."

Eldrin pulled his shirt back over his lean frame, shivering a little as the still-damp cloth touched his skin.

"You said you'd tell me how you learned about reading, and how you discovered that there were books in Tecoa." Challis gave Kallian a curious look. "Your people have no written language at all?"

"None. We didn't even know such a thing existed until last year, when a foundling showed up and was taken in by the Guardian."

"A foundling?"

"A young girl. Once I got to Tecoa, I wondered if she might not be from near there, because her manner of speech is much like yours. She and her parents had fled north when she was an infant, then been captured by people called the Samada who live between here and my home. The Samada killed her father, and she and her mother stayed with them until she was about six years old. Then her mother also died, and she feared for her life, so she escaped the Samada. She wandered alone in the forest, and only stumbled upon my home place when she was in the extremities of exposure and starvation. But she survived, and Syra—she is the Guardian of the Word—gave her a home. The girl taught us the rudiments of reading and writing, as her own mother had taught her."

He looked at the two people listening to his story. Eldrin's expression held interest, but nothing more. Challis's face, on the other hand, was still, nearly frozen, as if hearing about Lanya's fate had awakened in her some memory she had not thought about for years, and one she was reluctant even to bring back to mind.

"This foundling," she said, in a level voice. "What is her name?"

"Her name is Lanya. Lanya Desorla."

The frozen expression deepened to pure shock, and for a time, she didn't speak. When she finally did, it seemed as if she were almost unwilling, as if she didn't quite believe her own words.

"So that's what happened to them. Lanya Desorla. Daughter of Arlen Desorla and Azen Cheraskin."

"Cheraskin?" Kallian nearly shouted the words. "Syra's last name is Cheraskin."

Challis swallowed. "Arlen Desorla had a sister named Letha. Letha Desorla was my mother."

"Then you…"

She nodded. "Lanya is my first cousin. My mother was married to the High King Sweyn Acoca, although he is not my father."

Eldrin's head whipped around. "What?"

"My mother was executed when I was very young, and the whole Desorla family was disgraced and purged from the palace nobility. Arlen and his wife and child fled Tecoa seven years ago. We thought they were long dead."

"But you… you're not the King's daughter?" Eldrin's voice still held disbelief.

A tiny smile flickered around Challis's mouth, there and gone in a moment.

"You've seen King Sweyn. You really think he's my father? No. My father was Tanil Mazerine, the Twelfth Chamberlain of Tecoa. My name is Challis Mazerine."

The last words were spoken with a note of triumph.

"But… Cheraskin?" Kallian said. He hadn't completely followed all the family genealogy, but was still reeling with the knowledge that not only was Lanya connected to these people, but Syra was, too. He recalled the tales of Syra's mother, arriving in Klen under similar circumstances as Lanya had, nearly seventy years ago.

"The kings of Tecoa have a nasty history of exiling or executing people for any reason, or no reason at all. I do recall hearing…" She frowned, looking down for a moment as she searched her memory, then continued. "I remember my teacher saying that the Cheraskin family had a reputation for being seers. During the reign of King Sweyn's grandfather, several of them were killed or exiled. And one of them—her name was Thea—said as she was driven out that her heir would live to see the Acoca line die."

"Thea," Kallian said in a small voice. "Thea Cheraskin is Syra's mother. She, like Lanya, made her way north and was eventually taken in by our people."

"Does Syra have children?"

"No. But…" He thought about all of the lore he had learned, about prophecies that had come true—only if you interpreted the words figuratively. "I'm her apprentice. I'm the heir to the Guardian of the Word, and when Syra dies I will be the twenty-eighth Oracle of the line of the Blessed Mary of the Bridge." He paused, taking a deep breath. "Do you think Thea Cheraskin was talking about me?"

part four
the block of ice

twenty-eight

. . .

The pall of gray clouds looked close enough to brush the treetops, and a thin, chilly drizzle hissed against the litter of fallen leaves. Hadn't it been summer only days ago? It seemed to Syra Cheraskin like winter had descended without any of the slow decline of autumn, propelling them right into the damp, icy grip of December. She knew it was only an early cold snap, probably nothing more than a day or two before they'd be back in the warmth again, at least for a little while, but for her it felt like it was going to be forever.

Her mouth quirked into a smile. For her, of course, it would be.

She'd informed the other Oracles the previous day that she needed to speak with them, and they'd respected her wishes when she declined to answer what the issue was. It was a miracle to her how much that had changed over the past year. Those doubtful of her, even Bastian Nguyen, had come to accept her completely. He had merely nodded his head in acquiescence rather than arguing.

But now… now she was going to need to explain herself, fully. The thought made her heart pound. Even though she knew how they would react, knew the frozen past and future as if they were right in front of her, here in the ever-moving pinpoint of the present she was afraid.

Syra opened the creaking door into the Hall of Images. The other three Oracles had not yet arrived, giving her a chance to tend the fire, adding aromatic cedar branches to the brazier. The sweet-smelling smoke wreathed around her, and she willed herself to relax. She looked up at the nine statues of the Founders, reflecting that it was not only Bastian Nguyen's attitude that had changed in the year since she had become the Guardian of the Word.

She had finally become accustomed to thinking of herself as one of the Four Oracles of Klen. At first, it seemed presumptuous, almost heretical, to call herself that, but as she adjusted to her own position and saw herself gaining acceptance from the other three Oracles and the people of the community, she came to understand that the mantle had truly passed to her shoulders.

Even the statues of the Founders looked different to her now. As an apprentice, she had always found them forbidding, a little frightening, except for the figure of Blessed Mary of the Bridge, wearing her perpetual gentle smile of welcome. But the others had seemed aloof, distant, unreachable.

She looked up at Blessed Perry, his slim body draped in a long robe, pale hair tousled, his blue eyes staring at his slender hands, cupped before him as if receiving water poured out of a pitcher. Before, there had nothing in him to connect to. His visage had seemed disengaged from her, even unaware of her presence.

The day Leda Banfield died, something had shifted. At that moment it was almost as if Syra had been bodily turned around to see what had been behind her all along. The Blessed Perry was there with her, not just his statue but *him*, the real Perry, the remarkable individual who as a little child had used his oracular gift to save the lives of a dozen other children, many of whom went on to become the ancestors of the people of Klen.

The others were there, too, standing right next to her when she needed them most.

The handsome pair of lovers, Finn and Soren, their fingertips barely touching.

Emily and Colin, who went on to partner and from whom sprung, in straight lineal descent, both Leda Banfield and Kallian Dorn.

Quaice, who gave them the Sacred Language.

Julia, her eyes gazing over the people she led with stern but loving wisdom.

Finally Brandon the artist, with his paintbrushes clutched in one hand.

And of course Mary, dear Mary, who alone of the nine had perished before ever reaching the valley of Klen.

She gazed at them one by one. How had she ever found them frightening? They all stood there with her, an unbroken lineage, they and the others who had made that terrifying trek out of the wreckage of the Before Time. They were all here, even the ones not considered Founders themselves but who followed the Founders' leadership, and whose blood ran in her veins as well. Her own father, Davran Keene, descended from Trevor Keene, who had been one of the first to join with the Blessed Julia when her oracular gift came. They were all here with her, and their names were remembered, would always be remembered as long as there was a Guardian to commit their stories to memory.

Her smile faded. What of her own mother? Thea Cheraskin, born of an entirely different lineage. A cipher to everyone. The fact that Syra carried her surname meant that every time her name was spoken, everyone was reminded over and over that she was half an outsider, allied to… whom? No one knew. Syra had no memories of her mother, who had died when Syra was still an infant. To have no known heritage—to have left no memories whatsoever—could there be a worse fate? At least on her father's side, Syra could trace her lineage all those generations back to the Before Time. But her mother? Nothing, and no hope of ever learning it. That Syra didn't know her mother's origins meant, chillingly, that she would never know. If at some point she was to find out who her mother had been, her forward-facing knowledge would be aware of it.

No, whoever Thea Cheraskin had been, she was forgotten forever. Erased, lost as if she'd never been.

Syra shivered, wishing she were still snuggled under the blankets in her bed. The rain was falling harder now, pattering against the wooden roof. No matter. There were things she needed to see to, especially given what she knew. A little wet and chill was no reason to neglect her duties. She had decisions to make. Most importantly, when and how to tell the other Oracles what was to come.

She left Lanya finishing up her breakfast and preparing for the arrival of a handful of people, ages ten to sixty-three, who were interested in learning her amazing ability to read and write. The informal classes had begun two days after Kallian's departure, now almost a month and a half ago. It seemed like a good way to distract the girl from grieving the loss of someone who had become almost a brother to her. She'd taken to her role as teacher despite being younger than any of her students, and looked forward to the thrice-weekly classes, during which each student learned in their own halting fashion how to draw letters and numbers on flat boards with pieces of charcoal, memorizing the sound patterns and learning how to write lists of familiar words, short sentences… and their own names.

Lanya had explained to Syra that there was a thin, flexible, lightweight material called *paper* that her people used to keep more permanent written records, but she had no idea how it was made. The clunky wooden boards with their charcoal scrawls certainly weren't any kind of permanent way to keep records.

Syra tossed another branch into the brazier. Perhaps someone would eventually figure out how to turn their knowledge into a book, the way Lanya's people had, but if so, it would not be during her lifetime. Nothing in Syra's mind looked that far forward.

In some ways, she was glad of that. If they really did find a way to commit everything to written form, her own ability would be rendered useless. Why entrust all the knowledge of Klen to one mind, with its inherent frailty, if you could write it all down and make it equally available to all? It was a sad thought. Everything she had devoted her life to would be gone in one stroke.

Or, perhaps, that was the wrong way around. Maybe it meant that her role had been the most critical of all—to provide a bridge, a conduit between the old world and the new, to make sure that something at least of who they were would be remembered long enough to record permanently. Without the Guardians' commitment to remembering every detail of the collective knowledge of Klen, it would all have been lost during the years of plague and famine that followed the great floods and ended the Before Time. They would now be rootless, adrift, without any awareness of who they were and who their forebears had been.

Perhaps the role of the Guardians of the Word had been to bring them up to this point safely, then relinquish their charge knowing their sacred trust had been fulfilled. Even if that role was ending, it had served its purpose. And that was enough.

She closed her eyes, gave a silent prayer to the gods and to the spirits of the Founders to give her strength, and turned toward the door as it opened to admit the other three Oracles.

They filed in silently, only Elen Alleman giving her a quick glance and a nervous smile. Elen was of Blessed Perry's line. Did she already know what Syra was going to say? It was possible. Each of the Oracles guarded their own peculiar bits of foreknowledge carefully, judging when it was and was not appropriate to reveal, and maintaining silence if there was even a hint of doubt. Elen, too, was reticent by nature. Sometimes even when the four of them got together for discussion and decision-making, the matter would be concluded without Elen saying a word. She had a fine and incisive mind, however, and when she spoke, it was always trenchant. There was no doubt that the divine voice the Blessed Perry had heard spoke for her, too.

So she might well know. But it didn't matter if she did, not really. In a moment, they all would.

Syra and the others sat in the four wooden chairs, arranged in a semicircle around the brazier, and after a short silence, she began.

"My friends, it has been a year since I was invested with this office, and chose Kallian Dorn as apprentice. At his request, and with your blessing, he left on a quest to the south, and has now been gone for over a month. I believe he will be returning soon."

"You believe?" Bastian said. "You don't know?"

"No. I do not know." She looked at each of them in turn. "It is only a surmise."

Garlin Abraham gave a thin little gasp, as the import of those words registered, but he did not speak.

"His training was incomplete when he left," Syra continued, "but we deemed it a worthy enough cause to take that chance. Waiting until his training was complete would compound the risk. The more he progressed with learning what I know, the more could potentially be lost if he died along the way."

"I knew..." Elen said, her voice tentative. "I knew he wouldn't die."

"Why didn't you mention this when the decision was being made?" Bastian asked.

She shrugged her narrow shoulders. "I didn't need to. Had the discussion gone the other way, I would have spoken up. I knew that he needed to go, and that it must be then. He had to leave that day, not one day later. The timing was critical. Although I did not, and do not, know why."

"Nor do I," Syra said. "What is certain is that there are greater things at work here than one man on a lone quest to find lost knowledge. I cannot predict the outcome. It has been given to each of us to see a part of the whole, but not the entire. The four of us must trust in the others that together we can guide the people of Klen wisely and see to it that what should happen, does happen."

"We knew that much." A little of the old sharpness colored Bastian's voice. "It's no different than the vocation the Oracles have had for the past six hundred years. Why did you ask us to assemble here today?"

Syra suppressed a shudder. No amount of preparing them was going to make this any easier.

"I need your guidance to ready myself and our people, because there is a change coming. As I said, Kallian will return soon, and what he brings back with him will turn the course of Klen like a log falling across a creek. It cannot be stopped, but it can be prepared for. He will return with knowledge—the knowledge of the Before Time, and for good or ill it will alter the minds and hearts of everyone in this community. We do not know much about why the old world fell. Their machines and books and lives of plenty did not shield them, though, and their civilization collapsed. There must have been a reason even if we do not see it. Some of them—perhaps all of them—used what they had learned for evil purposes, and in the end the very lands and seas themselves rose up against them. If we can regain that knowledge and those abilities, it falls to you, and to our successors, to make certain that those deadly errors are not repeated."

"Perhaps it would be better not to relearn those skills, then," Garlin said.

"There is no stopping it. If Kallian had not rediscovered it, someone would have. Knowledge cannot be erased forever. Blessed Julia spoke of the Apple of the Tree of Good and Evil, that once eaten gave men and women understanding, but also condemned them to spend their lives in ceaseless pursuit of extending that understanding. Knowledge is both a blessing and a curse, a pleasure and an addiction. We cannot stop the flood Kallian will unleash, but we can direct it, make certain that for as long as possible, it is used to build, nurture, and heal, not to destroy."

"That is wise," Bastian said. "But you speak of this as if it is our task and not your own. You are still one of the Four Oracles, and he is your apprentice, is he not?"

Syra took a deep breath. Elen had closed her eyes. In that moment, Syra became certain that the younger woman already knew what she was about to say. "Yes. He is. But not for much longer. When Kallian returns, you must take over the task of his training. He has come far in one year, but he has further yet to go, and I cannot—I will not—be the one to guide him on that path. In three days, I will die, and by the time he arrives back in Klen, Kallian will be the Guardian of the Word. I commit him to your care."

twenty-nine

. . .

"Gátra-Skómna." *Leader of Falcons*. The emaciated man brushed his long, tangled hair, wet from the perpetual rainfall, out of his face as he hissed the words under his breath. Leader no longer, since the traitorous cur Thalaté engineered his downfall, and his vicious bitch Shisla mutilated and unmanned him. But he'd be damned if he'd give up the title, which had become his name. Gátra he was, and Gátra he would be until he died.

He continued dragging one foot in front of the other, his feet rustling in the wet leaves. Keep heading north; that was all that mattered. North, to where his final goal lay, and then it didn't matter what happened afterward. He reached down and scratched at his ruined groin, then winced. It was still painful. Infuriating that he couldn't wreak the revenge he dreamed of nightly on either of the ones who did this to him.

That much was made clear when his bleeding body was dragged out into the deep woods after the fight and its aftermath, and Thalaté spoke in his level, uninflected voice, looking down on him from what seemed a great height.

"It is all one to me if you lie here until the wild animals kill you, or drag yourself away and hide, and somehow survive. If after this you are seen by any of the Samada, ever, you will be killed on the spot." His mouth twisted, and he spat in Gátra's face. "Whatever happens, you are dead to the Samada. May your very memory be erased from our people's minds and hearts."

Then they turned and left him, barely conscious, like a heap of refuse thrown into the woods after a feast.

Only one person had come back, but not to rescue him. A young follower named Nydek, who skulked back at dawn, looking around furtively as if afraid he'd been seen and followed. Nydek gave him a sack of food, but when Gátra demanded that the youngster pull together other people still loyal and assassinate Thalaté and the other rebels, Nydek panicked, shaking his head and staring mutely, then turned and fled. Evidently giving Gátra enough food to survive was one thing, but helping him back to his rightful place was another.

Gátra screamed, as loudly as his weakened state would allow, "Traitor! All of you!" at the boy's retreating form, but soon he vanished into the trees.

No one else came.

Still, if it hadn't been for Nydek, Gátra would have died. The food only lasted a couple of days, but it was enough. By the time it was gone he'd regained sufficient strength to get up and walk, heading north and away from the Samada encampment, always north. Fortunately it was early autumn, and there were berries and other fruits plentiful enough to keep him from starving, but it was far from the rich diet of venison and fish he was accustomed to. He watched, day to day, as the weight melted from him, until so little was left few would have recognized him as the powerful fighter he had been. Leaning over a still pond to take a drink one morning, he barely recognized himself. His once ruddy complexion had gone pasty and yellowed. His dark eyes seemed to burn with a sick fire, but it was the only part of him that still looked alive. The muscles he'd used to power his fists and legs, the implements of his rage that had defeated so many strong men, had collapsed to fleshless ropes.

It was as if he'd become a ghost while still alive.

There was still a mission to accomplish, however, before he relinquished his life entirely. He had enough vitality left in him, despite having his body violated and being starved for nearly a month, to do what he needed to do. Even if the detestable Thalaté and Shisla and their accomplices were beyond the reach of his revenge, perhaps one other wasn't—the young man who had been the catalyst of it all.

Kallian Dorn of Klen.

Gátra's hollow face contorted into a leer. If that little whelp hadn't shown up, none of it would have happened. The boy had sweet-talked Shisla while he was fucking her, and won her sympathy somehow. Then they'd teamed up with Thalaté, who otherwise would never have had the courage to face Gátra down. Somehow Thalaté had gotten enough of the men of the Samada—and the women, too—on his side to ensure that Gátra's fall was permanent.

He continued to plod forward, never slowing. Start at first light, end when it was too dark to see, with his only company being his own thoughts. Not all of them were welcome. Amongst the jangling chaos careening through his mind were fleeting whispers that some of this had been his own fault. He hadn't seen the warning signs, had thought that his own strength and cunning would make it impossible for anyone to stand up to him.

Even nastier ideas slithered their way into his brain—that it wasn't just an oversight, it was his own arrogance that had done this. If from the beginning of his reign he had actually listened to the people he was supposed to lead instead of bullying the men and using the women as mere receptacles for his lust, if he hadn't thought his fists and his cock were all he needed to dominate everyone forever, perhaps he'd have had someone there fighting for him when Kallian struck him down.

Instead, once he was incapacitated, they'd all turned against him, almost as if the entire Samada people had been waiting for this moment.

Perhaps they had.

But he banished that thought from his head. No. He was the Leader. It didn't matter what they wanted, what they needed, what they desired. They were his to do with as he wished, to beat, rape, kill, whatever he decided. That was the Leader's right. His rule should never have been questioned. It would not have been had it not been for Thalaté, Shisla, and Kallian.

He continued his slow tread north, the rain streaming down his face like tears. He paid little attention to the ache in his groin, only using it to further stoke his rage.

What would he do to gain revenge against Kallian?

He had to admit that in his current state, he was no match for the boy. Even though Gátra had ridiculed Kallian's body when they'd stripped to the waist before the fight, he had to admit the younger man was fit and well-muscled, and with a few years and a little filling out, he would be a formidable fighter should he choose to be.

But now? Kallian had refused to kill when he had his first chance. He wouldn't make the same mistake again.

A slow smile grew on Gátra's face.

No, it wasn't enough to fight Kallian again and kill him this time. That was not even going to be possible. A more fitting revenge would be letting Kallian live for the rest of his life knowing what Gátra had done, what evil Kallian himself had brought down upon his community. Perhaps he couldn't harm Kallian directly, but he could take revenge against the people Kallian loved, the people from his home village.

What had the boy told him? His mentor, and the leader of his people, was some woman. The Guardian of the Word, he called her. He recalled the tone of Kallian's voice in speaking about her—loving, reverential, almost like the attitude of a child toward his mother. Perhaps it would be possible to get into their community and take his revenge on her. Unless Kallian had returned already, there was no one in Klen who knew who Gátra was. And even if Kallian *was* there, Gátra could still use stealth. Find the woman and kill her. If afterward they found him and killed him—even if it was Kallian himself who did it—it would still be worth it. His own death was a fate so likely as to be a near certainty, and he could accept that. If he was able to kill Kallian's mentor, the boy would never be free of the memory that Gátra had, ultimately, won their fight.

Plod, plod, one step at a time. He came to a little tumbling stream, and after taking a quick drink, walked across it. The icy water drenched his worn leather shoes and soaked him to mid-calf. He barely noticed it. A rock turned underneath one of his numbed feet, and he almost lost his balance, righting himself just in time. He glanced to the side. Where he'd have fallen was a large jagged rock. He'd have surely struck his head and knocked himself out, then tumbled into the creek's rushing water and drowned.

But he didn't. He dragged himself up onto the opposite shore, back onto dry land. Every near miss made him more certain that it was fated to be. He would keep walking north until he found Klen, and then he would finally conclude his fight with Kallian Dorn the way it should be.

Days went by. Gátra had no idea how many. If he'd known, he wouldn't have cared. The only things that mattered were continuing to walk north, to find enough food that he'd have the strength he needed, and somehow find the village of Klen. All he knew was it was north, and lay in a valley between the mountains and the ruined city from the time of the floods and famines and plagues, the city whose southward reaches he had glimpsed as a young man on his quest to find a name. He was weakening fast, but somehow he kept going. He was still tormented daily by the poisonous thoughts of having brought his fate on himself, but he used his pain and exhaustion and hunger to keep his mind focused on the anger that propelled him.

Of all the things he questioned, he never doubted that his slow, patient steps would take him where he wanted to go.

It was near midday—another sodden day, as if the skies themselves were weeping—that he came upon the double line of boundary fences, and he knew he had arrived.

He stood for a time, his hand resting on the rough barbed wire of the outer fence, looking in. Nothing seemed different on the other side. Trees, more trees. In the distance, he caught the dull gleam of a lake, silver-gray under the shifting canopy of rainclouds, framed by the dark greens and browns of tall fir trees. He edged his way through the pair of wires, only pausing for a moment to suck the back of his hand where one of the barbs had torn a scratch.

A bow's shot farther in was another fence. He crossed that one as well, and smiled. This was how these people thought to keep themselves safe? A child could get through them.

His head came up, like a deer scenting a hunter. A noise, coming in the direction of the lake. A child singing? At first, he thought it was his imagination, triggered by his thoughts, which more and more had seemed like voices shouting in his ears. But no, even above the din of his own mind, he could hear the light lilting of a girl singing, some sweet air in a language he did not know.

He crept forward soundlessly, from tree to tree, approaching the lake's edge like the predator he was. A slender figure was crouched over, and from her movements was washing clothing. She had light hair pulled back into a braid, but he could only see the curve of one cheek. Until…

She sat up to wring out the dress she'd been washing. In that moment, he knew her, and before he could stop himself, he gasped.

Lanya. Daughter of the woman Azen, the refugee from the city in the south whom he'd taken to his bed. Who was to give him a child, but died in the childbirth, along with the son he should have had, the son none of the dozens of other women he'd taken were able to conceive for him.

The girl looked up at the sound of his gasp, whirling around to face him. For a moment, their gazes locked, and then Lanya gave a thin scream, vaulted up, and sprinted away.

He stifled a curse.

How had the little brat come here? He'd thought she'd long since starved in the forest or been torn to pieces by wild animals. When he'd nearly fallen into the creek, he'd thought the gods were smiling upon him. Now his fevered mind twisted, screaming that the very fates were conspiring against him, sending to his enemies the one person who could have recognized him. Weak as he was, there was no way he could match her speed, so he had no choice but to follow the direction she'd run and hope by the time he got there, she hadn't already raised the entire village against him.

But as he went down the path, the expected clamor of voices, of the men coming out with weapons to meet him, never came.

The first house he saw was neat, built of hewn logs, with a small garden in front and chairs on the porch. He caught a quick glimpse of Lanya's face in the window, a face that seemed to be all eyes, there and gone in a flash, But then his attention was drawn to the figure sitting on the front step of the house, seeming not to notice the chilly rain pouring down all around them.

It was a tall, slender woman, perhaps sixty years old. She had long blonde hair, now streaked with gray so light as to appear almost silver. Her narrow face was relaxed. If she was afraid of this apparition from hell come to her front doorstep, she didn't show it. Her eyes were a light blue-gray. The resemblance to Azen, Lanya's mother, was striking. They could have been mother and daughter.

She stood slowly, and stepped forward to face him.

"I know why you're here." A level, quiet voice. She spoke the language of the Samada, just as Kallian Dorn had.

"Do you?"

"Of course. Do you know who I am?"

"I would guess you're the leader of this village, the one called the Guardian of the Word."

"That's right. You're the one who led the Samada."

"The girl told you that?"

"She didn't need to."

A thrill of fear coursed through his body. He'd encountered many adversaries in his life, and he'd seen bravery, defiance, fear, cunning, heroism, and outright terror, but this serene detachment, almost indifference, was something new to him. What he sensed in her was a supreme confidence that needed no bragging or swaggering. He understood why this woman was their leader. Compared to her, he felt himself to be no more than a wounded animal, weak but still capable of a pathetic, desperate viciousness. Under different circumstances, he might have met her and considered her to be a god.

But simultaneously, he rejected that knowledge. He saw her clearly; he hated her utterly. To be looked at, as she was looking at him, with grace and compassion, was intolerable. Anything was bearable except for being pitied. The pain when Shisla had mutilated him was nothing compared the knife-blow of the Guardian of the Word's gaze.

"I'm going to kill you." It came out as a growl.

"I know."

"Why aren't you running, or calling for help?"

"Tell me why I should."

He didn't answer for a moment. What she'd said was simple—only five words—yet it was so strange he thought he'd misheard her.

"Because no one wants to die."

"You think so?"

"It is the truth."

"You've been misled." She paused. "It isn't your fault. You learned very early to run, to keep running desperately as fast as you could, that if you ran and fought and hurt and killed others, you could somehow outrun death itself. What you didn't see is that there's nothing there to outrun. Death and life are not opposites. They're all one thing, seamless. You can no more separate life from death than you could separate day from night."

"And you're not afraid to die."

"I didn't say that. I am afraid, a little."

"Then why don't you get others to defend you? Or defend yourself?"

"Because this is the way things happened. It is my time to die, and I accept that. I have had a long life, in which I loved and was loved. I am content."

"Do you think Kallian will feel the same way?"

If she was surprised to hear Kallian's name, she gave no sign.

"Kallian will understand."

"Will he? You think he cares for you so little?"

Syra laughed. "No. It's the opposite. He loves me enough to let me go. To know that things happen the way they must. But you should know something else. You are doing this because of your anger and hurt, because you wish to strike at Kallian. You know you're too weak to assault him physically, so you think to wound his spirit by killing me."

Gátra's heartbeat was so loud in his ears he was nearly deafened. This woman… she *was* a god. She had seen into his mind, she knew who he was and why he was here, his soul laid bare. *And yet she did not lift a finger to save herself.*

He took a step closer to her, and she still did not flinch.

She shook her head.

"By killing me, you will cause a part of what I am to pass into him. You thought he was strong before? What you are about to do will make him stronger than you can imagine. It will bring down the skies upon your own head."

He reached for her throat, and she smiled. She actually smiled! His entire being was consumed with a desperate need to stop that smile, to cut off that patient, calm voice forever.

She closed her eyes.

"So be it."

The roaring chaos of his thoughts blended into a seamless wall of noise, joined by the terrified screaming of the girl inside the house and the incessant, maddening patter of the raindrops, falling from skies so dark it seemed the sun would never come again.

thirty

. . .

The rain had fallen endlessly since the day Kallian, Challis, and Eldrin crossed the Waterway. The only break had, fortunately, been the short respite allowing Kallian to build a fire and tend to Eldrin's wound. Soon afterward the clouds closed in again, the thin, chilly drizzle cascading down silently, soaking them all to the skin. Neither Eldrin nor Kallian had warmer clothes to wear, and the journey was a nonstop combination of helpless shivering and trudging through mile after mile of muddy fields and woods, stopping only whenever they found meager shelter. At least the pursuit seemed not to have followed them. The soldiers must have considered it not worth the time to pursue them into the wilderness.

"They probably figure we'll be dead soon anyhow," Challis said.

"Always the optimistic one," Eldrin said.

Challis shrugged. "Oh, I'm not planning to die." Her voice was cheerful. "And in any case, I'll risk death out here. Better than what the King had planned for us."

But that didn't make the present any more comfortable. They couldn't even build another fire. There was no wood dry enough to catch. They huddled together at night for whatever shared warmth they could manage to hold on to. Challis agreed to wrap Kallian's precious books and notes tightly in one of her pieces of clothing and stow it at the bottom of her satchel—as long as he agreed to take a turn carrying it.

Which was only fair.

They did have one warm, dry night, spent with Kallian's friend, the farmer Audris Galvan. Audris allowed them to shelter in his barn—the three of them were too many for his little cottage—but he fitted them out with some cast-off clothing, an extra pack, a knife, and as much food as he could spare. Compared with sleeping rough in the rainy woods, it seemed like opulence.

When Kallian exclaimed over his generosity, Audris gave them a friendly smile.

"I'll come out even. Kallian, your backpack and clothes and all are still at Bara's inn, right? Next time I'm in the city, I'll ask her for them. Consider it a fair trade."

Challis frowned. "Will she believe you actually gave us your own things? Won't she think you're trying to get something for nothing?"

"You royals. Trust no one, eh?"

"Pretty much."

"Hell of a way to live."

She laughed. "Why do you think I'm running away?"

Once in the dry, snug barn, Kallian unwrapped Eldrin's wound and did a cursory cleanup of the bit of blood that had seeped from it. "It's knitting well. You'll have barely a scar."

"Thanks to your skill."

Kallian nodded. "I'm glad to do it."

Challis bit into one of the apples Audris had given them, and gave Kallian an evaluative look.

"So, your people can see the future?"

"Not all of us. The four Oracles can, at least in some fashion. It works differently for each."

"Your mentor…"

"Syra."

"Syra. Syra Cheraskin." She sounded as if she couldn't quite believe hearing the name of a Tecoan noble family from someone living out in the wild north. "She knows what's going to happen? Everything?"

"Not everything. But her own life, and what will happen to her. If something happens elsewhere—another place, another time, outside her experience—she knows as little about it as the rest of us. But she sees her own past, present, and future as fixed, like it had all already occurred. She says it's like looking at a block of ice. You see the bubbles, frozen in place, never moving. From any angle, it's all the same."

"And her own death… is that one of the bubbles?"

"I would expect so."

"How terrifying."

"She told me that her foreknowledge took away all her fear of death, that our fear of death isn't really fear of the thing itself, it's fear of uncertainty. We furiously fight against it because we think that by doing so, we'll postpone it. Most of us act as if we could put it off forever." He paused. "For her, it's a known thing, no more frightening than knowing the sun will rise tomorrow morning."

"And when she does die, that gift passes to you?"

He didn't answer for a moment. He was still new enough to his apprenticeship that he had hardly given any thought to that eventuality. All his efforts had been put into learning everything he needed to learn.

But even that had been in preparation for Syra's eventual death, hadn't it? What would it be like to know, know for certain, every event of the remainder of his life? Would he even be the same person afterward?

No matter. It wouldn't happen for a long while. Syra

wasn't young, but she was strong and healthy. He would have many years to accustom himself to the idea of having such a perspective—and to assuming the duty of being the leader of the Four Oracles of Klen.

Days went by. Kallian passed landmarks he recognized from his journey south, and noted with some trepidation that he had passed into the territory of the Samada. He skirted west of the Samada encampment as carefully as he could, but was foiled by the terrain and the dense underbrush. He debated telling Challis and Eldrin about his encounter—and how closely he'd come to dying at Gátra's hands—but initially decided not to. Whatever the outcome of Thalaté's coup, it was certain that the geometry of the leadership had changed permanently.

Still, it seemed as if the others had picked up on his concern. They walked quietly, speaking little, as if everyone sensed the need for caution.

"I feel like we're being watched," Eldrin whispered, as they came across what was obviously a well-trodden path. "And this isn't just a deer path. Are there people living in these woods?"

Kallian didn't answer at first.

"What do you know that you're not telling us?" Challis said.

He glanced at each of them in turn. "Yes. There are people here. They're woods-crafty, and probably know we're here."

"Should we be worried?"

"I don't know for certain, but I don't think so. I had an… an encounter with them, on the way to the city. I believe I earned their respect. If we're seen, they'll certainly recognize me, and I hope they'll let us pass."

And indeed, as they continued north, the sensation of

being monitored gradually subsided. He never did see clearly the people who were watching them. Once, only once, did he catch a quick glimpse of a shadowed figure, still as a statue, back amongst a cluster of trees. He turned toward it, but it slipped aside and vanished.

Perhaps this was his thanks for helping them topple Gátra —that he and whoever was with him had free passage through the Samada territory.

Another day's walk brought them to the first of the boundary fences surrounding Klen.

Kallian's heart leapt in his chest. As driven as he'd been to make the quest to Tecoa, looking for knowledge, he was over-joyed to have a sight of home. He turned toward his companions.

"This is it! These are…"

He stopped mid-sentence, aghast, unable to move.

The whole world had frozen.

It wasn't that anything had stopped moving. The rain still fell, the light breeze still rustled the tree branches. But at the same time, there was no movement. He felt like the pivot, the still point of the entire universe, looking around at a scene that was locked in place, a tableau that had never moved and would never move again.

Challis put her hand on his upper arm. "What's wrong?"

"I…" He swallowed hard. "We have to get inside. I have to…" He shook his head, trying to clear the confusion. Nothing changed. "Syra Cheraskin is dead."

"Your mentor?" Her voice was thin with horror. "How?"

Kallian pulled upward on one of the fence wires, and motioned for Challis to crawl through.

"Just… when we get there. Stay back. Don't interfere. I know what I have to do, but… I don't want you to get hurt."

He took a long, uneven breath. He knew what was going to happen. He knew who was and was not going to get hurt.

It was there, right in front of him, as clear as his memories. But how could he explain that to them?

In the end, he silently held the wires apart for his two companions, and together they crossed the outer, then the inner, boundary fences toward what waited inside. Both of them looked at him with a combination of awe and fear.

He'd been right. He was changed, forever. But what he hadn't anticipated is that it would change everyone around him just as irrevocably.

He knew what he'd see as he approached the house that had been his home since his acceptance of apprenticeship a year earlier. Syra, his beloved mentor, the Guardian of the Word, slumped to the ground. The ghoulish, nearly cadaverous, figure of Gátra of the Samada crouched over her, just pulling his hands back from her throat. He heard their approach and turned, glaring up at them with a hateful glee, baring his teeth in a smile that had not the slightest trace of humanity. Without even being aware of it, Kallian shucked his pack, dropped it to the ground, and retrieved the knife he'd been given by Audris Galvan.

Gátra laughed when he saw it, standing up to face Kallian.

"What are you going to do, Kallian Dorn of Klen? Slit my throat? It's too late. Your Guardian is dead. You can kill me, but will it bring her back? Will it mend what *you* have done? Your actions made this happen. Bear that burden for the rest of your life. But as for your knife?" He laughed, a laugh that was half a snarl. "Kill me with it. I dare you. You didn't have the courage to do it before. You do not have it now."

Kallian stepped forward. A preternatural calm spread over him. Everything that was going to happen had already happened. There was nothing to fear, nothing to mourn. What was, simply was, and could not be changed. It was always this way since the universe had come to be billions of years ago, and nothing could alter anything, not the path of a mote of dust on the wind.

"You think I spared you before because I lacked courage?" He listened to his own voice. It was steady, tranquil, without any trace of a tremor. It was almost like listening to someone else speak. "It wasn't cowardice that stayed my hand. It was because I had no desire to become you. You never understood that rule through destruction is no victory. You never will."

"And yet I destroyed your mentor. Nothing you do will change that."

"I grieve her. She was my mentor and also my friend. But this doesn't mean you've triumphed. Syra understood that, and now—finally—so do I." Now he was near enough to Gátra to touch. The man seemed to have shrunk.. How had he ever been afraid of him? He was a wretch, more pitiable than deserving of hatred. "I will ask you once. Only once. Leave my village. Leave and never return. I don't care where you go. But this is your final chance to end things differently."

Gátra threw his head back and gave a howling laugh.

"Or what? Or *what*, you little cur? You'll stick me with your knife? You'll strangle me with your bare hands like I did to your beloved Syra? You dare not." His gaze locked onto Kallian's. "You dare not lay a hand on me. I would have killed you that night if it hadn't been for the help of the traitor Thalaté. But now? Now you have no one to help you, and you haven't the courage to strike your blade home."

In one swift movement, Gátra jumped forward, and grabbed Kallian's fist, the one clutching the knife. He jerked it toward his own bare, emaciated abdomen, and the blade pierced his skin. He grunted with pain, but yanked again, this time driving it deep underneath his own ribcage.

Kallian tried to let go, as the warm blood cascaded over his hand, but Gátra's grip didn't relax. The older man put his face next to Kallian's. There was a crimson thread trickling from his mouth. He said, in a hoarse voice, "I still win."

Finally his grip on Kallian's hand loosened. He collapsed to his knees, and pitched forward, face first onto the ground.

epilogue

. . .

eight months later

Lanya and Challis waved goodbye to the last of the students of reading and writing. The class had grown to include half of the village of Klen, especially now that there were actual books to study, books from the Before Time. Knowledge of history and science and mathematics that had been lost so completely no one even dreamed they existed, now open to anyone.

Some industrious people had used Challis's slim knowledge of how the people of Tecoa made paper to fashion some of their own, with limited success at first. The initial attempts were fragile, breaking apart when anyone tried writing on it. But subsequent trials were more fruitful. What they produced was nowhere close to the satin-smooth paper in the books Kallian had brought back from Tecoa, but slowly and steadily, their skill was improving.

As the students filed out and dispersed to their own homes, Kallian was working in the garden, tilling the soil and breaking up the clods in preparation for planting. He smiled as he saw Lanya approach.

"How was class today?"

"Good." She knelt, tugging at a clump of grass he had missed. "Bastian doesn't like being a beginner. He gets cross, but Challis doesn't let him get away with it."

He laughed. "Good for her."

"You like Challis, don't you?"

"Of course I do."

"No, I mean, really *like*. Are you going to ask her to be your partner?"

He leaned his shovel against the fence. "Do you think I should?"

Lanya scowled. "Of course. But you're being evasive. Isn't that the word? Answering a question with a question."

"Yes."

"Because you already know what you're going to do. You know what she's going to say. You know if you're going to be together and have children and so on."

"That's right. But she doesn't."

"So you can't say."

"Not can't. Won't."

"It doesn't bother you that you know everything that's going to happen?"

He frowned thoughtfully. "No. It doesn't, not really. I thought it would. But if you just accept that it's all the same thing—the future and the past—there's really nothing to be bothered about. Like Syra told me, it's just a change in perspective. Like looking at something from a different angle. It doesn't change the thing itself."

"I don't understand."

"I don't completely, either. It's just the way things are." A slow smile spread across his face. "But Lanya, I think you should run and fetch Eldrin now. Tell him I need to see him."

Lanya gave him a quizzical look.

"Go on, then. You come back with him, though, all right?"

She seemed to be debating asking him why, but finally said, "All right."

She jogged off toward the little cabin Eldrin shared with Indris Alleman, who had gladly taken the homeless young man in the previous year.

Kallian picked up his shovel and turned over a few more spadefuls of soil. Soon the garden would be filled with green and growing things, providing food for another season. With luck the barbed wire fence he'd erected around it would keep the deer out, a barrier made from the boundary fences they'd removed as one of his first requests after being installed as the twenty-eighth Guardian of the Word, Oracle of the lineage of Blessed Mary of the Bridge.

It was time for Klen to join the wider world, time for the isolation to end. Eldrin and Challis could not return to Tecoa, not that they had any inclination to. But there was no reason Kallian couldn't. Soon, he would lead a group back to the city, to see what more could be learned there from the Library. It had survived the fire—he knew that for sure—but even so, there was no certainty that it would be intact forever. All things had their time. Nothing was immortal, not humans, not books, not civilizations.

And that was as it should be.

One thing he still did not understand—the words of Thea Cheraskin, shouted in fury as she was exiled into the forest, that her heir would see the High King's line end. Nothing in his knowledge of the future said anything about such an occurrence. As far as he knew, King Sweyn was still ruling over Tecoa like some fat brooding spider, and he and his scheming nobles were still stabbing each other in the back with as much glee as ever. Maybe Thea's words hadn't referred to him after all. Perhaps not Kallian, but some heir to the Guardianship, was the one who would live to see Sweyn's line fail.

But whether that was a true interpretation, he did not know. Maybe she had simply said it as one last gesture of defiance, and it was no more true than many a person's final words before death.

Time alone would tell.

There was a noise, and he looked up from his reverie to see Lanya running toward him, Eldrin jogging along behind, his expression filled with curious puzzlement.

"Here he is," the girl said, unnecessarily.

"I see that." He turned to Eldrin. "I trust I did not interrupt you in anything important?"

"No. Culling last year's beans with Indris so we could start planting, now the weather's warmed. What is it you wanted?"

Kallian just smiled and turned his head toward the south, in the direction of the lake. A tall young man with several day's growth of beard, overlong blond curls, and stormy blue eyes was walking through the trees toward them. He wore travel-stained clothes and a heavy backpack, but as he saw the three of them standing there, he stopped for a moment, then broke into a run.

Kallian stepped aside to let the young man pass. He collided with Eldrin in a tangle of arms, almost knocking him off his feet.

Eldrin was able to gasp out only, "Leos... how..." before he burst into tears.

"Who's he?" Lanya whispered, tugging on Kallian's sleeve, watching the pair kissing, laughing, and crying all at the same time.

"Eldrin's lover. He thought he'd never see him again."

"And you were going to let me miss this?" Challis's annoyed voice came from the direction of the house. "I get left out?"

Kallian shrugged. "I knew you'd show up."

She snorted and gave him a playful swat. "Fine." She turned toward Eldrin. "So, this is Leos?"

"Yes." He wiped the tears from his cheeks with the back of his hand. "But... how? How did you find me? How did you find us?"

"With help. When the news arrived that you'd run away, I started to make plans to follow you. But the weather turned so foul I feared if I did, I'd die alone in the wilderness. I took trips up to Tecoa with my father, bringing his wares up for sale at the Midwinter Fair. I asked around quietly. Bara the innkeeper told me you'd escaped, with help from two people —Kallian Dorn, a scholar from the north, and your intended bride."

Challis snorted again.

"So I thought there was at least a chance that you had survived. I was determined that once it was traveling weather, I would follow you. I slipped away without anyone knowing, and made my way to Tecoa. Bara saw that I was well-provisioned, and from there I set off north. I met a farmer who'd seen you all..."

"Audris Galvan," Eldrin said.

"Yes. He thinks highly of all three of you and was happy to help me. And farther along, I was captured by some people..."

"The Samada."

"I don't know. I did not speak their language. But Kallian —they knew your name. When I said I was following Kallian... well, they must have understood that well enough. They not only let me go, but guided me to the spot you'd last been seen. A woman was with them—she wouldn't let me leave. She made me repeat a phrase over and over in their language until I memorized it. Then she kissed me and let me go." He blushed. "It was *Kaléska Kallian Dorn kés pélat lits'omem.*"

"Shisla. It must have been Shisla." Kallian took a deep

breath. "It means, 'Kallian Dorn has given us light out of darkness.'"

Challis put her hand on his upper arm and gave him a gentle squeeze.

"From there, it was only a day's walk. I... I feel as if the gods themselves guided my footsteps the whole way."

"It came," Challis said, "of treating people with fairness and loyalty. Offering them help when there is nothing to gain. Kallian did that over and over again. Acts like that create ripples that reach the farthest shore and the most distant reaches of time."

Kallian smiled, and picked up his shovel. The two lovers had a lot to catch up on. He, Challis, and Lanya had their own paths to follow. No one is guaranteed happiness, and nothing lasts forever. But in the frozen present, here and now, there was joy. Tomorrow, as the Blessed Julia had said, could look after itself.

The joy, and the mild breeze and sunshine, and the warming earth ready to sow for another season... they were enough. They would always be enough.

a request

Please do us a favor to help other readers find Gordon and his books.

On social media: likes, comments, and shares go a LONG way. Links are in the next section.

Follows and reviews are critical: If you liked this book, please tell the world! It just takes a moment of your time and will really help us out.

On Amazon: The Scattering Winds

On BookBub: https://www.bookbub.com/authors/gordon-bonnet

On GoodReads: https://www.goodreads.com/author/show/4779649.Gordon_Bonnet

And anywhere else you search for or buy books.
Thanks! - GB and CB, the Little Bustards

from "the chains of orion"

. . .

Book Three of Arc of the Oracles

T hurial Keene, the last Patriarch of the Holy See of Klen, stood up, trying not to let the ache in his knees and back show as he straightened his body to face the cameras. He knew he was old, and that his followers would forgive him the weakness and slowness that comes with age, but he was not ready to concede that much to himself.

He had been the Patriarch since he was forty years old, now almost three decades ago. It was hard to fathom that it had been that long. His mind was still sharp, and his memory of the day of his investiture, of accepting the jeweled orb as symbol of his high office, still had the clarity of cut crystal. Since then, he'd done his best to lead his flock and administer to the more practical matters of overseeing the care of Klen and its inhabitants.

Klen was like a country within a country, a tiny autonomous zone within the Kingdom of Cascadia. The Patriarch was not allowed to form any sort of military beyond personal guards for himself and his staff. Technically, the defense of the zone was the responsibility of the King, Lennis Acoca XII. The two men, who were almost exactly the same age and had been (respectively) invested and crowned the same year, lived in an uneasy truce. There were enough adherents of the cult of the Patriarch in Tecoa, capital of Cascadia, that deposing him would foment unrest. On the other hand, the Patriarch himself was grudgingly dependent upon the king—and the rest of Cascadia—to provide Klen not only with defense, but with food and electricity and goods to support its twenty thousand residents.

The King and the Patriarch didn't particularly like each other, and neither would have shed a tear if the other had suddenly dropped dead. But until that happened, there was nothing much to be done about it, not without altering the balance of power and creating an untenable situation.

This was why the Patriarch hadn't told anyone, not even his most trusted advisors, that he knew he would be the last to hold that office—and, in fact, since about five years ago, that one piece of information made up the sum total of his oracular gift, his knowledge of the future.

He'd only become aware of the loss gradually. It was like a river slowly drying up, becoming first a creek, then a shallow rill, then barely a trickle. The transition to a completely dry stream bed must have happened at some point, but he was damned if he could recall when.

It hardly seemed fair. His predecessors, so it was told, had complete knowledge of the past and the future, saw things so clearly they perceived no difference between the two. Seven centuries ago, one of the most famous of the Patriarchs—then called Guardians of the Word—one Kallian Dorn, was renowned not only for his foresight but for his strength, and if the legends were true, had singlehandedly defeated and slain a barbarian king who threatened his people.

Those were the days of renown. Things had been different then in so many ways. It was a harder time, when most people lived in what would now be considered poverty. Even the traditions, as timeless as they seemed, had evolved. For one thing, women had once been invested as Guardians. The shift to a patriarchy had been about two hundred years ago, by edict, ostensibly as a way of consolidating power to meet the growing strength of the king of Cascadia, and to narrow the rules of succession.

Sometimes Thurial Keene wondered if it wasn't simply because the men were afraid of sharing their power with women, but he didn't say it aloud.

And so much along the way had been lost. The Guardians had been respected, even revered. Now, the Patriarch himself was little more than a figurehead. When he was called upon to prophesy, he felt as if he were just mumbling vague words to placate his devoted followers, making it all up as he went along. Thus far, none seemed the wiser, although a couple of his advisors sometimes looked at him with suspicion when his pronouncements sailed too close to the wind.

They should have known. The thought was bitter. The Blessed Perry had said it himself, fifteen hundred years ago, during the Before Time, immediately before the Fall. The oracular gifts had come from the gods because the other means for knowledge were about to be taken away. They would last as long as they were needed, and then—when those paths to knowledge were rediscovered—might well vanish once again.

Who could look around at the cities of Cascadia now, with their FastRails and telescreens and electronic information storage and missions to the Moon, and think that the oracles were anything but a rapidly-fading anachronism?

Seemingly, though, no one did. Everyone still looked to him for guidance, as if he heard the voices of the gods as clearly as the Blessed Perry and the other Founders had.

And all the time, the knowledge burned in his mind. He would be the last Patriarch of Klen. That, and nothing else, was absolutely certain. He wasn't even certain what words he was about to utter to the waiting cameras, words that would be broadcast all over Cascadia, and probably farther still. Worse, he didn't much care. None of it seemed important, somehow, compared with knowing the end of his entire lineage was nearly upon him.

He tried to settle his face into some semblance of confidence and command, as if he had no doubt that the words he spoke were from the very minds of the gods. He gave a nod to the woman standing behind the nearest camera. Simultaneously there was a volley of clicks as buttons were pressed to begin recording.

"My dear people of Klen, and those of the secular realm of Cascadia who nonetheless look toward us for spiritual guidance and knowledge of the eternal, I greet you. Now, in the thirty-first year of my service as Patriarch of Klen, I have momentous news of a sort that has not been possible for fourteen centuries. Not only before our own time, but before the Black Years, when war and plague and famine nearly ended our entire species. We are on the threshold of a goal last accomplished by our far distant ancestors, in the Before Time of which only a few accounts survive."

He gave a long, dramatic pause. May as well try to stir up some excitement in his audience, even if he felt little for the enterprise himself.

"As you no doubt know, the king of Cascadia has seen fit to take on the challenge of exploring other worlds, and working in cooperation with scientists from his neighboring realms, the Intermontane Empire and the Republic of Darset, manned craft were sent to the Moon five years ago to establish a permanent base there. We have always given our blessing to this effort, as anything that furthers our knowledge of the universe within which we live is to the greater glory of the gods we serve. But now, one of our very own has been chosen to lead a survey mission into the unknown, charting the far-Earth side of the Moon—something we only know of through fragmentary records, of uncertain reliability, from nearly fifteen hundred years ago.

"A young man named Kallman Dorn will be responsible for this history-making venture, leading an intrepid band of young men and women who soon will leave behind the safety of our mother planet for the airless cold of space, coming back only when they have achieved their goal of broadening our scientific understanding. One day, perhaps, reaching the almost godlike levels of sophistication possessed by our distant ancestors, may their memories be blessed. It is perhaps significant that young Kallman is himself a direct descendant of one of our most renowned lineages, and traces his heritage back to the Patriarch Kallian Dorn and his consort, the Lady Challis Mazerine, and further back still to two of the Founders, the redoubtable Colin Dorn and his consort Emily Banfield, who together helped to lead a tiny remnant of our forebears out of the fire and flood and devastation that struck down the old world, and founded Klen, which still stands proudly as a testimony to their courage."

One camera operator made a circular gesture with one hand. *Move it along.* The Patriarch absently wondered if his predecessors would have tolerated being urged to brevity by a commoner, or if they'd have had the offending hand summarily cut off. Certainly King Lennis wouldn't put up with it. The thought made his mouth twist with annoyance, and it took an effort not to grimace. In any case, he couldn't do anything while the cameras were still rolling.

"So I hope you will join with me in a prayer for the brave men and women who are taking part in this expedition, which is scheduled to launch in three weeks' time from the Cascadian National Space Agency's site near Tecoa. And most especially our beloved representative Kallman Dorn. May the gods' hands shield him until he is safely back in Klen."

He bowed his head in what he hoped would look like a

gesture of sufficient piety to edify the watchers, as with another fusillade of clicks, the camera operators stopped recording.

Then they all started packing up and chatting with each other, without so much as a by-your-leave. The Patriarch had given his blessing. It was time to go get a quick breakfast and forget he even existed.

As Thurial Keene prepared to return to his office, his mind slipped into darker pathways, ones he'd been treading more and more often recently. Was there *anyone* left who actually believed? Oh, there were the Zealots, of course. There would always be Zealots. But where was the steady, clear-eyed acceptance earlier leaders of Klen had? Then, the belief of the common people in the pronouncements of the Guardian of the Word and the other oracles had been rock-solid and unshakeable. An enviable position. Why couldn't he have been born centuries earlier, when everything was so much simpler?

But, he reflected, back then what the Guardian said actually came from the divine.

What had happened that had separated him so strikingly from the source?

He trod the hallway of the Patriarchal residence, so familiar he could have found his way in the pitch dark, giving a longing look at the closed door of his quarters. How nice it would be to slip inside, turn the lock, spend the day reading in front of a crackling wood fire, letting the warmth seep into his body and chase away the chill he felt even on warm days. And not some theological tome, or even the latest scientific findings.

The science used to excite him. It seemed like new discoveries were being made every day, and that the people of Cascadia were perhaps finally approaching the knowledge humanity had achieved a fifteen hundred years ago, before the fall and the flood and the intervening Black Years during which so much was lost. They'd scraped together what they could from fragmentary records that had survived—much of which had come from the Great Library of Tecoa, which had somehow escaped the worst of the destruction—and reassembled the rest through nothing more than dogged determination.

But even that no longer thrilled him the way it once had. Mostly what he wanted was escape. To fall into some cheerful fiction, and forget for a time that his own life had become an exercise in fiction as well, but without the cheer.

No such luck today. Duty called, as it always did.

He continued the long walk past his private quarters to his office, where a pile of paperwork awaited him. Mostly formalities, needing only a cursory read and his signature. Land purchases and sales negotiated with functionaries from the king, trade agreements—same. A pledge to contribute to a joint effort toward scientific exploration of the geology of the region—same. A donation of money to aid people in the western part of Cascadia, near the ruins of the ancient city, whose homes had been damaged in an earthquake three months previous.

One he still had to consider—the possible commutation of a death sentence against a citizen of Klen who had made an attempt on the life of King Lennis. Since the man had been captured within the boundaries of Klen, by a previous treaty his fate was in the Patriarch's hands, not the king's. But still, it was a sticky issue since they were, at least nominally, allies. Even so, it bothered him to execute a man for attempting something when Thurial Keene would have been just as happy had he succeeded.

He opened his office door with a sigh, walked silently across the plush carpet, and dropped into the elaborately-carved chair behind his desk. The chair, an expensive gift from the king three years earlier, was uncomfortable as hell, but his inclination to have it burned was quashed by his Chief Minister, who worried—probably rightly—that word could get back to the royal ears.

At least it discouraged him from falling asleep.

The morning hours ticked away as he worked his way through signing documents, saving the potential commutation for last. He glanced up at the clock, wondering if he could justify breaking early for lunch before making a decision, when the door to his office burst open.

Chief Minister Andres Ballinger. His dark hair was in disarray. He looked as if he'd just gotten out of bed. Impossible, though, knowing the man's habits. Thurial had often wondered if the Minister slept at all. No matter what the time of day, he had the sleek, unruffled composure of a cat.

And he *always* knocked on the door before entering the Patriarch's office, even if he'd been summoned there.

"My lord," Andres gasped out.

"What's wrong?" Only then did Thurial notice that the Minister's sleeve was torn, and his right arm had a bleeding scrape.

The Minister stared at him, his expression somewhere between horror and disbelief. "You don't *know*?"

"I..." Thurial swallowed, their gazes locked. Here it was, then. "I want to hear it from your own mouth."

Andres took a deep breath, nodded, trying to regain some of his usual calm. "I... I bring foul news, my lord. There has been... significant unrest has begun in Cascadia. It is... it is worst in Tecoa, and martial law has been declared for at least parts of the city center. But agitators are active here as well, right in the heart of Klen. I was assaulted coming out of my home · this morning. I would have been here for your news conference. I apologize..."

Thurial waved this away. "Why? Who has started this?"

Once again there was a look of incredulity, and dawning

understanding, from the Minister. Thurial could read it in his eyes. *He didn't know. He didn't foresee any of this. His gift is gone... and how long has it been this way? How long have I been blind to the fact that the old man has been stumbling around, reaping the privilege of powers he no longer has?*

But the Minister only said, "The Zealots. The same men and women who have been protesting the corruption and wealth of the crown and the scepter for three years now. I did not—*we* did not—recognize how organized they are."

The switch to *we* registered immediately. The office of Patriarch, and before that the Guardian of the Word, had always been held by men and women whose foresight was respected and feared. It was understood that not everything they knew was fit knowledge for everyone, and that having a detailed knowledge of the future brought with it a responsibility to decide what parts of it were necessary to reveal. Everyone took it for granted that the Patriarchs and Guardians would use their foreknowledge and wisdom to protect the people of Klen.

That one word—*we*—told Thurial Keene that the pretense was collapsing around him, just as he'd feared for years. Andres Ballinger had figured out in one blinding flash that the Patriarch was only a quite ordinary doddering old man who loved wealth and ease and was no better equipped to safeguard Klen than anyone else. Whatever gift from the gods earlier Patriarchs had, it was gone, and they both knew it.

And the expression on the Minister's face said something else as well. *But this will be our little secret, because both our lives depend on keeping up the fiction.*

Andres cleared his throat. "My lord." He shifted his feet. "I hate to be the one who delivers such news to you, but... it is my opinion and the opinion of others on your council that you should be conveyed to a different location, for your own safety. Because... your friend and ally, King Lennis Acoca XII, was murdered last night as he slept in his royal residence. He has no heir. The kingdom of Cascadia is without a ruler."

Finish the journey with the Oracles of Cascadia! Order your copy of <u>The Chains of Orion here</u> or wherever you purchase books.

about the author

Gordon Bonnet has been writing fiction for decades. Encouraged when his story "Crazy Bird Bends His Beak" won critical acclaim in Mrs. Moore's 1st grade class at Central Elementary School in St. Albans, West Virginia, he embarked on a long love affair with the written word.

His interest in the paranormal goes back almost that far. Introduced to speculative, fantasy, and science fiction by such giants in the tradition as Madeleine L'Engle, Lloyd Alexander, Isaac Asimov, C. S. Lewis, and J. R. R. Tolkien, he was captivated by those writers' abilities to take the reader to a fictional world and make it seem tangible, to breathe life and passion and personality into characters who were (sometimes) not even human. He made journeys into darker realms upon meeting the works of Edgar Allen Poe and H. P. Lovecraft during his teenage years, and those authors still influence his imagination and his writing to this day.

This fascination with the paranormal, however, has always been tempered by Gordon's scientific training. This has led to a strange duality: his work as a teacher, skeptic and debunker on the popular blog _Skeptophilia_, while simultaneously writing paranormal and speculative novels, novellas, and short stories. Gordon explains this, with a smile: "Well, I do know it's fiction, after all."

He blogs daily, and is never without a piece of fiction in progress—driven to continue (as he puts it) "because I want to find out how the story ends." From historical fiction (_Kári the Lucky_), to murder mysteries (the Parsifal Snowe Mysteries, beginning with *Poison the Well*), to paranormal fiction with a humorous twist (*Periphery* and *Lock & Key*) to the truly terrifying (*Gears* and *Descent into Ulthoa*), Gordon's fiction has something for all tastes!

Find him conversing with his dogs (and perhaps his wife) in Trumansburg, NY, or the following platforms:

- Website *http://www.gordonbonnet.com*
- YouTube *https://youtube.com/@skeptophilia1509*
- Skeptophilia blog *http://www.skeptophilia.com/*
- Twitter *@TalesOfWhoa*
- TikTok *@LittleBustardBooks* and *@gordonbonnetauthor*
- Instagram *@skygazer227*

Or, ya know, the Google.

also by gordon bonnet

In the Midst of Lions (Book One of The Oracles)

Lock & Key

Behind the Frame

The Communion of Shadows

Gears

Sephirot

Descent into Ulthoa

The Shambles

Kári the Lucky

Kill Switch

The Fifth Day

Snowe Mysteries *(beginning re-releases 2023)*

Book 1: Poison the Well

Book 2: Dead Letter Office

Book 3: Face Value

Snowe Mysteries *(available now)*

Book 4: Past Imperfect

Book 5: Room for Wrath

Book 6: The Obituary Collector

Book 7: Slings and Arrows

The Boundary Solution Series (stay tuned for re-releases)

And More…

Stay tuned for releases *(and re-releases for ones you may have missed)*

Sign up for Gordon's Little Bustard Books Newsletter and Obscure Weird Tidbits at his website: http://www.gordonbonnet.com